Dead Soon
Enough

ALSO BY STEPH CHA

Beware Beware
Follow Her Home

Dead Soon Enough

A Juniper Song Mystery

STEPH CHA

MINOTAUR BOOKS

A THOMAS DUNNE BOOK

A THOMAS DUNNE BOOK FOR MINOTAUR BOOKS.
An imprint of St. Martin's Publishing Group.

www.thomasdunnebooks.com
www.minotaurbooks.com

Library of Congress Cataloging-in-Publication Data

Cha, Steph.
    Dead soon enough : a Juniper Song mystery / Steph Cha.—First edition.
        pages; cm
    "A Thomas Dunne Book."
    ISBN 978-1-250-06531-5 (hardcover)
    ISBN 978-1-4668-7206-6 (e-book)
    1. Women private investigators—Fiction.   2. Los Angeles (Calif.)—Fiction.
    I. Title.
    PS3603.H27D43 2015
    813'.6—dc23

                                                    2015017138

Minotaur books may be purchased for educational, business, or promotional use. For information on bulk purchases, please contact the Macmillan Corporate and Premium Sales Department at 1-800-221-7945, extension 5442, or write to specialmarkets@macmillan.com.

First Edition: August 2015

10 9 8 7 6 5 4 3 2 1

To Peter

ACKNOWLEDGMENTS

This book owes its genesis to a conversation in Lake Arrowhead with my friends Levon Paronyan and Lara Kalaydjian. Thank you guys for your support and enthusiasm, and for sharing your experiences as Armenian-Americans in L.A.

As always, thanks to my agent, Ethan Bassoff, for your hard work and friendship. We've gone through a lot together in the last five years, and I'm grateful for all of it.

Thanks to my editor, Anne Brewer, for guiding me through our third (!) book together. Thanks, too, to Shailyn Tavella, Jennifer Letwack, and the rest of the St. Martin's team.

Thanks to Phillip Burruel, for buying me lunch and sharing your stories.

Thanks to Ben Loory, for regular doses of clarity (for example, on how to handle acknowledgments).

Thanks to Naomi Hirahara, for your warmth and mentorship.

My friends—thanks for all of the hugs and drinks and conversations.

Mom, Dad, Andrew, Peter—thanks for your continuing love and support.

Thanks to my intern, Duke Charbabella, for your steadfast companionship.

Thanks to my husband, Matt Barbabella, for loving me even at my laziest and most self-loathing. You were right about that jigsaw puzzle.

"Who still talks nowadays of the extermination of the Armenians?" —Adolf Hitler, 1939

"I do, bitch. Hope it's a hot day in hell." —Nora Mkrtchian, 2012

Dead Soon Enough

One

❦

When I was twenty-two, I sold three sets of eggs for a total of $48,000. I was broke, bored, and quietly depressed, and had no strength to fight the call of easy money. It was a questionable decision, but I've made enough of those that this one doesn't keep me up at night.

I'd seen advertisements for egg donors in the Yale paper, but back then I was still on the payroll of a hardworking immigrant mom who saw no better way to spend money than to push her shitty kid through the Ivy League. The ads made a bit of a splash in cafeteria conversations, but as far as I knew, no one really responded. We had a whole campus full of prestigious eggs and, in aggregate at least, a brash imperviousness to financial pressure.

That changed for many of us soon enough. I left Yale with an attractive diploma, an unattractive transcript, and zero to negligible job prospects. I moved to L.A., not because I had dreams, or even family anymore, but because it was a city I knew, one that I liked better than others.

One day, after pinning tutoring fliers in coffee shops full of dead-eyed college graduates just as unemployed as I was, I came across a

New York Times article about Asian-American egg donors. Apparently, our eggs commanded high premiums for rarity on the market—Asian-American women waited longer than average to have babies, chasing those professional dreams with their biological clocks ticking softly in the background.

It was like a help wanted ad singing my name.

There was another reason, too, an enabling reason if not an actual impetus—despite my sadness and weakness of spirit I felt, in a way, invincible. It wasn't that I relished the idea of my spawn running the earth. The truth is, I didn't think about that much at all. I was young and cavalier, with a disregard for consequences that had almost nothing to do with reality, mine or anyone else's. Consequences were things that happened to other people. What happened to me was bad luck.

So I did some research and sold my eggs to the highest bidder. They went out into the world, and maybe some of them became people.

I hadn't thought about them in a long time, and then I met Rubina Gasparian.

It was a warm Tuesday in early March, one of those pre-spring Los Angeles days that knocked an unnecessary nail into winter's coffin. I'd had my private investigator license for almost a year, and during that time I'd made a steady, honest living, as free of mishap as any period in my adult life.

When I got to the office that morning, there was a woman waiting outside the locked door. She was standing straight, facing the hall, and when I looked up from my phone she was already watching me, waiting for me to acknowledge her. I nearly jumped.

She was a slim woman wearing a gray wrap dress and short, professional heels. I was almost a head taller, even in flip-flops, but there was something commanding in her presence that negated the impression of smallness. She was pretty in a brutal way, with a high forehead, straight black hair, and an immaculate gloss to her pale skin. Her eyes were sharp and dark, and by the time I got around to greeting her, they'd run their way right through me.

"Hi," I said. "Are you looking for Lindley and Flores?"

"Yes. I hope you don't mind my coming in so early. I don't have an appointment." She spoke quickly, but with a tentative, deferential tone of voice.

"Not at all. I'm Juniper Song," I said, holding out my hand. "I'm an investigator."

"Rubina Gasparian." She shook my hand with a firm grip, and I felt the press of a ring on my palm. Wrong hand for a wedding band, but I saw that she had one of those on, too. "It's nice to meet you."

I opened up the office and Rubina followed me inside. I sat down at my desk and, before I was able to offer, she took a chair across from me.

"So, Ms. Gasparian. What can I do for you today?"

"It's Doctor," she said, then added, "Though that doesn't matter."

"Sorry." I smiled, feeling mildly caught off guard. "*Dr.* Gasparian, what can I do for you today?"

She crossed her legs and folded her hands over the top knee. "I'd like to hire someone to follow my cousin."

"We can certainly do that," I said. "All three of us are seasoned tails. That's kind of the bread and butter of this job. What can you tell me about her?"

She produced a 4 x 6 photograph and pushed it delicately across the desk. It was a professional photo of Rubina in a wedding dress, with one arm around a younger woman in a lavender dress, unmistakably a bridesmaid. I took a long look at the cousin. She had the same pale skin and round eyes as Rubina, but she gave off a rugged impression, even in pastel chiffon. Her bare arms showed a colorful splash of tattoos, and her shoulders were broad and well honed. She wasn't as traditionally attractive as Rubina, but she would never fade standing next to her.

"That was taken on my wedding day, almost six years ago. The girl on my left is my cousin Lusig. I can e-mail you a more recent photograph—her hair's much shorter now, and she has a piercing in her nose, which I made her take out for the wedding." She paused and nodded, making a note to herself. "I've known her since she was in my late aunt's womb. She's a wonderful girl. I love her like a sister and daughter, and now, she's carrying my baby."

"How's that?" I asked.

"For a few reasons, chief among them that I am thirty-seven years old, my husband and I are unable to conceive. Since we want children, and adoption is out of the question, we decided on a gestational surrogate."

I wondered briefly why adoption was out of the question, and something in Rubina's eyes dared me to ask. It didn't seem like my business—not that that always stopped me—but I bit.

"Why was adoption out of the question?"

"Here are two clues," she said, holding one hand up in a V. "My married name is Gasparian. My maiden name is Balakian."

"You're Armenian," I said. Armenian surnames were almost as easy to spot as Korean ones.

"Very much so. And as an Armenian couple, Van and I would like to continue our bloodline. There are only so many of us left."

"Forgive me if I'm off track here. Been a long time since World History. But you're referring to a genocide?"

She nodded. "Of course. It's telling that you're uncertain. Not—" she added hastily—"telling of your ignorance, but of the Armenian genocide's status in history. But that is a long conversation, and we were already in the middle of another one."

"Right," I said. "You were telling me about a gestational surrogate. That means what, your egg, her womb?"

"Yes."

"And that surrogate is your cousin Lusig."

"Exactly." She smiled, lending a little warmth to her features. "Lusig wasn't ideal in every way. The perfect surrogate is a woman who's been pregnant before, who won't form an undue attachment to the baby. We think Lusig will be fine with giving him up, but this is her first pregnancy, and she had no familiarity with the process before she agreed to sign on."

"So why her?"

"First, she offered. She knew we needed help, and she said she was more than happy to. Second, Lusig and I are very close. She would be in the baby's life, as more than an aunt, if a little less than a mother. Third, Lusig has no desire to have children of her own."

"How old is she?"

"Twenty-six."

"Early to make that call, wouldn't you say?"

Rubina shrugged, a small, mechanical motion. "She's maintained this position for many years. Lusig is a headstrong, stubborn girl, and she is not known to change her mind. On top of which, she's unmoved by children, and thinks she would make a poor mother. Between you and me, I agree with her."

"Why's that?"

"Well, practically speaking, Lusig has never been employed for more than a year at a time. She has very little interest in figuring out her life, and I can't imagine she'd have room for a child anytime soon. And I know she's young, but twenty-six is not twenty-two."

I suppressed a smile. Rubina could have been describing me before I started working for Chaz. I'd spent my post-college years tutoring around the city for bursts of cash, just enough to pay rent and maintain my pantry and one shelf of my fridge. Pregnancy would have been a nightmare.

"What's she do?"

"This and that. Temp work, mostly. Sometimes she participates in psych studies and focus groups. She lives at home, with her father, so her living expenses are very low. We've been paying her a stipend while she carries the baby, so she isn't working now."

"None of this sounds particularly permanent," I said. "You think she'll always be unfit for kids?"

"I love her, but she's a selfish girl. She's a classic only child, not conceited but very self-centered. She's always surprised to recall that the world doesn't revolve around her."

"I don't think I'm especially selfish, but I would run far away if anyone wanted to borrow my body for nine months."

"Of course she's often generous. Maybe this is getting lost, but I think Lusig is wonderful. She's only fundamentally selfish."

I nodded, wondering how damning this was supposed to be. "Is that why you're here?"

She gave me a thoughtful stare before speaking again. "I suppose it is," she said. "I'm worried that she's putting herself before the welfare of my child."

"How so?"

"She's almost eight months pregnant, well past the initial touch and go. Not that this pregnancy could ever have been less than a deliberate, serious affair, with all the money and energy poured into it from the beginning, but my son is more baby than fetus now. He will be born. I'm going to be a mother." She looked pointedly at my left hand. "You don't have children, Miss Song?"

"I have not been so blessed," I said. "You can call me Song, by the way. Though 'Miss' is correct."

"I've always wanted to be a mother. I waited longer than I ever thought I would, but I went to medical school, then did my residency, then a fellowship, and before I knew it I was looking at limited options. If you're open to some friendly advice, I'd suggest you not wait too long."

The conversation was taking a weird turn. Rubina was not the type of woman who inspired quick and easy confidences, and I was more guarded than most. There was a clinical, universal tinge to her prescription, but it still struck me as somewhat intrusive. I ignored it and pressed on.

"So why are you worried about your cousin, Dr. Gasparian?"

"You can call me Rubina," she said. "I'm sorry I corrected you. It's a strange reflex."

"Sure. Rubina. Tell me your concerns about Lusig."

"She was a party girl. Through college, through her early twenties. And she's only twenty-six, so her early twenties were not very long ago. We've been Facebook friends for years, and I've seen all her pictures, drinking and carousing with friends. Nothing abnormal, understand, but she's always inclined toward the wild side. Nightclubs, vodka shots. I suspect some illicit drugs."

I pictured Rubina culling through her cousin's Facebook page, before and after entrusting her with her baby. The picture came easily.

"Drinking and carousing with friends seems pretty standard, really," I said, though I suspected as I said so that Rubina's youth had been tame and studious. "And from what you're saying I gather she got a lot of that out of her system well before she got pregnant. I imagine you wouldn't have chosen her if you had any doubts. What changed?"

She seemed surprised by the question, but recovered quickly. She tucked her hair behind her ear with a swift, precise motion. "Lusig's best friend is a girl named Nora. They've known each other since the seventh grade—they're both Armenian, both only children, and they stuck to each other from the beginning. I've met her several times, though I can't say I know her very well. In any case, Nora has been missing for almost a month."

I sat up a little straighter. "Missing? Like, officially? The police are looking for her and all that?"

"Yes, the police are looking for her. No one has said so, but everyone always suspects the worst."

"I see," I said, blinking hard. Murder had just entered the conversation.

Rubina broke the silence before it could set. "But I'm not here about Nora. I'm only giving you background. My concern is that Lusig has been acting strange ever since the disappearance."

"Strange, how?"

"She's been moody, and it's been hard for me to reach her."

"She's been off the radar?"

"Not exactly. Let me explain myself." She gave me a tight smile. "In general, I don't care what other people do with their lives. Lusig is my cousin, and we've always been close, but I haven't agreed with every one of her life choices. She hasn't asked me about most of them, and I've withheld unsolicited advice on many, many occasions."

I nodded. Something in her tone suggested unreasonable pride in her own restraint.

"But when you're pregnant, you don't *own* your body, at least not one-hundred percent. This might be especially true if you've signed on to be a vessel for someone else's baby."

My mind revolted against the idea, but I couldn't say it was without truth. Instead, I asked, "Then, who does?"

"Who does what?"

"Who owns your cousin?"

"Well, to be frank," she said, twisting her fingers together, "I think I do."

I let her statement ride a brief pause, and she let out a tight little laugh.

"I don't mean she's my property, per se. And I know in this day and age women have certain rights to their own bodies, which I support wholly. But in this situation, I believe I have an unusual amount of interest in the contents of her womb, don't you agree?"

"That's true," I said, and decided to get back on track. "So, your cousin hasn't been attentive to your demands as the mother of the child."

"No. She's been defiant and unpredictable, going on errands she doesn't care to explain and snapping at me when I ask where she's been."

"It sounds like she has some reason to be upset," I said.

"Of course she does, and I'd like to give her space to deal with her . . . grief, if that's the right word for it."

"On the other hand?"

She pressed her lips together. "On the other hand, I need to know if she's mistreating her body."

"Ah, so this is where I come in."

"I don't want you to bother her," she said. "Please just observe her, tell me what she's doing, take pictures as you deem appropriate or necessary."

"Sure, I can do that. Out of curiosity, though, what if I do find out she's slamming shots and sharing needles?"

"I will cross that bridge only if necessary."

I'd been surveilling people for a couple years now, and it had long since started to feel like a creepy second nature. I could follow any car across town at any time of day, and I developed a talent for blending into most environments, without the assistance of a trench coat or a fedora. Most people don't suspect they're being followed. After all, hiring a private investigator to solve a personal problem—sussing out infidelity being the classic case—is a somewhat nuclear option, one that many can't imagine using themselves. I couldn't follow a man into a public restroom and take a video of his stream, but anything short of that was more or less possible.

Still, some assignments were trickier than others. I wasn't quite ballsy enough to attempt a nighttime tail on a quiet road, but empty bars were usually manageable. Being an Asian woman worked in my favor—despite my height and somewhat unforthcoming demeanor, no one ever thought I was dangerous.

Lusig Hovanian was going to be an easier mark than most, and not because she was oblivious. Rubina, as I might have expected, kept her cousin on a short leash. Within a few hours of leaving my office, she e-mailed me a complete schedule of Lusig's day. She gave me the name and address of a restaurant in South Pasadena and requested that I eat there at seven o'clock. She gave me a fifty-dollar stipend—she'd researched the restaurant and determined that this was enough to cover dinner for two. She thought, correctly enough, that I'd stand out less if I wasn't eating alone.

There weren't too many people I wanted to meet for dinner, so I was happy that my roommate was free. Lori Lim was my best friend, an adopted younger sister of sorts, with whom I had almost nothing in common but a few shared episodes of extreme trauma. We'd been living together for about two years, in a two-bedroom apartment in Echo Park. I liked to think this arrangement was for her benefit, but we both knew I'd be lonely as all hell without her.

She was also pretty useful as a plus-one on stakeouts, not that she always knew when we were on one. She disapproved softly of my PI work, maintaining that it was unsafe. Fair enough, really, as I'd been drugged, threatened, and held at gunpoint since I'd met her, among other things. But even she recognized that my experience had been largely atypical, and most days she was content to leave me be.

Manhattan Bar & Deli of Pasadena was a cozy neighborhood place, and I guessed from the name that it was run by newish immigrants. I felt minorly vindicated when we were greeted by a middle-aged Chinese woman with halting, friendly English.

Lusig was already seated when we arrived. The restaurant was small and relatively empty, so I spotted her right away. She looked less fresh than she had in Rubina's wedding photo, though this, of course, was understandable. She was younger then, but I suspected the difference was due more to pregnancy and lack of makeup than to advancing through her mid-twenties.

Nothing about her appearance suggested an ideal surrogate mother. She looked slovenly and unnurturing, like she could hardly bother to take care of herself. Her hair was dyed crow black and cropped messily above her chin. It looked choppy and unwashed, with an oily shoe-polish shine. She wore a black T-shirt under a bulky military jacket big enough to hide a boar. Her ears were studded up and down with a spray of metal and stone. A tiny bright dot adorned one side of her thin nose, and above it, her huge, wild eyes were the focal point of the room.

Lori and I sat at a nearby table, within comfortable eavesdropping distance. I glanced at the young man sitting across from Lusig. He was clean-cut and handsome, with the kind of nonthreatening face that did well with mothers. He had dark hair, thick eyebrows, and sideburns that looked difficult to groom. Lusig had his full attention.

I ordered a hot pastrami Reuben and Lori got lox and cream cheese, which she formed into bite-sized bagel sandwiches, setting one on my plate. Fifty bucks left beer money, so I had a pint while Lori tucked into a milkshake. I told her it was my treat, and she thanked me with unnecessary enthusiasm.

She chattered about her job and her boyfriend Isaac, and I gave her the greater part of my attention while keeping one ear open to receive any revealing tidbits from Lusig's table. Lusig had a low, steady voice that cut across space without apparent effort. It was easy to track, even while carrying on my own conversation, and when I heard a change in tone and tempo, I pretended to devote all my energy to my sandwich. The small talk was over.

"I'm sorry I haven't been able to meet you till now," she said with a note of remorse.

The man laughed uncomfortably. "You're eight months pregnant, and I know this hasn't been easy for you, either."

"No, it hasn't. To be honest, it had nothing to do with pregnancy. There is nothing easier for a pregnant woman than to eat a pastrami sandwich."

He laughed again, but stopped when she didn't join him. "Okay," he said instead.

"Do you want to know the truth?" she asked.

"Of course." He didn't sound especially excited to know the truth.

"I was mad at you."

"Mad?"

She stared at him across the table, her eyes searching his. "You didn't keep her safe, Chris. You were supposed to be there for her, that was the whole"—she made a framing gesture with her hands, encompassing his figure—"point of you, and you didn't keep her safe."

He moved back in his seat, dragging his chair a few loud inches across the floor. "*I* didn't keep her safe? You have some nerve, Lusig."

She watched him closely, and then her expression softened, taking on the contours of contrition. "I'm sorry. I'm projecting, I know." She shook her head and looked disapprovingly at her dinner, then looked up again at her companion. "Where do you think she is, Chris? Where could our girl have gone?"

Chris was slumped over, looking helpless and crestfallen, and as I waited for him to answer, I noticed Lori was raising her eyebrows across the table.

"*Unni,*" she said. "Are you listening?"

I made a show of chewing and swallowing the bite of sandwich in my mouth. "Sorry, I zoned out a little."

She shook her head and bit her lip with her crooked tooth. "*Unni,* are you working right now?" she whispered.

"Shhhhh," I said, widening my eyes. "Jesus."

"I knew it."

"I'll tell you about it later, okay? Sorry, what were you saying?"

She twisted her lips, but I could tell she wasn't really annoyed.

She was used to my work mode after living with me for so long. Our friendship was also the only good remainder of a case that had left us both devastated, and she knew that the job stabilized me, even if she didn't understand how.

"I was just asking if you'd noticed how much time I've been spending at Isaac's."

"I am a detective, Lori."

She'd been spending most nights at Isaac's for the better part of a month. He'd moved into his own place downtown, and suddenly he was less interested in sleeping in my apartment. I hadn't seen his face at all for a couple weeks, and even Lori was scarce. His place was within walking distance of her job—she worked in human resources for an accounting firm—and she only seemed to stop home for an hour or two here and there to pick up clean clothes and make sure I had enough to eat.

"Do you mind?" she asked.

I smiled, a little wider than felt sincere. "You're an adult, Lori. I don't stay up all night worrying about you."

"I know, but you aren't too lonely?"

I shrugged. "No, not too. I'm good at being alone."

She nodded, still looking solicitous, but she changed the subject.

It wasn't long before Lusig reclaimed my attention, along with Lori's and everyone else's in the restaurant. Her voice was raised, and she was glaring at the waitress.

"Guess what's none of your fucking business," she said.

The waitress looked around the room. She was a small Chinese girl, about college-age, probably the owners' daughter. She wore a Manhattan Bar & Deli T-shirt over slim blue jeans and dainty shoes. Her face twisted into a look of scorn that searched for validation as she scanned the restaurant.

"You're acting very belligerent," said the waitress.

"Am I? I'm sorry. I just thought I could order a beer without being interrogated."

"I only asked if you were pregnant."

"Sure. Not a loaded question." She scoffed. "Of course I'm pregnant. Look at me. You knew I was pregnant, so don't fucking pretend you were just being curious."

"I don't know if I'm comfortable serving alcohol to a pregnant lady."

"It's *a beer.*"

"You're acting pretty drunk already."

Lusig stood up, rising a half head taller than the waitress, who seemed stunned to have this irate customer glaring down at her face. "I've had five drinks in the last three months, you judgmental cunt." She flung a twenty-dollar bill on the table. "Come on, Chris. Let's get out of here."

Chris gaped at the scene in front of him, and then stood up after Lusig, half bowing with apology. He left more bills on the table in a quiet hurry, then followed her out of the restaurant.

The door swung closed with a tinkle of bells, leaving an awed silence in its wake. The waitress stared at the door with her mouth hanging open.

I caught Lori's eye, and we both covered our mouths to suppress overt laughter.

"Oh, *unni,*" she said. "Please tell me you were here to watch them."

I shrugged, and a sly smile spread across her face.

"She's fun," she said. "This could be a good one."

I couldn't exactly leap from the table and follow Lusig to her car, so I texted Rubina to report that she'd left. I told her to let me know if she couldn't get hold of Lusig, and after a minute, she ascertained that her cousin was on her way home. I convinced Rubina she could wait for my report until I was done eating. I finished dinner with Lori and called from the car. She picked up immediately.

"Did something happen?" she asked by way of greeting. "She's in a terrible mood."

"She did storm out of the restaurant," I said.

Rubina sighed. "What did she do?"

I told her about the scene in the deli.

"I told you she was behaving strangely," she said. "She's always been a passionate sort of girl, but she usually has good control over her temper. She's not one to make a fool of herself in public."

"In my opinion, the waitress was being unreasonable and kind of insulting."

"That's no reason to make a scene."

"Are you upset about the beer?"

"Yes."

"I thought the occasional beer was pretty much harmless."

"I know what it says on WebMD, but I also know many, many doctors who have had children. Every one of them abstained during pregnancy."

I thought about nine months without alcohol, the first big sacrifice forced on new mothers. It seemed daunting to me, even with ordinary levels of stress.

"She said five drinks in the last three months. That doesn't seem dangerous or anything."

"It's the attitude. She's not acting like a woman putting another's needs before her own. And I don't really believe she's been careful enough to count."

"I don't know, she sounded pretty indignant. I'll bet she's been counting, even if it's with some measure of resentment."

She sighed. "And who was this man she was meeting? Did he look suspicious?"

I almost laughed. There was something childish in the question. "His name is Chris. I was going to ask if he was someone you knew." I paused and decided to add, "It sounds like he's involved with Lusig's missing friend."

"She didn't tell me she was meeting him."

"Who did she say she was meeting?"

"A friend from college." Rubina sounded dissatisfied. "Which wasn't a wholesale lie. She and Chris were at USC together."

"But not exactly the truth, I take it."

"No. He's Nora's boyfriend."

"It doesn't seem off or anything, that her boyfriend and best friend would spend some time together."

"Maybe not. But I know they aren't close friends on their own."

I pictured the two of them, Lusig with her tattoos and oily hair, Chris in his square gray polo shirt. They didn't look like two birds of a feather. Then again, I thought of my friendship with Lori.

"Shared experience counts for something," I said. "They both love Nora, and she's gone now."

"I would go as far as to say that they dislike each other."

"She's talked about him with you?"

"Many times. She adores Nora, and she has always thought Chris was a cold, condescending misogynist. Chris, on the other hand, seems to think Lusig is a deadbeat, a bad influence. He blames her for Nora dropping out of law school. I'm sure both of them have better shoulders to cry on."

There was something suggestive in her tone. "What are you worried about, Rubina?"

"I just wonder," she said. "Do you think she's looking for Nora?"

"I've seen her one time. You'd know better than I do."

"She was talking about her."

"Yes."

"And she was asking Chris where he thought she was."

"Yeah, that's true. But what else do you think she'd talk about with her missing friend's boyfriend?"

"Nothing at all." Her tone was clipped and a little impatient.

"Oh, I get it," I said. "You think she was pumping him for information. She thinks he knows something."

"Lusig must know Nora might be dead."

"And if Nora was murdered . . ."

"Yes. Exactly."

"You think she suspects him?"

"I don't know," she said. "But if that is the case, then she was going out of her way to meet a man she judged capable of murder. If she wants to endanger herself, that is one thing, but she is carrying my child."

"Rubina, I think it's important to maintain perspective here. She was getting dinner in a public place with a college classmate."

"You're right, of course." Her tone was gentle but unyielding. "Still, there's no harm in being watchful."

Two

❦

Chaz was in the office when I arrived the next morning, and I plunked into the chair across his desk with theatrical heaviness.

"It's hump day," he said with a *tsk tsk*. "Not slump day."

I looked up and raised an eyebrow. "Would you rather I humped the furniture?"

He smirked and shook his head. "Did not think that joke through. Don't go telling Art I harassed you."

"Okay, likewise then."

"So," he said, after an appreciative moment of silence. "Why the sighs, Girl Detective?"

"I think I've been hired to find a missing woman."

"Sure. We do that. But what do you mean, you think?"

"The client hasn't come out and said so, but it's the only thing that makes sense."

I gave him a rundown of the case, and he nodded along, paying attention.

"It sounds to me like you've got a neurotic woman who wants eyes on her most prized possession. What makes you think she wants any more than that?"

"She may not *want* any more than that, but it sounds like there's a big underlying problem. I mean, let's say you have a big scary mole and you go to a doctor to get it removed."

"Oh, you're a doctor now?"

"Come on, Chaz, it's an analogy."

"You know what I got on the SAT?"

"What?"

He smiled expectantly and let out a loud fart. "Okay, proceed."

I rolled my eyes. "So you have this nightmare mole, and you want it gone, but you kind of know there's a good chance something else made the mole pop up in the first place."

"Like cancer."

"Yeah, or whatever. But even if it's just a mole generator, what's the point of just treating the mole? Wouldn't you want to know the underlying cause? Isn't that kind of why you went to the doctor in the first place?"

"Okay, even I can tell this analogy is a mess."

"But you get what I'm saying?"

"I get it, but you're not a doctor, and an endangered baby is more serious in its own right than an unsightly mole."

"Do you remember Rusty Regan and the General? In *The Big Sleep*?"

"You always bring up that book like I didn't read it thirty years ago."

I nodded. "Fair enough."

"Anyway, what about the Rusty general?"

"The General is this rich old man who hires Marlowe to investigate a blackmailer, but from the beginning, Marlowe knows this guy has a missing son-in-law."

"Okay, that sounds familiar."

"Marlowe thinks he's been hired to find Rusty Regan, and the General keeps denying it and denying it, but of course, in the end, that's Marlowe's whole job."

"So you think you're supposed to find this best friend."

"I don't know. Maybe. It seems more like the kind of thing you'd pay money for than stalking a pregnant lady. Pregnant women can't be so hard to stalk on your own. You should see this girl. She is out to here."

"Your client— Does she seem particularly interested in what's happened to this girl?"

"Honestly? No."

"Is she callous?"

"She reads kind of cold, and yeah, maybe callous, but that isn't exactly it. She's interesting. I don't dislike her, but she is off. She has this almost socially feral quality, like she's been caged in her education so long she doesn't know how to deal with people."

"She's an actual doctor, right?"

"Dermatologist."

"Zit zapper?"

"Sure, but do you know how hard it is to become a dermatologist? You have to crush med school for four years, and then get through a three-year residency. She was probably thirty years old before she even got to breathe."

He shrugged. "She's a smarty-pants like you, is that right, Yale-bird?"

"Much smarter than me, probably."

"Don't be so modest. She's just less of a screwup."

I frowned. I'd gone to an expensive prep school and an Ivy League college, and it was true that I'd never dreamt of becoming a PI when I grew up. I was an introverted kid who had no talents other than studying, and my strict mother gave me a narrow, exalted vision of my professional future. Lawyer, doctor, rocket scientist. Something to let her strut a bit around other Korean moms. My little sister Iris had been less of a nerd, and my mom would've been satisfied if she'd become the head designer for Louis Vuitton or Chanel.

None of that quite panned out. Iris killed herself when she was sixteen after a disastrous affair with her history teacher. I was a fresh-man in college, and it was something of a miracle that I finished school at all. I still loved my mom—I never blamed her for what happened, and I was grateful she didn't blame me—but we weren't close anymore. She'd also adjusted her expectations on every cat-egory of my life prospects. When I started working for Chaz, she'd been amazed that I had a job with health insurance. If I'd nab my-self any kind of man, she'd probably shit herself for joy.

Chaz liked to joke that I was slumming it. Both he and Arturo, the other named half of Lindley & Flores, were products of the L.A. Unified School District. I met a lot of Angelenos in college—my school alone sent eight kids to Yale—but not a single one from our city's giant public school system, where a quarter of the kids didn't make it to graduation, let alone a four-year college.

Chaz wasn't a dermatologist, but he was a success story, more or less. He had a bachelor's degree from Glendale Community College, and he worked in IT for many years before he got into private investigation by way of computer forensics. He had a wife and two daughters, and he was one of the happiest people I knew. None of this prevented him from making fun of my expensive education, which I'd used to work as a part-time tutor before Chaz hired me to be his gofer.

"So, this doctor, what makes you think she's looking for the girl?"

"Couple reasons. First, she keeps coming up. Her disappearance is the whole reason Rubina's even worried about her cousin, and I can't seem to untangle one girl from the other."

"And let me guess."

"What?"

"The second reason."

"Sure."

"You think you're marked for the job."

I had to smile. When I'd first met Chaz, I'd thought he was an oaf—he'd been tailing me, and I thought he looked like one of the bumbling stooges who got bumped in detective novels. He was bald and fleshy, and he wore high white socks with white tennis shoes every day. He acted like a textbook corny white American dad, telling bad jokes and embarrassing me at every opportunity. It was easy to forget how smart he was, and his quiet bursts of insight still took me by surprise.

"I've had a good break since my last gnarly case. It just seems like the universe has been a bit nice to me, don't you think?"

"Maybe, but you've been unluckier than most," he said. "We don't catch a lot of homicides in this business."

"I know," I said, "but I have a feeling."

"Yeah, I'm sure you do. Coincidentally, I think you want to go look for this girl."

"Hey, it's not like I'm dying for excitement here. I've had enough of that for a lifetime." He narrowed his eyes at me and I shrugged. "But I guess I can't say I'm not curious."

I googled Nora from my desk. I didn't have her last name, but she was easy enough to find. There weren't too many missing Armenian Noras in the L.A. area.

I found a spate of news articles on her disappearance, dating from almost a month earlier. As I read up, the facts started to sound a bit familiar, and I thought I might have heard about this case on the radio. The story hadn't attracted a lot of national attention, but it wasn't hidden under any rugs, either. I wondered if it would explode if a corpse showed up.

Her name was Nora Mkrtchian. She was a twenty-five-year-old L.A. native, the daughter of Armenian immigrants who'd left the Soviet Union in the late '80s. She ran a Web site called *Who Still Talks*, a popular niche political blog devoted to discussion of the 1915 Armenian genocide. The *L.A. Times* called her "a firebrand Internet activist" with a strong following among young Armenian Americans.

She'd started *Who Still Talks* two years ago, when she was a 1L at Loyola Law School in downtown L.A. When she'd generated a following, she dropped out and devoted herself to the blog, posting several times daily while applying to graduate school for genocide studies.

She was last seen on a Friday night in February, when her roommate stated that Nora had appeared "agitated" before leaving the apartment for what was supposed to be only a few hours. Her car was still missing with her, but foul play was suspected.

If the police had any leads, they were evidently not sharing them with the press, but the political blogosphere was abuzz with speculation. Nora had been the target of some serious online harassment. This had been a constant throughout her blogging career, but it had intensified in the months leading up to her disappearance.

I found a link for her Web site and clicked through. It had a simple design, with a few slight embellishments that showed an effort at departure from the standard blogger template. "Who Still Talks" was printed at the top in a thick, crisp-edged font that suggested hip professionalism, millennial savvy, minimal bullshit. Then, in the middle of the page there was Nora, middle finger extended at the top of her last post. I started reading.

Hey guys, today we're going to talk about me. "But, Nora," you say to your laptop, "Don't we *always* talk about you?" And because I can pretty much hear you, I'll say: Yes, we do, to an extent. This is my blog house run by my blog rules, and in my blog house, we talk about things that are dear to my heart, and as we all know, I am a raging narcissist. You all know what I care about; my screaming Armenian blood, my conflicted feelings on System of a Down. You all might feel like you know me reasonably well, and you know what? You probably do.

But I don't talk about some stuff here. I don't talk about

my love life, my family. I could have four kids for all you guys know. (I don't have four kids.) Believe it or not, I show some restraint. I try not to get too trivial about sharing the day-to-day shit, though you know I #can't #fucking #resist posting pictures of pancakes from time to time. But honestly, I do think about the things in my life that might help or at least entertain other people, and despite all the random junk that gets through the filter, you guys should know that I do have a filter.

Which is why I didn't address the harassment till now.

As some of you have noticed, we've had a few uninvited guests over the last month or so. I don't always respond to comments, but I do try and read them all, and I've seen you guys engaging these shithead trolls. I want to say thank you to everyone who's defended me. At first I thought it would be better if we all just ignored them, as a family, but to be honest it felt good to see you guys stick up for me so I just tried my best to stay out of it and let you all do your good work. But it's gotten to the point where I can't ignore this shit anymore. These people have gotten so fucking noxious that I'm just gonna go ahead and call them out right here.

Here's what happened, for those of you who don't read the comments. (And by the way, I know in general the rule is, Never read the comments, but that hasn't been true of this site until pretty recently. Most *WST* readers are respectful, funny, etc. etc. *mwah mwah mwah*.) Last month, I ran a post on the anti-memorial lawsuit, condemning Thayer White for representing genocide deniers. That got cross-posted on *HuffPo*, and even now, when you google Thayer White, that post comes up. (Suck it, you soulless mercenary motherfuckers.) Thanks to all that attention, I got a few exuberant new readers, who took it upon themselves to plaster my comments sections in straight-up hate speech. It got ugly and personal really fucking quickly. At first I thought they'd get bored after a while, move on to the next hateable woman on the Internet. That didn't happen. It got worse and worse, and it's still escalating. It goes without saying that I get rape threats on the daily. I've actually stopped checking my e-mail because some of this comes straight into my in-box. (This is also why I made my e-mail address private a few weeks back, but once you put that shit on the Internet, I guess it stays accessible. Anyone who had it before would still have it, and could share it further.)

I don't want to go into too much detail, but I will say that I've been threatened in a way that extends out of the Internet. It's been a nightmarish couple of days.

But listen up, you horde of disgusting anonymous cum wads: Enough is enough. I'm coming for you.

The post had been reblogged thousands of times, and there were over eight hundred comments. I checked the dates—the post had gotten a reasonable amount of attention when it was first posted, but it went semi-viral when Nora's disappearance made headlines. I started reading the comments. Most of them were positive wishes from strangers, praying for her safety.

The comments were unmoderated, with no apparent filter, because a large chunk of them was obvious spam. There were several comments in some version of English somehow both wretched and robotic, gushing about hot dates with older men, and friends who were making hundreds of dollars an hour working from home.

I scrolled through quickly, but one brief comment snagged my attention. It was written in all caps, indicating anger and ignorance, and it said, "I HOPE HE RAPED U FIRST."

I felt a visceral stab of disgust. The anonymity of the Internet seemed to bring out the worst in people, who were assholes often enough to begin with. I wondered what kind of mask this commenter presented to the outside world.

With sick curiosity, I scanned through the rest of the comments, my eyes alert for more unrestrained hate. I didn't have to look very hard. About a quarter of the comments were in the same malicious spirit, and it was starting to look like a targeted campaign. There was a lot of name-calling, with particular concern for Nora's perceived unattractiveness and rampant promiscuity. Some commenters lamented not having the chance to rape her. Others promised to kill her if she happened to turn up alive.

All of these comments were met with condemnation and outpours of support for Nora, if she was reading, from first-time visitors to the site, as well as friends from both the Internet and the real world. The positive voices outnumbered the threats and insults, but even just a few of those remarks would have flavored the pot. As it was, the remarks were far from few, and I suspected there was some sort of organized effort to mob the missing girl's Web site. I wondered what kind of person would undertake such a project.

I rooted around her archives to get a sense of Nora and her work. She was the sole writer on *Who Still Talks*, though she interviewed and cross-posted other bloggers regularly. Her posts were frequent, ending abruptly the day of her disappearance. Not every update was serious or even political. The blog had a strong personal bent, with a surprising number of selfies for a Web site with any mainstream credibility. There was also an orange cat that commanded a lot of screen time.

Nora was thin and pretty, with straight, dark hair and large, dark eyes perpetually ringed in black liner and several coats of mascara. She put a lot of evident effort into her appearance. She was in full makeup in almost every picture, and she wore beautiful, expensive-looking clothes, favoring low-cut tops that showed off a rack out of all proportion to the size of her body. There was nothing bashful about this girl.

The Web site wasn't about her, but its writing and content emitted an easy vanity that was slightly off-putting. It would have been downright obnoxious if it weren't also pretty insightful. Even the undisguised narcissism had a strain of womanly defiance, some of which was clearly reactive.

Nora's main focus was on the need for universal recognition of the Armenian genocide, a topic that was still controversial in many parts of the world. She'd started *Who Still Talks* as a passion project to keep her going in law school, but when she attracted thousands of readers, she decided she'd found her calling. She became a powerful voice for Armenian-American youth, particularly in Southern California.

I felt some embarrassment at how little I knew about the genocide, though it was, apparently, a more obscure topic than I would have thought given the scope of atrocity. Since I was hesitant to get my facts from a blog, even one as established as Nora's, I decided to go to my number-one source for everything from dog breeds to the lives of serial killers—the often reliable Wikipedia.

The facts of the genocide made my stomach turn. The death toll was almost inconceivable, as was the pure evil of a regime set on eradicating an entire religious and ethnic minority. The genocide had apparently been the answer to an "Armenian Question"—a question of this Christian minority's place in early-twentieth-century Turkey. A ruthless answer, one that afforded human life all the respect due to dust bunnies. The genocide was minutely organized and executed with devastating cold-blooded efficacy. The Turkish government even tried to collect on life insurance policies for the Armenians it had exterminated, on the assumption that their heirs were dead, too.

By the time I emerged from this Internet wormhole, it was two o'clock and I hadn't eaten lunch. I also hadn't heard from Rubina, so I went for a sandwich and called her on her cell phone.

"Is there something wrong?" she asked.

It struck me that Rubina was a woman who lived in constant expectation of bad news.

"No," I said. "Sorry, I'm at the office. I've just been doing some research."

"What kind of research?"

I hesitated. "You won't be charged for my time or anything. I had a slow morning and was waiting to hear from you."

"Does it relate to me?"

"Sort of," I said. "I was just reading about Nora, and I found her Web site."

"Oh." There was a startled flutter to her tone. "We are all terribly worried about her."

"Do you know where the police are on her disappearance?"

"I don't know much more than what's in the papers," she said neutrally. "Are you very interested?"

I bit my lip. "I'm concerned," I said. "It seems like she has a lot of enemies."

"Yes, she does. She's an attention-seeker and a rabble-rouser. It's only natural that some people don't take to her."

"Do you think she's"—I paused, looking for the most delicate word—"alive?"

"I don't know. I'd like to think so, but she has been missing for a long time."

"Do you know that she was the victim of an online harassment campaign? These—"

"I know about that," she interrupted. "You're beginning to sound a bit like Lusig."

I colored at the admonishment. "I'm sorry. It's hard not to be interested in this kind of thing."

"That's okay, but let's keep things clear. Whatever happened to Nora has no bearing on me or my baby unless Lusig lets it claim her.

I've hired you so I can make sure that doesn't happen. That's all. Do we understand each other?"

"You mean, do I understand you."

"Excuse me?"

"You asked if we understood each other, but I haven't asked you for anything. If you're going to reprimand me, just reprimand me. No need for the royal 'we.'"

"I'm sorry. I've been told I can be condescending, but that is not my intention."

"No problem," I said. "And yes, of course I understand. I am committed to your case, and I won't do anything that could impair my ability to work for you."

"Thank you."

"So what's next?"

"I'm concerned about her behavior last night. I want to know if it's part of a broader pattern. Is there a way that I can put Lusig under full surveillance?"

"Depends what you mean by 'full.' Are we talking 24/7, Big Brother Is Always Watching You surveillance?"

She forced a small laugh. "Is that available?"

"No," I said. "We don't have God powers."

"What is available?"

"I can keep a steady tail on her within reasonable bounds. I need to sleep, eat—well you're a doctor, so you know these things."

"Can I hire two of you?"

"We're a small outfit, just three investigators. I can ask Mr. Lindley and Mr. Flores to fill in some gaps, but I think it would be hard to keep two of us on this one case at all times. That being said, I won't hold it against you if you want to reach out to a bigger outfit. Obviously, anything you've told me I keep in confidence, and that goes for the fact that you even walked into my office."

"No," she said quickly. "Believe it or not, it was difficult for me to talk to you in the first place. I'd rather proceed with whatever you can provide, as long as that's moderately comprehensive."

"Of course. If you want, I can even see about getting a GPS tracker on her car."

"That won't be necessary."

I could tell by her breathing that she had something to add. "It won't?" I prompted.

"I've already attached one."

"Oh." I laughed. "You're prepared. Are you sure you even need me?"

"I don't care particularly where she goes. It's what she's doing that concerns me."

"It sounds like you haven't bugged her phone or apartment. I wonder what's stopping you."

I must have sounded snider than intended, because she dropped her voice to a quiet, sheepish tenor. "You must think I'm mentally unstable," she said.

"No, sorry, not at all. Didn't mean for it to come across like that."

It was true enough that I thought she was extreme, but I'd never had a client who wasn't a bit more willing to indulge paranoia than the average goon on the street. In any case, I took their money and let them use me to probe, invade, spy, whatever. Their paranoia was my cash cow.

"It's very important to me that Lusig take care of her body. I cannot have her acting out where I can't see her. It won't do." She sighed. "However, there are certain barriers I can't cross—that is, not directly."

"Are you worried that Lusig would find out?"

"Yes, there is always that chance, though I try not to worry excessively about things that might never happen." She paused, perhaps catching the irony. "But even if I knew Lusig would never find out, I would feel guilty and uncomfortable about spying on her with my own eyes and ears."

"Which is why you contacted a mercenary." I smiled. I'd spent years romanticizing the literary private detective, but now I wore the badge, and I knew more or less what I was.

"Yes. Do you understand my position? I think all this is quite necessary, but I have no intention of betraying Lusig's trust where I can avoid doing so. If you overhear her talking about me, or my husband, for example, you don't have to tell us that. I only need information pertaining to her obligation to me."

"Sure."

"Song," she said, pronouncing it slowly. "Is that a Korean name?"

"Yeah. So is Juniper."

"Oh, how so?"

"Sorry, I was kidding. Though I guess only an immigrant would name her kid that. Anyway, what about it?"

"I don't know how things are in your culture, but Armenians are very family-oriented."

"Koreans, too." I didn't mention that my own family was all but entirely disintegrated.

"Of course, no one would describe her culture as non-family-oriented, but the standard American model is to put the individual first, and that is not the case for Armenians. Do you know what I mean?"

"Yeah, it's an immigrant thing."

"Yes, exactly. In our family, at least, the lines that divide us are very fluid. And within our family? Lusig and I are bonded as strong as sisters."

I knew the feeling of being lied to by a sister, of wanting to know when I wasn't being told.

"Now, add to that that Lusig and I are both mothers to the same child. I feel that she would forgive me a decent level of intrusion." She paused, and when I didn't insert my agreement, continued. "Not that I need to defend myself, of course. I just don't like to be thought of as unpleasant."

"Don't worry, Rubina. I don't judge my clients."

This wasn't strictly true—most of my clients weren't great people, and I was generally aware of their various flaws. It was part of my job to account for them, after all. But one thing Philip Marlowe and Sam Spade let you forget was that private investigation was a service job. The renegade PI was an interesting figure, but it was no accident that Marlowe never made any money. I was beholden to my clients, not just for services rendered, but for a baseline level of courtesy. I wasn't obsequious, but I was too old to take pride in being an asshole.

So while I couldn't avoid forming general impressions on my clients, I maintained a fiction of impartiality, like the kindergarten teacher who loves all her students equally. My judgments were compartmentalized to the point where they couldn't offend.

"The GPS tracker, have you been using it?"

"Lightly," she said. "I was thinking it would be a good supplement to your service."

"Is it a real-time tracker?"

"Yes."

"Do you want to give me access to that?"

"That would be fine."

"Alternatively, we can use the tracker to cut down on my hours. Not that I wouldn't love to bill you for time spent reading a novel outside of her apartment, but maybe you don't want to pay me when I'm not going to see anything."

She was silent for a few seconds, and I worried she thought I was being lazy.

"I guess that isn't exactly 24/7," I said. "But think about it. She's not trying to sneak around. I don't think she'll be beating on your baby when she's alone in her apartment."

"Yes, you're probably right. I suppose I was overzealous."

"How about this? We can start with some spot surveillance. If she's going anywhere of interest, I'll make sure to follow. Where does she live, by the way?"

"Koreatown."

"Close to the office," I said. "Ah, is that why you picked us?"

"That is how I found you, yes."

"Convenient for me."

She gave me an address and detailed notes about Lusig's schedule, like an anxious parent instructing a new sitter. I was glad I wouldn't have to change any diapers.

We hung up with the understanding that I'd check in at regular intervals, and I went back into my idle Internet research, just in case.

Three

❦

I spent the next few days chasing after Lusig. I tried to monitor her tracker, but I was never as fast as Rubina, who texted me every time Lusig's car woke up. I trailed her to the grocery store, watched her eat frozen yogurt and pick up Chinese takeout. She seemed to stay put most of the time, behaving like a woman encumbered with an eight-month-old fetus. If she had any social interaction, it didn't involve stepping outside—Rubina was pretty light on the trigger, so I gathered her cousin didn't leave the house much at all.

I stayed in the office during business hours, keeping my eye on my phone. Chaz called it the baby monitor.

At the end of my second morning spent reading the Internet at the office, Chaz pulled a chair up to my desk. "Are you disappointed?" he asked with a wink.

"What?"

"It's been three whole days and you're still not chasing a murderer."

"No, Boss, I'm not disappointed."

He pulled his chair up next to me and reached his hands over my keyboard, fingers wiggling and hovering.

"Mind if I take a look at your browser history?"

"What?" I laughed. "Yeah, I mind."

"Too bad. This is part of your hazing."

Chaz and Arturo had voted to make me a partner just over a month earlier. I'd been working for them for over a year and had built myself something of a profile, in part due to my involvement in a Hollywood murder scandal—long story. Chaz made the announcement with a lot of fanfare, and he decided that as a "newly made guy" I'd be subject to a certain amount of hazing. He'd gotten the idea from *The Sopranos*, and he was a regular Paulie Walnuts about it, corny and annoying, though to be fair, toothlessly respectful and harmless. I'd had to buy beers exactly once, and Chaz had made an extra show of looking over my shoulder while I worked. Since I relied on him for advice anyway, there was no real change except in the mock bully face he made when he asked me questions. I knew he'd back off if I asserted my need for privacy, but in this case, I didn't have much on my browser history to hide. I rolled my eyes and scooted over.

He scrolled through, chuckling and shaking his head. "Let me guess. The missing girl, is her name Nora Mkrtchian?"

I'd read every article on her disappearance I could find, and looking at the browser history, it looked like there were a lot of them. I shrugged—I was letting him make his point, but I didn't have to help.

"And have you always been so interested in the Armenian genocide?"

"Yeah, yeah, I know what you're getting at. But come on. It's a news story, and it's legitimately interesting. And the genocide, Jesus. I'm ashamed I knew so little about it before."

"Yeah, what did they teach you in school anyway?"

"Very little, apparently. And they about skipped this genocide altogether. I mean how much do you know about it?"

He crossed his arms. "I've heard the words 'Armenian' and 'genocide' together before, but that's about it. Long time ago?"

"Hundred years this year. So yeah, history, but not ancient history. World War I. Less than thirty years before the Holocaust, and no one's in danger of forgetting that one."

"Six million people died in the Holocaust."

"A million Armenians died in the genocide. The word 'genocide' was coined to describe it."

He whistled.

"What's crazy is that there are tons of people who deny that it was a genocide at all."

"I'm guessing there's a body count that needs explaining."

"Oh yeah. I mean some of these accounts, Chaz . . . there were bodies lining the streets, sometimes stacks of them. There were definitely plenty of bodies." I shook my head. I'd seen a few corpses, but it was hard to imagine evil and destruction on such a large scale. "The official Turkish position is that it wasn't ethnic cleansing, it was just a byproduct of World War I. Basically, 'It was a confusing time for everyone.' It's all bullshit though. Armenians were an annoying Christian minority under Muslim rule, and they were systematically targeted."

Chaz nodded appreciatively. "You're pretty worked up, huh?"

"It's just so ludicrous that the status of the genocide is controversial a hundred years later. I mean I know there are Holocaust deniers, but everyone knows they're more or less crazy people who think the president is hiding Martians in the White House dungeon." I sighed.

"I have yet to see proof that he isn't."

"Har har," I said. "Anyway, as you can see, this shit is interesting in its own right. It's not all about Nora Mkrtchian."

"Not all, sure. Fifty percent?"

I smiled. "Maybe thirty. Doesn't hurt to be prepared."

Rubina called me on Friday morning to tell me she'd be spending the better part of the day with Lusig, and that I was free to do what

I pleased until further notice. Further notice came early Friday afternoon.

"Sorry," Rubina said quickly when I picked up the phone. "I did mean it when I called you earlier. I was supposed to pick Lusig up for her doctor's appointment, but she texted me two hours ago to say she didn't need a ride, and now I'm in the lobby waiting for her, and she is not picking up her phone."

"Do you know where she is?"

"I know her location. I don't know what's there, and I don't know what she is doing."

Dark images flashed through my head—her dark blood, her dead eyes, her studded ear bent against cold concrete. I had a morbid streak dating back to my childhood, well before I had any reason to have one. I knew from experience, now, that imagining the worst wasn't always a safeguard against its realization.

Still, I kept my paranoia to myself. Rubina didn't need egging on.

"Where?" I asked.

"Sixth and Grand, downtown."

"I'll track her car. I don't think that'll be a problem. But my guess is she'll be really hard to find from there. Unless you have some idea where she could be running around?"

"Try the library. Isn't that right there?"

"Sure," I said. "I just want to manage your expectations here. Downtown is big. It's not the kind of place where you park right in front of wherever you're going."

"Understood. Please hurry."

I drove straight down Sixth and started looking for a lot as I approached Grand. There were two aboveground lots on the block, for $10 and $15, and a driveway to an underground garage. I drove as slowly as I could, looking for Lusig's car. I pulled into the $10 lot—I didn't see why any sane person would choose the pricier lot on the same intersection.

Lusig drove a black Prius, not terribly distinctive unless you happened to have her license plate memorized, which I did. I found her car in the northeastern corner of the lot, parked in plain view. It was empty, but I hadn't expected any different.

She was parked as close as possible to the library, within that lot. I stared up the back stairs climbing up into the skyline, and decided to park and follow Rubina's hunch.

The Central Library was one of my favorite buildings in Los Angeles. I'd fallen in love with it as a sophomore in high school, when I spent a weekend inside doing research for a history term paper. It was a beautiful, imposing 1920s building, with a central tower topped with a mosaic pyramid that looked out like a watchful eye. At some point it must have been one of the taller buildings downtown, but nowadays it was a short one, standing in the shadow of the US Bank Tower, the tallest skyscraper west of the Mississippi.

The library was a favorite among the downtown work crowd, as well as bookworms and the numerous homeless who made do within a mile radius of the building. It was a big, gorgeous space, with a wide atrium strung with colorful chandeliers. Escalators ran up and down multiple stories, each one crammed with stacks and stacks of fragrant books. I'd gotten stuck in those stacks, seated on the carpet with cracked spines fanned out around me, losing hours without missing them in the least.

Even if Lusig were in the building, it could take all day to find her. It was possible, too, that she wasn't there at all. Still, I had to give it my best shot.

Rubina must have had a reason for sending me to the library, and I wondered what she thought might make her cousin want to study.

I looked for her in the news section, where newspapers and magazines hung from bamboo dowels. When she wasn't there, I remembered she was an adult woman in the twenty-first century with probable access to affordable Internet—she was unlikely to get her news from a public library, especially not one miles from her apartment.

I sat down at a computer and opened up the library catalog. If Lusig was choosing research over a doctor's appointment, it had to be related to Nora. I ran a few searches and found the call number for the Armenian genocide.

I took the escalators to the history floor and found the corresponding aisle. There was no one there—it had been a long shot. Then again, I wasn't sure what Rubina expected when she gave me the intersection of a downtown parking lot. I could follow up on hunches, but there wasn't much more I could do.

I found the call number anyway—956 for Armenia in general, 956.6 for the genocide. It had been a long time since I'd browsed these shelves, and once I had a call number in hand I couldn't not track it down.

The aisle was rich with the smell of aging paper. Most of the volumes were old and dusty, with that soft binding particular to long-standing libraries. Several were newer hardcovers, with clear plastic jackets to keep them in good condition. I scanned the titles and picked three books to check out and read at home.

I did a walk-through of the rest of the library, but Lusig was nowhere in sight. I fought down a strange feeling of disappointment, even of mild surprise. It was unpleasant to remember that decent intuition and random strokes of luck weren't quite enough to find everything I wanted.

I exited the library on the northern side, where business casual people carried take-out bags and iPhones, walking on straight trajectories with averted eyes. I looked up at the US Bank Tower, at Bunker Hill and the rest of commercial downtown—I couldn't count the buildings, let alone the offices, the rooms, the people, people, people. Lusig could be anywhere, doing anything at all.

I walked back to my car feeling a little deflated. Lusig's car was still there, and I'd at least be able to catch her return. I called Rubina.

"No luck," I said. "You haven't heard from her?"

"She's supposedly stuck in traffic, coming from lunch on the Westside."

I looked at Lusig's car and winced. A lot of my clients hired me to spy on people with things to hide. Sometimes the marks were squeaky clean, but when they weren't, there was always a definable oh-shit moment when they were caught in a lie. "Oh," I muttered. "Shit."

"She is lying to me," Rubina said quietly. "I can't believe it."

Despite her persistent suspicions and active mistrust of her cousin, there was genuine surprise in her voice.

"What would you like me to do?"

"Wait for her," she said. "Wait for her to come back, then call me."

"Are you still at the doctor's office?"

"Yes, but I will go home shortly. There is no point in waiting when the appointment has been given up."

She hung up, and I felt the force of her anger and irritation. If I were Lusig, I would have been very scared.

I sat in my car and lit a cigarette, but I knew I wouldn't have to wait long. If Lusig was supposed to be caught in traffic, she'd have to leave downtown within half an hour unless she was bold enough to invent a crazy fatal accident that shut down the 10, and any idiot with Internet access could prove her a liar with a few clicks. She might not suspect her cousin of sticking a GPS tracker and a private investigator on her car, but if she had any insight at all, she'd have to know Rubina was high-strung enough to ask questions when Lusig had missed an OB/GYN appointment.

I picked up one of the books and opened it up to the title page. It took a few seconds for me to process what I was seeing—tucked snug against the inner spine was a business card with Nora Mkrtchian's name on it.

The card was bright and a little bit gaudy, with three horizontal stripes in red, blue, and mustard yellow. The Armenian flag, if I had to guess. *Who Still Talks* was emblazoned over the red stripe in black, and Nora's name, URL, and e-mail address were printed in the yellow. I picked up the other two books and found identical cards wedged in their first pages. I was fairly confident I'd find similar cards tucked into every volume under the same call number. It would have been clever marketing if enough people would end up seeing it.

My head was buzzing with the enormity of this coincidence but I had a hard time extracting any meaning. I shook my head and started reading instead.

The genocide was consuming my imagination. A million people. A third of a race. My mind skimmed around the edges of these figures, and their reality in flesh, in life, flickered in lurid flashes. It didn't seem possible, and each link in the chain that led to it came off sounding over the top and absurd. Yet there was the death toll—there was nothing more ridiculous than that, but that was very real. Even the genocide deniers didn't contest that many, many Armenians had died, well before their times. And here was Nora Mkrtchian, her name wedged firmly in their histories.

One cigarette and several pages later, Lusig came into my field of vision. I'd been keeping an eye out for her approach, but she'd gotten within signal distance of her car without drawing my attention. She was coming from the direction of the library, walking slowly on a pair of low professional heels. The heels didn't square with the image I had of Lusig, but they went with what she was wearing. I hadn't noticed her because she looked like a different person entirely. Instead of the big army jacket, she had on a black blazer, black slacks, and a pastel blouse that gave her pregnant belly a demure definition. Her hair was washed and neatly styled, and the only piercings she wore hung from the centers of her earlobes.

She teetered to the Prius and climbed into the backseat with apparent effort. Her eyes darted all around her, scanning her surroundings with furtive curiosity. I watched her without staring, afraid of making eye contact. I wondered what she could possibly be doing.

A few seconds later, she shrugged and lowered herself further into the seat, and she seemed to squirm and struggle against herself.

She was changing. Her movements had the awkward quality of getting in and out of pants without exposing underwear. When she straightened back up she pulled a hooded sweatshirt over her fancy blouse and got back out of the car. I was right—now she was wearing jeans and ratty loafers that slipped off her heels when she walked. She maneuvered herself back in the car, this time in the driver's seat.

She flipped down the mirror, then mussed up her hair and reattached her piercings.

It was a strange transformation to witness, from order to calculated dishevelment. It was even shady enough to justify Rubina's vague suspicions.

What was she doing that had to be done in a suit and heels? She'd come from the direction of the library, but I doubted she was spending her afternoon reading in her pregnant professional finest. She must have had business above Fifth, maybe in one of the office towers on Bunker Hill. Whatever it was, she meant to hide it from her cousin.

She was making a phone call now, and I called Rubina and got a busy signal. I started my car and drove it into the cul-de-sac between Sixth and the library, where I could wait for Lusig to come out. Her car nosed out of the lot, and I followed it down Hope, keeping a safe distance.

Rubina called almost as soon as I'd started moving.

"Looks like you heard from her," I said.

"Yes. Did you see her?"

"I see her right now. She just left the parking lot."

"Do you have anything to report?"

"She was wearing a suit," I said. "She changed when she got back to her car."

"A suit?" she asked with genuine puzzlement.

"Any idea as to what she might have dressed up for? I'm guessing she wasn't going on a job interview."

"I haven't the slightest clue."

"What did she say to you when she called?"

"She said she would be at the doctor's in ten minutes. I told her I was on my way home, and that she could forget about the appointment. She apologized."

"Sincerely?"

"Yes. She did seem very sorry."

"So, what now?"

"I've asked her to come to my house."

"She's going there now?"

"Yes. And I would like for you to come as well."

I felt my eyes widen. "Are you sure?"

"Yes," she said. "I would like to confront her."

I pictured the jagged family scene and wanted to object. "With me there?"

"You can say no," she said.

"I'm aware."

"But I would like to have you there. Please."

There was no supplication in her voice, only the neutral tone of a stated preference. I found it difficult to resist.

"Sure," I said. "Should I follow her?"

"No. I would like you to beat her here if possible."

She gave me an address in Glendale, and I sped ahead of Lusig.

Glendale was technically its own city, a separate entity from neighboring Los Angeles, though surrounded on almost all sides. It was heavily Armenian, even more so than Little Armenia, which was smaller and less defined, sharing most of its space with Thai Town. It wasn't far from where I lived, but I rarely ventured that way unless I had a pressing need to visit a Nordstrom Rack or an Ikea.

Rubina's place was a mansion in the hills, a beautiful white house with a perfect lawn trimmed with perfect flowers. I didn't know too much about real estate, but I guessed this house cost a few bucks more than my apartment. I parked and stared at it for a few seconds before plugging the address into Zillow. A cool two million, sold two years earlier. Someone here had more than young doctor money, or at least ready access to generous parents.

I rang the doorbell and Rubina let me in within two seconds. She was wearing a smart, conservative gray wool dress with low black heels. She could have been a politician's housewife.

"Nice place," I said. "You could raise five kids in here."

"One will do for now."

I gave her a tight smile and cracked my knuckles. The entryway echoed with the pop of my bones.

She wrinkled her nose and sniffed. "You've been smoking."

"I didn't know meeting Lusig was part of the plan."

I flapped my shirt to air it out, and she frowned. "Well, come in," she said. "I'll make us coffee."

She led me into an immaculate kitchen, where she bade me sit in a breakfast nook that was too new and spotless to be quite cozy. She stepped across cold tile to a massive chrome-colored espresso maker, then pressed a button and brought the sleeping beast to life. Its groan displaced the silence in the room.

"Milk? Sugar?"

"Black's fine," I said. "Thanks."

She sat across from me and folded her arms on the table, keeping her back straight.

"So," I ventured. "What's the plan here?"

"I'm going to come clean, then I will ask her where she went."

"Are you sure this isn't a private conversation?"

"Are you not a *private* investigator?" She forced a smile and I saw that this was as close as Rubina ever came to cracking a joke.

I dropped that line of inquiry. "So I just sit here and what, like, testify when called?"

"Yes," she said. "Essentially."

I sipped at my coffee. It was unusually good, and it gave me something to do.

I was almost relieved when the doorbell rang and Rubina sprang up to answer it. I geared myself for an unpleasant scene, making sure there was enough coffee left to fill a few pauses.

"Where have you been?" Rubina's voice traveled loudly from doorway to kitchen.

"I told you," said Lusig. "I was in Marina del Rey."

"What for?"

"Lunch. It ran long, and then there was terrible traffic."

"Who with?"

"Derek. I don't think you know him."

"Where'd you eat?"

"We had burgers. What is this?" Lusig's tone was annoyed now, even righteously petulant. If Rubina didn't have proof her cousin was lying, Lusig's tack might have worked. "Why are you interrogating me about my lunch? Lay off."

"You missed the appointment. I have a right to know why."

"I told you why, and I said I was sorry. Now will you get off my back? I have my own life. I am literally just doing you a favor and that gives you permission to be on my ass all the time?"

"We had a doctor's appointment!" Rubina was shouting now. "And thank you, by the way, for reminding me of your favor. As if I *wanted* to leave this to you. As if there were any chance I wouldn't be happier carrying my own baby to the doctor."

Lusig was silent.

"Please don't lie to me," Rubina said, in a calmer tone of voice. "Where were you?"

"I was getting lunch with Derek," she said, enunciating each word.

"Come here."

"Hey, ow!"

I looked up and saw Rubina march in, dragging Lusig behind her by the wrist.

"I know you're lying to me," she said.

A strange pallor came into Lusig's complexion, and I could see it turn into a shade of recognition, an acceptance of defeat. "How?"

"I didn't trust you, so I've been tracking you."

"What does that mean?"

"I put a GPS device on your car."

Lusig's eyes widened, and she started to say something before breaking into a loud, indignant laugh. "What? Are you serious?"

"Yes, I'm serious. And I know you were in downtown half an hour ago. You lied to me."

But Rubina had given up her advantage. I could see the emotions running across Lusig's face—if there was any contrition there, it was drowned out by betrayal and fury.

"You *spied* on me. That's crazy."

"I was right to spy on you. You're hiding something from me."

"I'm entitled to live my life however I see fit."

"You have no right to run around town endangering my baby. Now, tell me. What were you doing?"

Lusig shook her head in disgust, and she looked at me, registering my presence for the first time. "Who's this?" she asked with a sneer.

"She's my friend. I asked her to be here."

"You don't have friends," she said coldly. "What is she, some kind of intervention expert? This is bullshit."

I winced. My sister had been dead for years, and I'd almost forgotten the tone of open cruelty that entered certain familial disagreements—the abandonment of restraint that results from assured forgiveness, the bitter truths spoken in anger, shot with unerring aim. I recognized it immediately.

I took a long sip of my coffee and cracked my thumbs.

"Hi," I said, getting up, when it was clear Rubina wasn't about to introduce me. "I'm Juniper Song."

"And *what* are you, Juniper Song?"

I smiled. "Korean?"

"Not what I meant." She colored. She had white liberal written all over her, and I'd knocked her off-kilter.

"Rubina? It's your move."

"She's been following you," Rubina said with a light sigh. "For me."

I raised my hand in a brief wave. "I'm a private investigator."

Lusig turned white, then red with anger. "You're a *what?*"

"You know, like a detective?"

She turned to Rubina with a vicious stare. "You care so much about this fucking baby? How about sparing me the emotional stress of an ambush?"

Rubina let out a quiet panicked sound that might have been the compression of a shriek. She pulled out the chair across from me and commanded, "Sit down."

I half-expected Lusig to stand until fainting to make a point, but she sat.

"So," she said, looking at me. "You're a professional snoop, huh?"

I shrugged. "That's more or less accurate."

"You feel good about yourself?"

"I sleep okay. How about you?"

"I sleep like shit, what do you think? I'm up to my throat in baby."

"Lusig," Rubina interjected. "Stop being a snot."

I smiled. There was something humanizing in this whole exchange, and I realized Rubina was a different person with Lusig in the room. She couldn't manage to be formal, and her emotions, so skillfully checked on the phone with me, were ranging around in a way that was downright messy.

Lusig took a deep breath, and I saw for the first time that she wasn't much more than an exhausted pregnant woman. "You had no right to spy on me, Ruby."

"I did what I had to do."

They spoke in reasonable tones for a few minutes, before anger reentered the conversation. I sat with my coffee while their argument ebbed and flowed, retreading the same hurt dignities, the same defenses. By the time they noticed me again, I was pretending to sip from an empty cup.

"You have to tell me what you were doing," Rubina said. "Song saw you get in your car downtown."

The mention of my name wrenched me back into the conversation, and I nodded attentively.

Lusig shrugged, her upper lip sulky.

"Take your sweatshirt off," Rubina said.

Lusig laughed. "Why?"

"I saw that you changed," I put in. I didn't feel like listening to a five-minute fight about her sweatshirt. "You were wearing a suit. You're still wearing that blouse."

"You saw that I changed? You mean you watched me change."

"Sure," I said. "I watched you change in a public parking lot. For my own pervy gratification."

She rolled her eyes. "Whatever."

"Tell me what you were doing," Rubina said again.

Lusig sat in sour silence for a full minute.

"I have a guess," I said.

"Please." Rubina was trying to recuperate her formal tone.

"She was looking for Nora."

Lusig's eyes met mine at the mention of her friend's name.

"Downtown?" Rubina asked, glancing from me to her cousin. "Why would she be downtown?"

"Not like, hiding in a library carrel. I mean *looking* for her, trying to track her down. Sort of like what I do. Am I right?"

Lusig was silent, but she bit her lip in an expression that looked acquiescent.

"Lu?" Rubina nudged with a suggestion of gentleness.

"Okay," Lusig said. "I've been looking for her."

Anger spread across Rubina's face. "You're eight months pregnant! You shouldn't even be lifting heavy objects, and you're running around town, piling on physical and mental stress?"

"This is why I didn't want to tell you. I'm being safe, okay? I'm not actually running, and I'm definitely not lifting any heavy objects. Plus, you want to talk about mental stress? My best friend has been missing for a month. Have you maybe thought that this is how I'm dealing with that?"

Her speech touched and chilled me. I'd started my career as an amateur sleuth, wrapped up in the problems of people I loved. Those people were all dead or dead to me now, and I knew firsthand that I'd taken beatings in search of bad truths.

"I have thought about it. I've thought about it constantly, Lu, of course I have. Which is why I have a proposal," Rubina said. "For both of you."

I raised an eyebrow.

"Lu, you can't keep doing this to yourself. It's too hard on you, and it's unfair to me." Lusig started to object again and Rubina stopped her. "Just hear me out. I just told you, didn't I? Song here is a private investigator."

My heart rate jumped. I realized I'd been sitting there, quietly, waiting for this.

"I remember. What's your point?"

Rubina widened her eyes and slumped her shoulders in mild exasperation. "I'm willing to hire her to find Nora."

Something like ecstasy coursed through my body, a strong and immediate relief from a tension that had built up inside me for days.

"The police haven't been able to find her. Why would she?"

"And why would you?" Rubina retorted.

"Because I give a shit and no one else seems to."

"What a terrible thing to say. We're *all* worried about Nora."

"Who's we all? The Armenian collective? They can take kebabs to Mrs. Mkrtchian all day, but it won't do anything to help Nora."

"I'm telling you I care. I want her found. I just don't think you have to be the one to find her. You're eight months pregnant, Lu, and the baby you're endangering isn't even your own."

"Jesus, I'm well aware of how pregnant I am. And like I said, I'm not endangering anyone's baby."

"Please. For my peace of mind. Isn't that worth anything to you?"

Lusig bit her upper lip as if to seal it shut.

"I know what that's like," I cut in.

"What are you talking about?"

"To lose someone and need answers. I can't tell you how many people I've lost."

"What do you mean, 'lost'?"

I hesitated. There was no reason to call attention to the specter of murder when there was no body to confirm the worst. "I wasn't always a PI. I only got my license after I threw myself into something that turned out to be a case. A really personal, debilitating case. So I speak from experience when I say it's not worth it. You should let me handle it. I'll listen to whatever you need to say to me, and I'll keep you posted. Rubina, does this sound okay to you?"

"I don't expect Lusig to forget Nora is out there. I only want her out of harm's way."

I nodded. "Lusig?"

The sound of an engine floated into the kitchen, followed by the rolling rumble of a garage door opening. Rubina and Lusig grew visibly attentive.

"Someone coming home?" I asked.

"That'll be Van," said Rubina. "My husband."

"Does he know about all this?" Lusig swirled her index finger in a way that indicated something distasteful that encompassed my presence.

Rubina opened her mouth, then looked down with a wry smile I hadn't seen on her before. "I was going to tell him eventually. This day didn't go exactly as I'd planned."

She looked up again and met Lusig's disbelieving eye, and after a tense moment, the two cousins broke down laughing.

"Oh, shit, Ruby," said Lusig with a mirthful sigh.

"Honey? Is somebody here?" They fell silent under the disruptive call of this masculine voice, directly followed by the entrance of a man.

Van Gasparian was in his late thirties or early forties, with the tired expression of an older man. He kept his black hair short, but I could see it was sparse and speckled with gray. He was tall and wiry, about six-foot-one, even with bad posture. He had dark eyes, dark brows, and a dark complexion, and in spite of evident wear and tear, he was compelling, if not decidedly attractive. I wondered if my assessment was influenced by the knowledge that he operated on brains for a living—I was raised by a Korean immigrant, after all.

His eyes found Lusig and widened in startled surprise, before turning to me with some puzzlement. "What's going on here?" he asked.

"Hi," I said, in my second awkward first encounter of the hour. "Juniper Song. You must be Mr. Gasparian."

"Doctor," he said.

I smiled. "Sorry, my mistake, Dr. Gasparian."

"It's all right. Reflexive, I suppose. It's just that 'Mr.' is inaccurate. Anyway, how do you know my wife and cousin?"

I looked at Rubina. I felt like the voyeuristic producer of some soapy reality show.

"I'm hiring Song to find Nora," she said. "For the safety of our child, Van."

Van blinked at his wife, and his face twisted into an incredulous smile. "You're what?"

"She's a private detective. She's been very devoted so far."

"Let's talk upstairs," he said. "Nice to meet you," he added curtly, glancing back at me. Then he turned around and left the kitchen.

Rubina followed him, leaving me and Lusig sitting at the table. I decided I'd help myself to more coffee.

I walked to the machine and asked, across the kitchen, "Do you want any?"

"No thanks." She scowled. "No caffeine."

"Right." I smiled tightly and walked slowly back to my seat.

She watched me intently while I drank, trying not to avert my eyes. It was another minute before she spoke.

"So you think you can find her, huh?"

"I can't make any promises," I said. "I can't say I'm smarter than the entire LAPD."

"I sure hope you are. They're a bunch of fucking losers."

I shrugged. I didn't particularly care for the police. Every month it seemed like a cop was Tasering, or pepper-spraying, or raping someone or another. They were definitely frisking minorities every day, sometimes killing them for nothing. But the one police officer I'd ever really dealt with seemed decent enough, and was definitely sharp enough to inspire some confidence. I made a note to call her later, though I doubted she'd want to hear from me.

"What I can tell you is that I'll stick to the case and it'll eat me alive if I can't get to the end of it. I'll give it every ounce of my attention. No cop can do that. And honestly, no pregnant woman should."

She grimaced. "Just so you know, I do care about this kid. Ruby's like a sister to me. Pain in my ass, but I do love her. I wouldn't endanger her baby. I'm not a monster."

"You don't have to be a monster to underestimate your limitations."

"I know my limitations fine, thanks."

I shook my head. "Take it from someone who's lived a bit past where you are. You have no idea what this shit can do to you."

"What are you, like five minutes older than me?"

"I've been down more roads. Look, your best friend is missing. That is fucking awful, and I'm sure you think you're suffering as much as humanly possible. Want to know what happened to my best friend?"

"What?"

"He was murdered. In cold blood. Trying to help me."

"Jesus."

"And I needed to know who did it. That's kind of how I got into this job."

"So what happened?"

"I found out."

"Was it satisfying?"

"Yeah, in a way, but it didn't bring him back. What it did do, is it almost got me killed."

"How did it almost get you killed?"

I smirked. "I got kidnapped at gunpoint, so there's one way. And then instead of waiting around to get clipped, I forced a car crash. I was wrecked, but you should've seen the other guy."

"What happened to him?"

"I stilettoed him in the nuts to get him to lose control, and then the crash kind of brained him. He survived, but not really. He'll never miss his nuts."

She stared at me and blinked twice. "If you're trying to impress me, I guess I'm impressed."

"Not the point," I said. "What I'm telling you is that if I'd been pregnant while looking for answers, that baby would've left me like a log going over a waterfall."

"You went after a murderer."

I nodded. "That's true. I knew he was dangerous. But honestly, Lusig, what are you looking for here? Do you think it's likely that Nora is just on a secret vacation?"

She closed her eyes tight. "I don't know."

"As long as she's out there, she could be alive. But we have to ac-knowledge that she could be dead, or at the very least, in pretty grave danger."

A bright tear seeped out of her left eye and rested, without falling, at its corner. "I want to find out she's okay."

"You can't control the outcome, Lusig. And you can't go after it prepared for nothing but the best-case scenario."

She looked up at me again, and I hoped my expression was as earnest as I felt.

"Let me help," I said.

The sound of a door opening reached us from upstairs. Whatever argument had taken place behind those doors had been resolved, for now, anyway. Rubina came down alone, looking tired but resolute.

"You're hired," she said to me. "On one condition."

I crossed my arms. "Yes?"

"Not for you, for Lusig."

Lusig crossed her arms. "What now?"

"You have one more month until delivery. That's no time at all, but it's crucial to my baby's health and safety."

"And?"

"I want you to live here," she said. "Until that baby is born, I don't want you out of my sight."

Lusig looked like she'd been slapped, and for a second, I thought she was gearing up to let out a scream. Instead, she bolted up, grabbed her purse, and exited the house without another word.

I excused myself after that, and Rubina was shaken enough that she didn't mind seeing me go. She told me to hold off on my assignment for now, but the admonition wasn't too strong. I wasn't about to bill her for legwork, but she couldn't stop me from continuing the research I'd started on my own time.

Four

❧

I spent the whole weekend watching my phone, waiting for word from Rubina. I tried to keep myself occupied, but my mind went around the case in tight circles. Chaz invited me over for dinner with his family on Saturday night, and Sunday afternoon I took a long walk, looping around the Echo Park Lake and reading about genocide while sitting on a series of benches.

When I came home, I opened my apartment door to a full-on assault of intricate, spicy, mouthwatering smells. Lori was cooking, and I could tell right away that she'd been at it for a while.

I heard the clatter of a wood spoon on the cooktop, and Lori came around and smiled at me while I took off my shoes. "I'm making a lot of stuff, *unni*. I hope you didn't eat a big lunch."

"It smells amazing in here. Do you need any help?"

She laughed. "Maybe you can wash the rice? Don't touch anything else."

I felt a little bit like the bumbling husband In an outdated sitcom, but it was true that cooking was not one of my talents. Lori had tried to teach me, but she was in the unfortunate position of having to eat whatever I made. It didn't take too long for her to abandon her zeal for instruction.

Washing rice I could handle. No discretion, no chopping, no real room for error. Just cold water and a lot of rinsing, letting whatever impurities clung to the grains fall off, turning the pot water a murky off-white.

I set to work and watched her cast her eyes over several active pots with intense concentration. I could tell she felt me looking at her, and I knew right away that she was pretending not to notice. She had something to say to me.

I put the washed rice in the cooker and opened the fridge. "Do you want a beer?" I asked.

She shook her head. "I got some chardonnay. We can open that if you want."

I scrunched my lips and nodded. I'd offered her beer as a formality; Lori didn't drink casually at home.

I poured out two glasses of wine and handed one to her. She took a big sip and smiled at me when she saw me looking.

I laughed. "What's going on, Lori?"

"Nothing," she said. "Do I need a special reason to make all of your favorite foods?"

I looked at the stovetop and saw that every pot held one of Lori's greatest hits. She was a master chef of Korean comfort food, and she must have been standing there for hours, braising beef and prepping stews.

"Is it something bad?" I asked, sitting down at the kitchen table. "Should I get out the hard stuff?"

"No, nothing bad," she said quickly. "Here, dinner will be ready in like half an hour. You can relax until I'm ready."

I shrugged and went to my room, where I read in bed with my drink in hand. I finished the glass and picked up a refill.

When I wandered back out, she was setting the table, and I helped her carry a dozen plates and pots from the kitchen. There was enough food for a dorm full of Korean girls, and it crowded the table until I worried it might collapse.

I handed Lori a pair of chopsticks, and she took it with a sad smile.

"Okay, Lori, I can't take this. What do you need to tell me?"

She shook her head and raised her left hand to her head, tucking her hair behind her ear with a slow, delicate movement. A movement that showed off the glint of a diamond.

I put my chopsticks down. "Oh my God."

Her smile widened into a blushing grin. "I was wondering when you were going to notice."

"When did this happen?"

"Last night. He took me to dinner and proposed at the restaurant."

"Took a knee and everything? Were there other people around?"

"Yeah, they all clapped. Someone sent us champagne."

I wondered if I was a bitter old lady for thinking that sounded like a nightmare. "Was it a total surprise?"

"No," she said. "I mean yes and no. I didn't know he was about to do it, but we'd talked about getting married."

"I guess I knew that, but wow, still surprised." I felt a slim needle of hurt push into my happiness. Lori had other girlfriends, and I had a feeling she gushed to them about Isaac more than she did to me. She must have edited herself in consideration of my spinsterhood. "Congratulations. That's incredible."

She was glowing. I laughed. "You should see your face right now." I pulled up my phone and took a picture. "Here, I'll send this to you and you can show Isaac."

We started eating and she showed me her ring and gave me the details. I had never seen her so joyous, and I was happy, too. She deserved all the good in this world.

"So why the doomsday prep? Did you think I'd be upset?"

"No, I knew you'd be happy for me. It's just . . . ." She bit her lip.

"Don't tell me I have to get married first like we're in *The Taming of the Shrew*. Wrong genre."

She laughed. "No, it's just, we're moving in together."

I felt my smile crack. It was out of my control. "Oh. Yeah. Obviously. When?"

"As soon as possible." She bit her lip again, and I stared at her crooked incisor. It had been the first thing I noticed when I met her three years earlier, the sweet humanizing flaw in her angelic face. "I'll keep paying rent until you find someone, but I'm actually going to start moving out now."

I was stunned, and as I sat there trying to process this change, Lori's eyes started to fill.

I snapped back to attention and willed myself to smile. "Oh, don't cry, Lori. This is really great news."

"I'll miss you," she said, two big tears escaping down her cheeks.

"It's not like you're leaving the country. You're moving into Isaac's place?"

She nodded.

"I think I can manage visiting you downtown. It's what, a mile from here? I can even walk. It'll be good for me."

"Will you be okay? What will you eat?"

I laughed. "I used to live alone, remember? I know my way around a microwave."

Her face started to crumble, and I sang a line of Korean proverb: "If you laugh and cry at the same time, you grow hair on your asshole." And she laughed.

We spent the rest of the night drinking and reminiscing, allowing ourselves to get downright sloppy and mawkish. We'd been through a lot together, after all.

I meant to fall asleep as soon as I hit the mattress, but I couldn't keep my eyes closed against the increasing burden of my dread. I was feeling grave, and that gravity moved through my body, building an ache in my chest and filling my limbs with a drunk, sluggish weight. I didn't cry. I was determined to be happy for Lori, and I hated to indulge in self-pity. But I couldn't fool myself all the way.

I wondered whether I was becoming a bitter lonely hag. I wasn't even thirty, but my stars were aligning to form a convincing picture. I could count all my friends on the fingers of one hand, and when Lori moved out, I'd have to find a stranger to help pay the rent. Not only did I not have a boyfriend, it had been years since I'd even slept with someone I legitimately liked as a person.

It wasn't too late, in theory, to meet someone, have kids, do the whole thing. Time wasn't the issue, or if it was, it wasn't the main one. The problem was more essential. Looking at my past and my present and extrapolating to my future, I just couldn't summon up a visual of my life as a wife or mom.

I'd had one serious relationship, and I'd ended that unilaterally when I was a sophomore in college. That was almost a decade ago, and I wasn't any closer to marriage, or children, or any of that other mid-phase stuff. I felt like an adult in my own way, but when I thought about my future I tended to see myself alone. I could get a dog one day, I supposed, but so far I'd proven incapable of keeping a plant without leading it to an early, brownish death.

My mind wandered toward my long-ago donated eggs. I'd given them so cavalierly, without any notion of attachment. But now that I was thinking about them out there in the world, I felt a strange hesitation and unease that hadn't plagued me when I was twenty-two.

All my donations had been closed, an option I'd chosen with alacrity. The thought of maintaining fuzzy relationships with donee couples had made me feel too apprehensive. I might have felt differently if I'd been a true donor, relinquishing my eggs out of the goodness of my heart. As it turned out, I was more of a vendor.

Which was fair enough, really. Egg donation was a lot of work.

There were countless e-mails and phone calls and a rigorous screening process. I submitted pictures, both current and ancient, and drilled through my medical history with an obsequious woman from the fertility center. She needed a promise of good, clean genes, and I did my best to oblige. I had to give up smoking for a year and paint optimistic pictures of my mental health. My sister had killed herself a few years earlier, and I hadn't quite risen out of the anhedonic funk that followed. But I answered all questions honestly—there was no history of clinical depression in my family, at least—and at the end of the day, people wanted my Ivy League Korean eggs.

I spent a lot of time in doctors' offices that year, and I never even had my own doctor. The actual retrieval took something like half an hour, but it was a bigger deal than I'd thought at first. All it took to give sperm was erotica, privacy, and a receptacle. I had to go under to let a doctor spelunk up my birth canal and retrieve my genetic material like it was made of diamonds. Actually, diamonds would have cost less by weight. Life being priceless, and all that.

Somewhere, years ago, women I didn't know had stared at my picture, noted my SAT score, and we'd synched up our cycles so I could transfer a part of myself. I wasn't romantic about progeny, but this was literally true. I'd parted with something internal, and I didn't know what had become of it.

Schrodinger's donated eggs: fertilized or not, children or waste matter.

I'd donated dozens of them. It seemed unlikely that not a single one had served its purpose. I envisioned the spread of my genes, my self, a secret army of my broken-off pieces that might linger behind me when I was gone.

I wondered how much of Nora was left in this world.

I woke up the next morning fresh off of a vivid dream about her. It was pretty uneventful, as dreams about missing strangers went. She was over at my place, and we were chatting about nonsense while she painted her toenails. I wasn't even sure we were using actual words, until the end, when I asked her where she was and I woke up. Maybe if I'd stayed asleep a minute longer I could've changed careers and become a TV psychic.

It was later than I'd thought, almost ten, and Lori was already gone for the day. She'd left a note on the dining table saying there were bagels in the fridge. I was unreasonably moved by her handwriting. I hated to think about the headache and sadness of finding a new roommate to split the rent.

I scarfed a jalapeño bagel and headed into the office, wondering when I'd get a reprieve from case limbo.

I decided to give Veronica Sanchez a call. I had yet to make her regret giving me access to her cell number.

"Juniper Song," she said, her voice pleasantly sarcastic. "It's been a while since we tangled."

"Did you miss the headache?"

"Now that you mention it." She laughed. "How've you been?"

Veronica Sanchez was a murder detective with the LAPD, a sharp-eyed, quick-witted woman I'd met on one of my first cases as a private investigator. I'd been an uncooperative pain in the ass on that case, but by the end of it, Veronica and I had built a weird camaraderie. She didn't know I'd protected a murderer, but for the most part, neither did anyone else. I'd had no real choice in the matter, not that that helped me sleep at night.

She used to work with Arturo, and she let some of the respect she had for him rub off on her attitude toward me. Over the last couple years, we'd developed a casual friendship that I enjoyed enough to let override my feelings of guilt. It also didn't hurt to know a murder cop, with the number of murders I seemed to run into.

"Can't complain," I said. "Staying out of trouble, as you've noticed."

"You didn't call me for a pat on the back."

"No," I admitted. "I've stumbled onto something that might be in your department."

"A murder?"

"Not exactly. A missing girl. I'm sure you've heard of her. Nora Mkrtchian?"

"Ah, the Armenian sweetheart. Where are you hiding her?"

"I wish I were hiding her. Then I could stop. I'm looking for her, sort of."

"What's that sort of?"

"Well, technically, I haven't quite been hired."

She chuckled. "But crime and intrigue are like magnets to your bit of lead."

"Hey, be fair. I've been behaving myself."

"And now you're getting restless."

I rolled my eyes. Veronica had a way of reading me that was uncannily intuitive and as smug as possible. If she liked men and Chaz weren't married, I might have introduced them. They could have made a formidable team of annoying parental surrogates though, to be fair, Veronica was only in her late thirties.

"I'm being practical. I'm like a phone call away from being put on the case."

"I guess it makes no difference to you that the LAPD is already on it."

"I don't know what you mean by 'on it.' There hasn't been any progress, and she's been missing for a pretty concerning amount of time. I just met her best friend. She's been going crazy trying to track her down on her own. She didn't seem particularly impressed with the heroic efforts of our boys in blue."

"Another amateur sleuth, huh? I'm sure that's what we all need."

"Well she's eight months pregnant, which is why I suspect I'll be taking over soon."

"Detective work is tough on the body. It's best handled by old maids, huh, Juniper Song?" She clicked her tongue in a verbal wink.

"Speak for yourself," I said. "I'm practically drowning in husbands."

"Ha, I wasn't even speaking for myself. I got a nice lady. Young and pretty, teaches grade school."

"Nurturing type. No wonder you're so damn friendly. You must've met her last week."

"It's been three weeks. That's three years in lesbian time."

"Congratulations," I said. "From the bottom of my heart."

"How did we get on this topic?"

"You wanted to rub your happiness in my face."

"Oh yeah." She laughed.

"Joke's on you. I'm happy you're happy. Maybe we should get dinner this week, and you can tell me more about your happiness."

"My happiness and maybe a little information, I take it?"

"How ungenerous," I said, taking a tone of exaggerated indignation. "Don't you miss my face?"

She sighed. "Sure. How's Wednesday, seven?"

"Okay. How's Korean food? My treat."

"Perfect," she said. "In the meantime, I guess I'll see what I can do for you."

I went into the office and found I had nothing to do. I had no other cases on my docket, and the phone didn't ring all morning. There was no point trying to follow Lusig around—that jig was up, and I needed my cue to start dancing the next one.

Arturo came out of his office at around one in the afternoon. I had my head down on my desk, and I was listening to the amplified sound of my fingertips drumming by my ear.

"Hey, Song," he said, his authoritative voice startling me upright. "Are you busy right now?"

I looked behind me and saw him standing in his doorway with

the shade of a smirk on his face. I shook my head. He knew I wasn't busy.

"What's up?" I asked. "You have something for me?"

I felt a tick of anticipation. As the ex–homicide cop on our team, Arturo brought in the most interesting cases, discounting a few outliers. He handled death threats, high-stakes security; he tracked down missing people. If there was a single PI who embodied my old conception of what this job entailed, it had to be Arturo Flores. He was a handsome bachelor in his mid-forties, a little gruff, with a subtle, dry sense of humor, and an honorable streak the length of Los Angeles. He had the experience and air of competence to land quality work, and I'd learned a lot under his supervision on a variety of jobs. Chaz made a point of giving me chores and buffing up my basics, but Arturo passed me the sexy stuff. I always preferred Arturo work to Chaz work.

Arturo liked to use me as a tail because no one suspected the Asian girl, and he'd even gotten me to strike up conversations with targets, mostly in bars, with the occasional staged encounter at a bookstore or Target. On one long assignment, he'd had me move into an apartment in Reno and befriend a woman who'd worked for a building manager and run off after cashing a month's worth of rent checks. I'd stayed there for over a month, gathering intel at gambling tables and feeling like a goddamn spy.

I hoped he had something good for me. I hoped it'd be good enough to let me forget about a missing activist. If I had a tail, it probably would've wagged.

"I wouldn't ask if you had anything better to do, but . . ."

My mental tail stopped wagging; my expectations deflated like I was a disappointed heiress in an old English novel. Excitement converted to a sudden dread of drudgery, roiling in protest in my stomach. I could feel a bad task coming.

". . . I need some trash pulled."

I stifled a groan. I would've let it out if Chaz were the one asking, but I knew there was no complaining when Arturo asked for a favor. I didn't point out that this was Chaz work.

Of the many boring and unpleasant things that came with the job, the trash pull was probably my least favorite. There was nothing metaphorical about the phrase, as I'd hoped when I'd first heard it—this trash wasn't digital, it was actual garbage placed in actual garbage containers placed on actual curbs fronting actual homes. It looked like garbage, it felt like garbage, and it sure as hell smelled like garbage. Of course, the garbage sometimes contained valuable information, the kind of stuff private investigators might go to humiliating lengths to find. The other advantage was that this brand of stealth snatching was legally sound—trash was no longer private property once it hit the street for collection.

What few illusions I had left when I started this job dispersed at the smell of my first trash hit. I was looking for signs of infidelity, and one of the first steps was a visit to the alleged mistress's house. Chaz went with me, and he laughed at my discomfort as I pulled the heavy bags out of their containers, holding my breath and tugging delicately with gloved hands. He laughed harder when the husband showed up and started fucking his mistress while we hid with her garbage in my car. We put it back, and the sorting part became a lesson for another day.

I sighed. "Sure, Arturo. Tell me where and when."

"Trash gets picked up tomorrow morning, so it'll be out there tonight. Here's the address. I think it's near you."

The address was in Silver Lake, a quick drive from my place. Not that distance was a major impediment after midnight.

"What am I looking for?"

"Just get the bags and bring them in tomorrow. I'll sort them myself, unless you're having another slow day."

He almost gave me a smile. He knew damn well I was scheduled for another slow day.

We made a policy of leaving trash pulls until dark, so I had the rest of the day to kill before I had anything I had to do. Chaz and Arturo were both busy, so I couldn't even burden them with my frustration and boredom. I'd have to figure out how to keep myself occupied.

Was there any harm, I wondered, in doing a little light digging?

It wasn't hard to find Nora's boyfriend online. I remembered his face, and I matched it to a man named Chris Oganian in Lusig's friend list on Facebook. From there, it was cake to find out where he worked, at a hedge fund in Century City. His company bio listed his résumé under a picture of him in a nice suit, crossing his arms and looking all business. He went to Wharton. I might have guessed as much.

Century City was a pretty deep drive from Koreatown. I couldn't exactly step outside and run into Chris by accident. I tried to think of a valid reason for me to cross town, but I more or less knew I didn't have one. I couldn't remember the last time I'd gone to Century City. It was a business center with a big mall, so there wasn't much for anyone who wasn't employed there or currently in high school. I used to go when I was in high school, to watch movies or hang out at Abercrombie, which was as close to a club as any of us knew of when we were fifteen. At some point in my adult life, I realized that this hot spot of my youth had nothing to offer me anymore. I wasn't working there, and there was nothing interesting about the neighborhood.

It was also impossible to get to from the Eastside, or from anywhere else, really—the only people who were happy with their Century City commutes were the rainmakers who built their offices there in the first place. They came from Beverly Hills or the Palisades, while their underlings trudged in from less extravagant zip codes. There was a Metro extension in progress that would include a Century City stop, making things easier for workers to get to their jobs. The Beverly Hills school district had succeeded in delaying it with groundless petitions and bad-faith lawsuits. The line was set to run under the high school, and there was a panic about the safety of the children—never mind the profitable oil drilling that was already in place beneath the same campus. The real reason seemed much more obvious and sinister—classic fear and disdain for outsiders.

Icarus Capital was right on Avenue of the Stars, at what looked like a desirable address, a short jaunt from the mall. Did I need anything from the mall that I couldn't get at a closer mall?

I was about to ask Chaz to talk me out of or into unnecessary snooping, but he was on the phone and had been for almost an hour. I was the only idle body in the office, and I knew I could go home if I wanted. In which case, what was the harm in plumbing my own curiosity, on my own time?

I sent an e-mail to Chris's company address, introducing myself as a friend of Nora's and Lusig's. I asked if he was free for coffee in the afternoon and left the office as soon as I sent the e-mail. I hoped he'd respond, but I'd see him either way. I wasn't going to Century City for nothing.

I left a note for Chaz on my desk, in case he wondered where I'd run off to: "Circumventing death by boredom." He could call me if he needed me, or just pick up the Post-it and roll his eyes alone.

As I sat in an unwarranted afternoon traffic jam, driving with all the speed of a kayak headed upstream, I remembered why I never traveled this far west. I thought of the poor tourists with their rental cars sitting in traffic from Brentwood to downtown, from Hollywood to Disneyland, going home to cold climates and rejecting sunny California because of a fundamental misunderstanding of this city. Our United Neighborhoods of Los Angeles, each one its own universe if not its own island. I'd spent more time in Connecticut than I ever would in Venice, even if I died a white-haired woman fifteen miles away.

But for now, I was stuck in this sluggish crosstown caravan, bristling with impatience, checking my e-mail at every stoplight. I kept an eye out for word from Chris, but it was mostly to curb my boredom. I turned the radio on and listened to NPR at low volume, getting irritated when it started up with a traffic report.

Then, like a sign from heaven, a story came on about the upcoming Armenian genocide centennial. I raised the volume and shook my head, letting the timing take on maximum significance.

The story started with a rundown of the events of the genocide, and I marveled at its precarious status in our understanding of world history. The reporter introduced the murder of a million people as if it were a subject that could lie outside the knowledge of an informed public radio audience. I guessed I couldn't be too surprised—until this week I'd known almost nothing about it. And I was an Angeleno, in a city where Armenian-Americans were prominent.

The reporter segued into a brief note on the legal battle over the genocide memorial, and when she mentioned Nora Mkrtchian, I found that my ears had already been waiting for the name. There was no news on the missing girl, but I wasn't the only one sitting in a car, still wondering where she'd gone.

I arrived, at length, in Century City and parked at the mall, where I could cross a walkway to Chris's building and get validation on my way out. I didn't want to mess with office building rates, and I had a feeling Chris's company wouldn't spot me for parking.

I kept my eyes on my phone, but I hadn't heard back from Chris by the time I reached his work address. It was one of the tall office buildings that made up the Century City skyline, one of those block towers surfaced by reflective gridded windows that looked more LEGO-built than full of human life. There was something forbidding about all this structure, and I felt suddenly shabby as I put my hand to a door of bright polished metal and glass.

The lobby gleamed with veined marble, like a giant five-star hotel shower. The elevator banks held the chrome fixtures. Icarus Capital was on the nineteenth floor, and I spotted the right set of elevators, for floors 12 through 20. I'd been naïve to imagine walking right in and pressing the button. There was an electronic turnstile in the way; past that, a security guard who was starting to pick up on my stilted presence.

I sat down on one of the low beige chairs designated for waiting. It was almost offensively uncomfortable, with expensive buttery leather wrapping a thin cushion that did nothing to make me feel welcome.

The colossal security desk was about twenty feet away, and there were two people behind it on rolling chairs jacked up to meet its height. Both wore suits and blank, smiling expressions. They looked like they'd take secret pleasure in walling me out.

Or maybe I was being unnecessarily antagonistic. After all, most visitors to this building probably had legitimate reasons for being there. I thought about turning around and going back home. The lobby was sparsely populated, and I would be conspicuous if I waited hours for Chris to come out, not to mention burning a big chunk of my day for nothing but curiosity. No one had asked me to come. Was it so important to talk to Chris that I'd be willing to try and pull one over on the security guards? Was I so tantalized by this case that I would turn into a fanatic?

I went outside and smoked a cigarette, leaning against a high stone planter with one eye on the lobby through the glass wall. I was almost done when someone called my name. "Juniper Song? Is that you?"

I looked up and saw a small Asian woman in a blue sheath dress, approaching with evident caution. My eyes went straight to her belly, which was three times as wide as the rest of her. I knew this woman, but it took me a long second to place her—she was a high school classmate I hadn't seen since graduation.

"Kelly Pak?" I asked with relief at the recognition.

"Yes! I thought it was you."

I stubbed out my cigarette and moved toward her, trying to leave the smoke behind me. Unless she'd gained weight in a very weird way, she was at least five months pregnant.

"I take it you're not here for a cigarette break," I said.

She laughed. "No, just searching for a snack."

Kelly and I had been friendly in high school, but all potential intimacy had been sabotaged by a current of fierce competition. We were the two high-achieving Korean girls in our grade, and had a lot of classes together throughout our years of schooling. The way I remembered it, the competition had been mostly on her end—she managed to find out my scores whenever tests were returned, whether by looking over my shoulder or asking directly. Strangely, this didn't bother me, even if it did mean we would never hang out off campus. I was happy for her when she went off to Harvard, though maybe it helped that I happened to know she was waitlisted at Yale. I had to admit, I hadn't been above that kind of thing, and it was possible Kelly remembered me as the instigator in our rivalry.

"Well what are the odds, huh? Not every day I run into Greenwood folk."

"It's every day here, pretty much," she laughed. "Jeff Bloom works in this building. Molly Richmond works next door. There are at least a dozen of us on this block."

I nodded, as if I remembered who she was talking about. I should have figured, in any case. My prep school churned out professionals with impressive reliability, and professionals clustered in Century City.

"It's like the old days at the mall."

"Basically, yes."

"And you work here?" I asked, though it was clear that she did.

"Yes! I work at Goldman."

"Doing what?"

"I'm an I-banker."

I whistled. "Tough job for a pregnant lady."

She frowned. "I'm not pregnant," she said after a long pause.

My mind blanked and I had to stop myself from bringing a hand up to cover my open mouth.

She laughed loudly, slapping her thigh. "Oh my God, your face! Of course I'm pregnant!"

"Jesus. Still a joker," I said, as if Kelly Pak had ever been a joker.

"I'm sticking around until baby, and then we'll see. Maternity leave is generous. What're you up to?"

I smiled. "I'm a private investigator."

"Wow!" she said. "Now that you mention it, I think I might have heard something about that. You were always interested in that stuff, weren't you? Did you always want to do this when you grew up?"

Her tone was suddenly a note too cheerful, and I almost winced as I registered the condescension. It disappointed me.

"Actually I wanted to be a ballerina. Barring that, an I-banker."

She laughed. "Touché, Song."

"When's it due?" I asked.

"July 4, my Independence Day."

"That joke only works if you're planning to sell it once it's born. Boy or girl?"

"We're waiting to find out."

"That's some willpower," I said. "When'd you get married any-way?" I asked, noticing a rock on her finger the size of an almond.

"Let's see, we bought the house in 2013, so . . ." She tapped on her chin like she was thinking very hard. "It's been three years. How about you?"

"Widowed three times, unfortunately. Series of freak accidents."

She scowled. "I can't tell when you're joking, Song."

"Okay. That was a joke. Here's the punch line—nobody loves me."

"That's not true," she said, too quick and too reproachful.

I laughed. "I know."

"So what are you doing in Century City?" she asked, changing the subject abruptly.

"Private investigation," I said, as gently as I could.

"Of course. Well," she said with a smile. "I guess I'd better get my snack."

We hugged, and the hug felt unnatural, especially with a fetus in the way. She left and I resumed smoking.

It bothered me that Kelly Pak felt sorry for me, and it bothered me that it bothered me. I could imagine her going home to her husband and telling him that she ran into an old classmate, one who'd made interesting life decisions. I wasn't jealous of her—it was hard for me, even at my most self-pitying, to envy a pregnant woman of any kind—but I didn't like for her to see me as a failure, to breathe deeply in her sense of a life well lived at my expense.

My mind was swirling unpleasantly in this slow, useless pattern, when Chris Oganian appeared in the building lobby, walking from the elevator bank to the coffee kiosk just inside the doors. I took a long drag off my cigarette, then stubbed it out to make my way in.

I had no good way to approach him without making it clear I'd been waiting for him to show up. I felt suddenly self-conscious, like I was about to ask him to spot me two dollars to help me get to the airport.

I walked in and went up to him by the kiosk, where he was tapping a packet of Splenda into his coffee. I tapped his shoulder, and he flinched at my touch before turning around with a look of displeasure.

"Hi," I said, trying to sound reasonable and apologetic. "My name's Juniper Song. I'm a friend of Lusig's and Nora's. I e-mailed you earlier?"

He blinked sharply and nodded once. "Yes, I saw that. I'm sorry, I was planning to respond later this afternoon."

His demeanor was stiffly professional, and I saw that this stance worked to my advantage. I held out my hand. "Sorry for accosting you in this way," I said. "Pleased to meet you, regardless."

He took it, cautious but obedient, and I knew I'd secured the interview.

"Would you mind speaking with me for a few minutes?" I asked, before fully releasing his hand. "It's about Nora."

He took a sip of coffee and pulled his phone out of his pocket, checking the time. "I can talk briefly," he said.

"Great. Outside?"

We retreated to the stone planter, where I was apparently taking meetings now. I wondered what kind of clients I'd get if I put out a shingle right there.

I sat on the edge of the planter, where he rested his coffee while he stood, looking distinctly uncomfortable. "How did you know Nora, again?" he asked.

"Sorry," I said. "I should clarify. I don't know her directly. I'm a friend of Lusig's. I'm helping her find Nora."

"She's looking for Nora?" There was a tinge of hurt feelings in his voice, like he hadn't been invited to a birthday party.

I cursed myself mentally. Lusig hadn't meant to include Chris in her investigation. Maybe she just didn't like him, but it seemed likely that she suspected him of having something to hide. "This is a new thing," I said, reassuringly. "She just asked me because I have some experience with this stuff."

He nodded. "I wish I could help."

"Maybe you can."

He shook his head. "I couldn't help the police."

"When did you last see her?" I asked, launching into questions before he could demur further.

"It was the day after Valentine's Day. A day before she disappeared."

"Did anything unusual happen that day?"

He took a sip of coffee and shook his head. "She spent Valentine's at my house, and went home the next afternoon."

"Do you know if anyone saw her after that?"

"Yes. At the very least, her roommate saw her on the afternoon of the sixteenth."

"How long were you together?" I wondered if he'd contest my use of the past tense.

"Four years," he said.

Nora was twenty-six years old, which meant she'd spent the most significant part of her adult life with Chris, who I'd gathered from his bio was thirty-one.

"Wow," I said. "That's a long time."

He nodded, starting to look miserable.

"How did you meet?"

"Our mothers are friends," he said. "Not close friends, but they know each other. The Armo community is fairly tight."

"They set you up?"

"Yes. I had a good job, and she was starting law school. Our mothers thought we would make a good match."

"And they were right. You hit it off."

"We did."

"Was the idea that you guys would get married, have kids, the whole thing?"

"It was always a possibility."

"You didn't live together after four years, huh?" I realized I was asking a very personal question, and I tried to make it sound as casual as I could.

"Religious thing," he said vaguely.

"But I take it your lives were pretty intertwined?"

"Of course."

"Did you participate in any of her activism?"

He drew in a quick breath—this was apparently the touchy subject. "No, I did not. I thought it was stupid of her to push it as far as she did."

"The blog?"

"The blog, the Twitter, her whole attention-grabbing thing."

"Was this a source of conflict?" It was the closest I could get to accusing him of anything. I wondered if the police had given him the full suspect treatment.

"No, I wouldn't say conflict." He sighed. "But she wasn't the same girl anymore. She was this firebrand—wayward, opinionated, passionate. If she'd stayed in law school, kept herself quiet, no one would have had any reason to hurt her."

"Can you think of anyone who might have had reason to hurt her?"

"No." He seemed to bristle at the question, as if he'd finally caught that I was interrogating him. "No one by name."

"Are you talking about the Internet trolls? The people who were harassing her?"

"I told you. I don't know any of those people."

A pause entered that lingered a second too long, and I found myself glancing around us until I saw two men dressed in business casual, staring at us without pretense. I made eye contact with the more blatant one, holding it until he turned away with an embarrassed expression.

"Do you know those guys?" I asked.

Chris glanced over, and they waved at him with smiles that were too wide, revealing a caught sheepishness. He waved back, though without enthusiasm. "Yeah, they work on my floor."

It occurred to me that Nora's disappearance was the most interesting thing that had ever happened to Chris. It was probably the most interesting thing that had ever happened to his coworkers.

"This must be hard for you," I said. "But I promise I didn't just track you down for a cheap thrill. I'm going to find your girlfriend."

A look of open pain crossed his face. He dumped the remnants of his coffee into the planter and crumpled the cup. "I'm sorry," he said. "I can't talk about this anymore. I don't even know you."

"You're right," I said, shifting back into my most businesslike tone. "Thank you again for your time."

Five

❦

I went back to the office instead of heading home. I wanted to talk to Chaz, and I was afraid of what I might feel when I got to my apartment and found Lori gone or packing.

He was at his desk when I got there, and he made a show of puzzling over my Post-it as I walked into his office.

"I see you aren't dead of boredom, so I guess whatever remedy you found must have worked. I hope no one else is dead for it."

"I've spent half the day sitting in traffic, so not quite in the clear. And, later tonight, Arturo has me doing a trash hit."

Chaz laughed, a little too happily, barking with amusement. "Oh, you poor woman. Tell me, would you have signed on for this job if you'd known about all the garbage?" He hooted some more, clearly pleased with this joke that was barely a joke. I thought of the prank he pulled on one of my first trash hits, when he made me save at least six blue-knotted Baggies of dog shit.

I shrugged, not giving him the satisfaction of even feigned annoyance. "It's not all bad. I wasn't bored today."

"Yeah? Where have you been, anyway?"

I told him about my errand in Century City.

"I thought your current status on that case was minding your own business."

"Kind of," I said. "But I didn't have any other work to do until midnight."

"What's wrong with sitting at your desk and numbing your mind on the Internet like the rest of us?" He shook his head. "Sometimes I think you like this job too much."

I put my head down on his desk and sighed. I acknowledged the seed of melancholy that had been sprouting in my chest, playing it up for my audience. "I've got nothing else going for me, Chazzie. I'm like a sad bachelor cliché. No one would notice if I slipped and broke my head in the shower."

He laughed. "Oh, that's not true," he said, patting the top of my head. "Lori would need to use that shower eventually."

I looked up at him, resting my chin on the edge of the desk. "Lori's engaged. She's moving out."

"Lori Lim is getting married? Do you hear that?" He put a finger up and made a show of listening for a distant sound. "That's the chorus of a thousand hearts breaking."

"I feel for them. Mine's probably wailing the loudest."

"I believe it," he said, striking a tone that invited confidence.

"I'm only half joking, but you don't have to worry," I said. "You don't happen to know any cool people my age who might need a place to live?"

"Song, you are the youngest person I know who is not technically a child."

"Really?" I said. "What are you, like a boring dad?"

"A very boring dad."

"You must have a distorted image of my generation."

"Everything I know about millennials I've learned from you. I gather you are all dogged chain-smoking PI types."

I nodded. "And none of us have figured out how to grow up, or how to feel good about staying who we are."

"You're plenty grown up," he said. "I hope my daughters are as mature when they're your age."

"That's very sweet of you," I said, trying not to fight the compliment.

He saw that I didn't believe him. "Look, Song, what is it you think you want? What do you think you're missing?"

I shrugged. "I don't know, the barefoot, pregnant life?"

He slapped his desk and guffawed. "Give me a break. You wouldn't trade places with a barefoot pregnant woman if she were married to Philip Marlowe himself."

"Okay maybe not barefoot and pregnant, but maybe pregnant one day? Maybe not alone forever?"

"Are you whining about not having a boyfriend?" He grinned. "Carry on if you are. It's fascinating."

"Why is it so cool to be a lone wolf, and so lame to be lonely?"

"Who said it was cool to be a lone wolf?"

"Movies, TV, everyone. Marlowe was a lone wolf. Spade. James Bond. Every outlaw cowboy."

"Okay, I see your point. Lone wolves. Bad boys."

"You know what it is? Men stand on their own. A single man standing tall against the world—that's something we know to romanticize. But single women? Who's ever told us to look at a single woman and say, 'She's cool, she's whole, I'd like to be like her.'"

He opened his mouth to say something, then thought better of it, his lips knotting and his shoulders deflating in thought.

"Men without women are men. Women without men are pathetic. I'd like to feel like this isn't true. On one level I *know* it isn't true. So why do I feel pathetic?"

"Well, girl detective, it's 'cause you read too many books. If Marlowe were real, he would've gotten lonely and horny just like anyone else."

"You think Arturo gets lonely?"

He gave me a sideways look. "Hey, don't go making a mess of things. We got a good situation here."

I rolled my eyes. "Jesus, not what I meant."

"Okay, I have some gossip for you." He beckoned for me to lean in.

I scooted forward in my chair.

"Arturo doesn't sleep alone these days. He's got a lady friend. She's a recent divorcée. He got the money shot for her lawyer."

He leaned back, drummed the desk, and started singing "Everybody Needs Somebody to Love," eyes closed with his hands to his ears like he was supporting a set of headphones.

I laughed.

"Feel better?"

"Sure."

"Just remember, Arturo's in his forties. You're a baby, Song, practically wet from the womb. If you want a husband, children, all that, you've got time." He came forward again, falling back into his confidential pose. "And look, Song, here's a secret: Any idiot can have a child. The dumbest, most worthless people in the world can bump up on each other and reproduce. Sometimes they do this multiple times. Hell, I've managed two kids and I have just enough competence to wipe my own ass. You've got talent. Passion. Not everyone can reproduce that."

"So what you're saying is, that if my passion is to be a mystery-solving busybody, then I should embrace it, maybe including tonight."

"Why, what were you planning to do tonight?"

I shrugged. "I was thinking maybe I'd talk to the roommate. What would you do?"

"It's six o'clock. I'm going home to have dinner with my family. But if I were you? I'd maybe talk to the roommate."

* * *

Nora Mkrtchian's last address was a two-bedroom apartment in Little Tokyo, on the eastern edge of downtown. Her building was one of the new ones, a large beautiful complex that couldn't have existed in the area even five or six years earlier. Her roommate was a woman named Hanna Bloom. She'd been Nora's classmate in law school, and they'd been rooming together for over a year when Nora disappeared. I gathered this much from a set of Facebook pictures from their housewarming last January.

I parked on the street and made my way to the front entrance of the building. I found Hanna Bloom's name on the giant intercom. She occupied apartment 118. I clicked through and found Nora still listed on the directory.

I buzzed up to the room, and a few seconds later, a woman's voice answered. "Hello?"

"Hi," I said. "I'm sorry to bother you. Are you Hanna Bloom?"

"Yes, this is she. Who is this?"

"My name is Juniper Song. I'm a private investigator, and I'm looking for Nora Mkrtchian." I didn't feel any need to mention that I was investigating on spec. "I was wondering if we could talk."

She was silent for a long beat.

"Hello?" I prodded, in case she'd hung up.

"I'm here," she said. "What do you want to ask me?"

"I just want to talk to you about her. What she was doing, who she was seeing. Anything could help. Are you available now, by any chance?"

She hesitated. "Are you outside my apartment?"

"Yeah," I said. "Sorry, I didn't mean to be creepy. I just know this was Nora's last address."

"That's okay," she said, her tone still uncertain. "We can talk in the lobby, but I don't have long. I have plans tonight."

"Actually, if you don't mind, I'd like to see the apartment."

"Look, don't take this the wrong way, but I'd like to see your face before I invite you into my home. We've had some nightmares in this apartment."

"Of course," I said.

"I'll be right there, okay?"

A minute later, Hanna Bloom came to let me into the building. She wore a reluctant, skeptical expression, as if she spied religious pamphlets spilling out of my purse. It was evident that I was imposing on her time, energy, and peace of mind.

She was a pale, freckled white woman with a round face set off by a pair of hip, rectangular glasses. She dressed very well for a woman sitting alone at home—she wore a knit V-neck sweater and tight blue jeans that showed off a plump, curvy figure. Her reddish brown hair was short and well maintained.

"This is my face," I said, extending a hand. "I promise I'm only here out of concern for Nora."

She shook it and yielded a wry smile. "Trust me," she said, "if I didn't share that concern there's no way I would've let a stranger into my building."

She led the way through a modern lobby that looked like it could have belonged to a Hollywood hotel. We left it to enter a courtyard with a large swimming pool and several alcoves with lounge seating. There were a few other people in the courtyard, but the place was calm enough. It was a Monday, and the chill of night had arrived.

"We can talk here," she said, sitting down on a cushioned bench.

"This works." I sat on an adjoining bench.

"I've already spoken with the police. It probably says something that they caught me off guard less than you did." She managed to state this without sounding hostile.

"When was this?"

"Last month, a few days after she disappeared."

"Do you mind rehashing some old territory?"

"Sure, but what is this for? Why are you looking for her?"

I bit the inside of my lip. "I've been tentatively working for a friend of hers," I said. "But I shouldn't say more until it's official."

"Ah, it's Lusig, isn't it," she said, without rising intonation.

"I can't say." I had to stop myself from stuttering.

"You don't have to. I know it's her. She bought me dinner last week and quizzed me for details, anything she might have missed about Nora's life."

I pictured Lusig, heavy and outraged, slipping away from Rubina's grip long enough for this interrogation. My coyness felt suddenly stupid.

I noticed an ashtray on a low coffee table in front of us. I pulled a Lucky Strike from my purse and asked, "Do you mind?"

She shook her head. "Go for it."

I lit the cigarette and waited for the ritual of it to put me at ease. It worked, if only slightly. "Are you friends with her?" I asked.

"Lusig? Not close friends, but I know her. Everyone who knows Nora knows Lusig, more or less. They're kind of a set."

"Do you consider Nora a close friend?"

"I do," she said. "We met in law school and hit it off. Became roommates even though she dropped out. Our lives were very different, though. We had our own groups of friends. Lusig is part of her group."

"Armenian friends?"

"Some of them. They went to middle school and high school together, so they have non-Armenian friends, but they both got into church, and activism, so I guess heavily Armenian. But in some ways, Lusig *is* her group. Or at least a large segment of her social life. Lusig is kind of her shadow."

"Interesting word choice," I said.

"I guess that came out a little snide. I didn't mean it that way."

"Is that the dynamic? Does Lusig follow Nora around?"

"I guess you never met Nora."

"No, I never heard her name until a few days ago."

"Have you read her blog?"

"Obsessively," I admitted.

"She has something, doesn't she? A spark? What Tyra Banks might call that je ne sais quoi?"

"She's pretty."

"It's not just pretty, though that is part of it. She's magnetic. I've always felt a little bit lucky to be her friend, maybe even possessive of her affection."

"Would that make you and Lusig rivals?"

She smirked. "I get the sense that Lusig felt cheated when Nora and I started rooming together. It was purely circumstantial—I'm sure Nora would rather have lived with Lusig, given the choice. But it's probably fair to say Lusig was jealous."

"I noticed Nora's still listed on your apartment directory."

She stiffened a bit, adjusting her glasses to fill a pause. "She is, yes."

"Does that mean you haven't filled the room?"

"I have filled the room," she said evenly. "Subletter moved in on the first."

I nodded. I registered just then that Hanna waffled between past and present tense when talking about Nora. "You don't have to feel defensive," I said. "She's been missing a long time."

"It's weird not to know," she said. "Sometimes when I hear the key in the door I think she's going to walk in like nothing happened and get upset that I thought she was dead."

"Do you think she's dead?"

She took a deep breath, letting it out with a shudder. "Yes, I do. Dead, or as good as dead."

"Just because she's been missing so long?"

"That's part of it. I've done the research. I know that when someone's missing for over seventy-two hours, they're often missing forever. And what's missing forever but functionally dead?"

"What's the other part?"

"She was in a state when I last saw her. Wild, agitated, on a mission. I was worried about her."

"Why?"

"Not because I thought she would get killed or, Jesus, I would've stopped her. She just seemed a bit out of her mind."

"Do you know where she was going?"

"I wish I did. I've been thinking about it nonstop. But all I have are guesses, and those haven't done the police much good."

"What's your guess?"

"That it had something to do with her stalker."

"Stalker? Just one? From what I gathered, she had several vehement admirers from the Web."

"She did. There was no way to count or keep track of them. And every one of them was completely vile. But there was one guy who kind of stood out from the rest."

I thought back on the stream of nasty comments—the tirades, the insults, the rape threats. They blurred together into a slimy pattern of malice and misogyny. Then I wondered what they might have said to her—done to her—if the whole of the Internet weren't watching.

"He found her in real life?"

She nodded. "I don't know how he got this address. That was the one thing we were truly afraid of—that one of these anti-Armenian groups would get ahold of our home address and make it public. That's been known to happen. We were afraid we'd be raided, that we'd have to move. But that didn't happen. Not on that scale."

"Just one person?"

"We think maybe he saw her in real life. Her face was public, and she was easy to recognize. He could've seen her anywhere and followed her home."

"I was able to get this address pretty easily. If she wasn't trying very hard to hide it, it would've been a cinch to obtain. It's just how things are these days."

"That's a scary thought."

"Most people are more constrained by the usual run of social norms." I didn't add that I wasn't most people, in this case.

"It started with letters. Crazy handwritten letters."

"Do you still have these?"

She shook her head. "The police took those."

"Right," I said. "They didn't figure out who they were from?"

"If they did, they didn't tell me."

"What did they say?"

"You saw the comments already, you said?"

"Yeah, couldn't look away."

"A lot of that stuff—accusing her of having an agenda, being a liar, and obviously a slut, too."

"That's so weird."

"It is weird, but it's also the most everyday thing on the Internet. If you're a woman with an opinion in a public space, someone's going to call you a slut. If you're hot, anyway. If it were me I guess they'd just call me fat." She shrugged matter-of-factly. "Nora's hot. Worse, publicly hot. Worse, publicly hot and unavailable. She's very much into displaying herself and being admired—it's kind of her thing, this exuberant narcissism. It doesn't bother me, but it enrages a lot of people. Men and women. But women don't get scary in the same way."

"So this stalker—" I prompted.

"He was scary. He hated her, and was clearly obsessed with her. He took the name-calling to a whole other level, every disgusting gendered insult you can lob at a woman, he lobbed right at her. And you could just tell, reading all these notes, that he had a serious, angry hard-on for her. As we all know, there's no bigger whore than the hot girl who won't sleep with the lonely guy on the Internet."

"But he wasn't just a guy on the Internet. He was a guy leaving letters in your mailbox."

"And the letters got worse than the comments pretty fast. It was bad enough they were showing up, but he'd put in details about what Nora had done on a given day, where she'd been, what she'd been wearing."

"How fast was this escalation?"

"He left the first note in early December. She got three more that month, then six in January, three in February, all before she disappeared. Every one this year included some kind of signal that he'd been watching her. The last few were dropped directly into our mailbox. None of them had return addresses, obviously, but the last set didn't even have postage."

"Jesus, this sounds like a horror movie."

"It gets worse." She pointed to a window facing onto the courtyard. "That's our place. First floor. Convenient and vulnerable."

"What happened?"

"This was just before she disappeared. Nora was up late, hanging out on our couch. It must have been around two in the morning. I was asleep in my room. And you know, she'd been jittery since the letters started, constantly looking over her shoulder, afraid to even go outside alone. But even she didn't expect a face in her window."

"You're kidding. He tried to break in?"

"Not quite. He talked to her through the window."

"Jesus."

"She was sitting on the couch in just a T-shirt and underwear, with her laptop on her lap. We've had blinds since we moved in, and always kept them closed at night, but never got around to curtains. We didn't realize you could see through the blinds if you stood with your nose right up against the window."

"That's what he was doing?"

"Had to be. We tried it the next morning. Closed blinds aren't completely opaque, it turns out, but you need a straight downward angle to see past them."

"What did he say to her?"

"Same shit, except more sexually explicit. She said he was moaning."

"What a fucking nightmare." I shook my head. "What did she do?"

"She just froze. When we talked about it later, she had all these ideas about what she should've done. Should've gone up to the window, smashed it and sent glass right into his eye. Should've grabbed a kitchen knife and gone out to the patio. Should've at least opened the blinds and looked him in the face, taken a picture or something to show the police. But in the end these were all fantasies."

"Like staircase wit."

"She couldn't move, or even talk to him, let alone turn around and try to see him. She was literally petrified. She just waited for him to shut up, which he did, after about fifteen minutes. When she hadn't heard anything for a long time, she got up and said out loud that she was calling the police. She didn't even try to get me until then."

"Makes me wonder what I would've done."

"Same. But the thing is, before this happened, I would've guessed Nora would kick his teeth in through the window, or at least come up with a great way to shame him, publicly and permanently online. I think she would have thought so, too."

"Did she end up calling the police?"

"Of course. And they came, and by then he was long gone. Within a week, so was Nora."

"I can't imagine they didn't follow this lead when she went missing."

"They must have, right? But she's still missing. There's been no arrest, no word at all, and she's still out there somewhere. How can that be?"

"I don't know," I said. "Some people are never found."

She sniffled, and in the half-light of the courtyard I saw her eyes fill with hopeless dark.

We sat quietly for another minute, and I stared at the window. It was a black rectangle. I guessed it was curtained now.

"Hanna," I said, pressing my inquiry into the softness of her gloom. "Can I see the apartment?"

She nodded with an air of resignation. "Why not. Who knows how many perverts have seen it, anyway."

She stretched her arms and cracked her neck, and I cracked my knuckles in unconscious response. The courtyard echoed with the sound of bones. When she rose, I followed, and she led me down a hallway that smelled like flowers and car freshener.

Her apartment was at the end of the hall, and as I followed Hanna I saw her as a stalker might, framed by the close walls and closed doors of neighbors she might never see or know. Had someone walked this way before, hyped up on malice and anger and nerves? Did Nora see him coming for her, or did he deny her even that power?

Hanna applied her attention to the door, undoing at least three locks with a series of brassy thuds and clunks. It took about thirty seconds—not a standard apartment setup.

"Sorry," she said, jamming a key into a tight lock with a metallic crunch. "I've been feeling a bit paranoid lately."

"That doesn't surprise me."

"These locks are brand-new. Nora and I talked about getting them put in but she disappeared too fast to do anything about it. Not that they would've helped her." She shook her head. "You can't lock yourself in a fortress forever, and it's not like she felt especially safe inside. Someone wanted to get to her, so he got to her. We are all fundamentally unprotected." She shoved the door open, speaking in a tone that suggested a mantra. "We are at the mercy of the decency of men."

I followed her into the apartment, her words playing musically in my head. It was a nice apartment, with a thickly decorated living room boasting full bookshelves and an assortment of picture frames hanging on the walls. Nora peered out from one of them, with her arm around Hanna. The rest were clearly Hanna's pictures, showing a big family and an assortment of friends.

"I took her pictures down," she said when she saw me looking at the photo wall. "I thought they would creep out the subletter."

"Understandable. Is she here?"

"No, Tinder date." She sighed. "She's kind of obnoxious, to be honest. She actually said to me, 'I hope he's not, like, a murderer.'" Her voice went high and she rolled her eyes.

"Does she know about Nora?"

"Yup."

I sucked air through my teeth. "That's pretty bad."

She shrugged. "At least she's too clueless to be uncomfortable here. She's renting the room furnished."

"Really?" I couldn't suppress a spike of excitement.

"Yes, but if you're thinking Nora's room is as she left it, that's not what I meant."

"Right." I smiled and admitted, "That is what I was thinking, but only for a second."

She walked into a small bedroom and turned on the light. "This is it," she said.

The room was plain, with a bed and a desk and nothing on the walls. The bed was rumpled, but not by Nora. The desk held a laptop, also not Nora's.

I tried to gather a sense of her from the sterile remains of her room. I didn't believe in ghosts, or ghostly remainders, but I thought I might feel something, a kinship, maybe, to tell me why I was there, to tell me where to go next.

Instead there was nothing, just a temporary room belonging to a stranger. Wherever Nora was, it was clear she wasn't here.

"What'd you do with all her stuff?" I asked.

"Police took anything they thought might help them. Her computer, her phone, anything she might have written on. The rest is with her parents."

"Where are they?"

She hesitated. "Nearby. Glendale. But it'd be best if you didn't bother them. I know you're not in the tact industry, but they're having a rough time, from what I could tell."

"When did you see them?" I asked, making no promises.

"When I dropped off her stuff. They had already talked to the police, and were pretty devastated."

"Is Nora close to her parents?"

"In her own way, I think. They wanted her to stay in law school, get a stable job, live with them until she married Chris. She didn't do any of that, and she resented the expectations."

"Rebel girl."

"By their standards, definitely. But they love her. You should've seen her dad crying. It was like the dad in *Twin Peaks*."

"Bad example."

"Yeah, shit. Not intentional," she said. "In any case, maybe hold off on interrogating them if you don't know what the police are up to. No reason to make them run through everything twice if it isn't necessary."

"That's fair," I said. "I guess I'm the third person to interrogate you."

"Oh, I don't mind, really. I can handle it. Anything I can do to get her back."

It was almost ten when I got home, exhausted by chasing a missing girl who wasn't mine to chase. Lori was gone, at Isaac's for the night, and I noted with resignation that her room was starting to look uninhabited. The desk was uncluttered and a stack of dresses lay on the floor, ready to be packed and whisked away. Pretty soon there'd be no sign of her left. Nothing to indicate that we'd spent two years sharing a wall.

I woke up my computer and started the business of finding a new roommate. I'd never had to do it before—I'd lived alone since college, until I moved in with Lori. It crossed my mind that I could return to that solitude. I'd never hated it, really, and it was preferable to living with someone annoying. But there were practical concerns. The lease wasn't up, and besides, I liked our apartment overlooking the Echo Park Lake. I was used to it, and I didn't warm to the idea of leaving it behind.

I posted solicitations on Facebook and Craigslist, seeking a roommate who could move in as soon as possible. I looked at other postings to get an idea of the format, and discovered a lot of optimistic people attempting to design their own roommates, as if they might get all the traits they asked for like toppings on a pizza. Sociable, cleanly, responsible. Educated, liberal, shared taste in music a plus. I wondered who I'd want to live with, and couldn't think of a ready profile. I described the room and noted candidates must be okay with smoking.

I hit Post and lay in bed, refreshing my e-mail and killing time before the trash pull. The apartment was peaceful and empty—I was aware all at once that I didn't fill it. I closed my eyes and thought of Nora. I wondered if we would have gotten along.

I waited for midnight to start getting ready. Arturo had given me a roll of white trash bags, a match for the ones I'd find in the bins— Arturo had done his research, at least. He'd lifted the lids before shoving the rest onto me.

I changed into a sweatshirt and sweatpants, both black, and snapped on a pair of latex gloves. I gathered all the garbage and recycling in the apartment and stuffed it into two bags. I would need a lot more volume.

It was garbage day on my street, too, and I went down and raided two of the blue recycling bins on the curb. These bins weren't clean or anything—the plastic containers collected a lot of dust, dirt, spiderwebs, plant life—but they beat plain old garbage. There were a lot of dog walkers on my block, and I knew the black bins got shoveled full of dog shit. This shortcut meant I would end up sticking some recycling bags in a non-recycling can, but I hoped it would all get sorted out in the end. Even if it didn't, whatever altruism I had stopped short of lovingly subbing in garbage for garbage.

I packed the new bags full of recycling, double bagging to protect from anything wet, sticky, or sharp, then loaded them into the trunk of my car over an extra layer of empty trash bags—protection from stains, spares in a pinch. I drove to Silver Lake and switched my lights off before turning onto the right block. There were no other cars driving by.

I found the address, a small house up a hill about a mile north of the freeway. I parked in front of it—no one would notice my car without first noticing me, a dark figure raiding garbage in the night. The bins were where Arturo said they would be, and they were full past the brim, with bags spilling out and preventing the lids from closing.

I brought the decoy trash from my car and placed it by the containers, where I was sure I wouldn't mix them up with the real ones. Then there was nothing else I could do. I held my breath and dug in—the faster I got it over with, the less likely I was to get caught, not to mention the faster I'd get it over with. I filled the bins back up, using every bag I had and lifting a couple extra from a neighbor to pad the bottoms. Then I hauled the waste into my car, where it was sure to stink things up for a good while, especially since it would sit there ripening overnight.

I tried to picture Philip Marlowe Dumpster diving, decided it didn't fit his image. He dressed too well and cracked too smart. He would be the guy who shook his head at the other guy for spending his hours sifting through garbage when he could solve a mystery by drinking whiskey and evading seduction from dames.

When I got home, I took a thorough shower and went to bed. I hoped to God that Rubina would call the next day.

Six

❧

I was still tired when I woke up, just after nine. I made coffee and took my time getting ready for work. I tried to block out the garbage smell in my car as I drove to work.

Arturo was in his office when I arrived, wearing the same clothes as the day before. This happened at least once a week, and I wondered if it was because he slept at the office or at his lady's. I would've believed either, but I wouldn't have dared to ask.

I walked in and set up the tarp before going back to my car for the garbage bags. I snapped on a new pair of latex gloves and got to work. It took three trips, and Arturo and Chaz watched in amusement as I traipsed back and forth. Neither offered to help, and by the time I returned with the last batch, they were standing in front of the tarp, arms crossed and grinning.

"It's like the good old days," Chaz said to Arturo. "Back when she was an intern."

"I was never an intern," I said, doing the call response to one of Chaz's favorite jokes. "You paid me."

"Did I?" He scratched the back of his neck, then turned to Arturo, squinting. "Did I, really?"

Arturo nodded. "We both did. And that's why she's a garbage professional."

I laid out the trash on the tarp. "You guys are free to help."

"We're busy," Chaz said, giggling.

"Sure, you look totally slammed." I squatted in front of the spoils. "Well, I don't mind. I've got nothing better to do. What am I looking for?"

"Client is a rich man in his fifties," said Arturo. "Target is a penniless woman in her mid-twenties."

"Oh," I said, swinging my arms together in a mock swoon. "This sounds like a love story."

He nodded. "Our client, who is paying us lots of money— something to keep in mind if he happens to visit the office while you're here—is gearing up to buy a fat piece of Harry Winston."

"And before he signs up for a hefty future alimony, he wants us to check out his potential wife's character?"

"Very good. That's exactly it."

"He's worried she'll want to marry him for something other than his shining personality."

"That's part of it."

"And he has just enough self-awareness that he knows he can't ask for a prenup."

Arturo smiled and rocked on his heels. "Not quite. He already asked."

"And she cried and asked why he'd even want to marry her if he didn't trust her? Actually, it's a good question."

"That's exactly what happened." He turned to Chaz. "Is Song as smart as you say she is or are we all just that predictable?"

I felt a blush come to my cheeks, the praise momentarily negating the smell of garbage, still waiting for my exploring hands.

"Combination," Chaz said. He winked at me, sharing my pleasure at the compliment. "Song's a smart lady, but this client is fresh from central casting."

"Who is he?" I asked. "Do you have a picture?"

Arturo smiled, and I knew he'd indulge me. "I don't have one on me, but his name's Harvey Emmanuel."

I took off my gloves and googled him while Arturo and Chaz watched. I found a company photo. He was a CPA at KPMG, round, balding, and mottled. His head rose straight out of a blue suit—he had as much neck as your average snowman. I passed my phone to Chaz and he squinted at the screen then put it down, laughing.

"He's no Brad Pitt," he said.

"He's not even Paul Giamatti." I turned to Arturo. "Well? I know you have a picture of the girlfriend."

Arturo nodded and passed me his phone, the photo in question already enlarged on the screen. "This is Brandy."

"Of course it is," I said, staring. She was a young tanned blonde with balloon tits straining against what must've been a Baby Gap tank top. "This is the picture Harvey sent you?"

Arturo nodded.

"Daddy must be really proud," I said. I looked closer. She had a pretty face, not extraordinary but well above average. "I think she's selling herself short. She could probably nab an accountant her own age. Maybe I should send her an anonymous tip, tell her to hire a PI to run down his finances. He can't make more than a couple hundred thousand a year."

Chaz laughed. "Look at Miss Moneybags over here. All three of us together don't make two hundred thousand a year."

"And I don't see anyone trying to marry us for our money. Arturo, does he have an ex-wife? Any kids?"

"One ex. Two kids."

"So I figure he takes home, what, a hundred and twenty? And I don't know how much child support is, but I imagine it's not nothing. We're talking take-home pay of maybe $80K, and that has to do for both of them. She has to sleep with *this*"—I held up my phone screen—"for limited use of eighty-thousand dollars a year. I hope she has a friend who's laying out the math for her."

"As much as I share your concern for this moral paragon," Arturo said with a smirk, "our job is to audit her, not the client."

"Okay, okay," I said. "Just anything that looks like dirt?"

"Yes, anything that might embarrass him, or give him pause about marrying this woman."

Chaz laughed again. "Didn't *he* send *you* that picture?"

"How do we even know what stuff is hers? She can't live in that house by herself."

"You're right, she doesn't. She lives with her mother. But generous Harvey sent mother out of town, a ten-day vacation to Mexico. He decided it was a good opportunity to get some eyes on his girl."

"A real sweetheart."

It was amazing what you could learn about someone by sorting through her trash. Habits, lifestyle, even values came through in the garbage, the waste telling stories about the lives that produced it, sure as shit gave a window into diet. After an hour of dirty work, I had a pretty good handle on Brandy.

I started with the recycling. I learned right away that she didn't know how to cook. She'd gone through a lot of microwave dinners in the past week. I sympathized, though even I'd left Hot Pockets back in college where they belonged. She drank Diet Coke but never finished the cans, and the warm liquid splotched almost everything in the bags.

She was also a potential compulsive shopper. I found ten paper shopping bags and over twenty receipts, all dated within the past week. There was one for groceries, where I found the bulk of her frozen meals, but most were for random frivolous purchases, made at various shops around town. Tops, earrings, cosmetics, housewares. There was one receipt for a felt fedora. None were for more than $50, but they added up, I tallied, to over $600. There was also a cardboard box from Amazon—at least one online purchase, which wouldn't have generated a paper receipt.

The trash was grosser and trickier to sort. I was thankful that I was right in my initial assessment—that she wasn't much of a cook. None of the wet egg shells or pungent oils that made trash hits truly terrible. There were some wrinkled Luna Bar wrappers, vegetable packets from instant noodles discarded whole. The few takeout boxes were more or less empty—just rice grains and a localized spill of cornstarch-thickened sauce. A couple of black banana peels looked and smelled well over a week rotten, but that was the worst of the food.

The used condoms were easy enough to isolate. There were three of them, and I nearly retched at the thought of fucking the neckless accountant three times in one week, though there was no way to know whether they all belonged to him, unless Emmanuel wanted to test the sperm. I noted the number, at least, assuming he'd know how many he'd been responsible for. I checked them for holes, just for good measure. I'd never actually seen a sabotaged condom. There was no evidence of other birth control, or of a menstrual cycle, but most of the trash from these things was limited to specific windows. I was happy enough to miss out on tampons.

There was a lot of bubble wrap, packing foam, and ripped plastic, the molted remains of newness. There was also an empty tube of purplish lip gloss and an empty container of foundation. Might have been coincidence, but it seemed likely that she went through makeup a lot faster than most women I knew. I didn't wear much, and even Lori, who always looked perfect, rarely finished using a lip gloss before she'd had a chance to lose it. This had the look of an expensive habit, though probably one that Emmanuel would have to be willing to maintain.

I separated out the true junk, and photographed it in a few wide group shots. I separated out the condoms, the receipts, anything else I thought might be of any interest to the client. I photographed these items individually. When I was done, I had Arturo scan over what I'd done, and he gave me leave to take out the bulk of the trash. The whole process took about an hour and a half.

He patted me on the back. "Thanks, Song. That was a big help. Do you think you've got time to write it up?"

I heard Chaz belly laughing in his office.

I was wrapping up the write-up and thinking about lunch when my cell phone rang, the caller ID showing an 818 number. I didn't make a habit of answering unrecognized numbers—I'd gotten too many cold calls from Yale and the Democratic Party, asking for cash— but I couldn't risk missing a call from Rubina or even Lusig.

"This is Song," I said, with a sharp saccharine note of hopefulness in my voice.

"Hey, it's Lusig. I'm sucking it up."

"You mean you're taking Rubina up on her offer?" I kept my voice neutral and pumped my free fist.

"That's right. I dance for her and you dance for me."

"Happy to."

"I'd like to start as soon as possible. Are you free at all today?"

I didn't have to open up a calendar to know my day was scheduled full of quiet, excluding whatever grunt work Chaz or Arturo might push on me. "Sure. Coffee?"

She laughed. "We can meet at a café, but Rubina doesn't want me drinking coffee."

"Really?" I said. "Okay, so you tell me. You can't drink booze or caffeine. What exactly can you do?"

"I can eat like a beast. I feel deprived if I go two days without a bucketful of pastrami."

We arranged to meet at Langer's at one, leaving me about half an hour in the office. I finished the write-up and walked into Arturo's office, trying not to beam.

"I'm on a job again," I said. "It's going to take most of my time, I think."

Arturo raised his eyebrows to look up at me, more or less indifferently. "Good for you, Song."

"I just e-mailed you the trash write-up. Do you need me to do anything else on that case? Protect this noble client from his temptress's wiles?"

"You're free to go, but don't make me feel like I have to protect my client from you." He pointed at me with a ballpoint pen. "Remember, you're a professional. And none of us make our bread by choosing our own clients."

I nodded, slightly chastised. "I know, Arturo. I was just trying to get off the hook, to be honest."

He smiled. "I know that."

"I have a winner here," I said. "A case I can really get into."

"Chaz told me about your missing activist. Congrats, Song. Don't go crazy."

I visited Chaz's office next, letting loose my grin of triumph.

"Uh oh," he said. "Looks like someone just handed this cat the canary."

"I'm back on," I said.

"I heard," he said. "Hey, Art," he called through the wall without raising his voice.

"Chaz," Arturo called back.

"I'm happy for you," he said, turning back to me. "I'm glad you have a proper avenue for your obsessions again. Juniper Song stressing out about men and children was a bit too *Twilight Zone* for my taste."

I laughed and changed the subject. "You're some kind of computer genius, aren't you, Chaz?"

He gave me a broad, crooked smile that said he was in the mood to be flattered. "I don't know about genius, Song. I can't keep up with you kids these days. I haven't made any apps."

"I need a favor."

"What else is new, huh?"

It was to my advantage that Chaz loved doing favors for the grateful. He had a paternal streak, and he cherished the idea of his own indispensability.

"Can you find anonymous commenters from a Web site?"

"What kind of anonymous commenters?"

"You know, the usual. Racist pests, harassers of women, the riff-raff that hang out in the dark corners of the Internet."

"Have you been reading the comments on YouTube?"

"On a political site. Nora Mkrtchian's. Can you help?"

"It depends," he said, twisting his mouth. "I'll tell you right off the bat that sometimes it's downright impossible."

"I thought all this stuff was trackable. You know, like Edward Snowden and all that?"

"Do I look like the Pentagon?" He chuckled. "Even if everything is accessible to some people, which, I'm not sure that's true either, I can tell you there are barriers for a working snoop."

"Can you try?"

"What do you think?"

"You'll try."

"Anything for you, Girl Detective."

I took the subway from Koreatown, something I liked to do when it made sense, maybe once every few months. Langer's was in Mac-Arthur Park, across the street from a Metro station. I liked to think the Metro station was built as a portal to Langer's.

The train was dingy and somewhat crowded, with just a few empty seats on the far sides of passengers who looked like they'd sigh loudly if I asked to climb in. Some days I would have punished one of these commuters, but I was too restless to sit sandwiched between a resentful stranger and a subway car wall.

I held on to a pole and looked around as the train rumbled through its tunnel. The L.A. Metro was less essential to the daily life of many of its citizens than transit systems in comparable cities. Its lack of reach and general shittiness were, in fact, one of the greatest strikes against L.A. in the opinions of annoying outsiders.

A black-and-white sticker caught my eye on one of the windows next to an empty seat. I squinted, trying to make sure of the text, and then I made my way through the aisle. I looked at the scowling man beneath my nose. He was thickset with heavy eyelids, and he smelled less than fresh from a few feet away.

"Sorry," I said. "May I?"

He got up—I'd known that he wouldn't scoot in—and I crammed myself up against the window. On it was a bumper sticker, about three inches square, with white text touting *Who Still Talks*. There was another sticker next to it, which I hadn't been able to read from a distance. This one had the URL for *Who Still Talks* written in one corner. The rest of it was devoted to the words *FIND NORA*.

I snapped a picture on my phone and wondered how these stickers were circulated and how many of them were around. I was not such a believer in coincidence that I thought I'd stumbled on a message, a clue designed to reach me alone. I wondered if Lusig knew about the stickers. It was even possible that she was behind their printing.

The train stopped a minute later at the Westlake/MacArthur Park station, and I made my way around my fellow commuters and got out into the sunlight.

MacArthur Park was a notoriously dangerous part of town still awaiting its turn to gentrify. The park had seen a lot of crime, and the wide lake, so pretty in daylight, suggested shady possibilities. In the public imagination, the lake was clogged up with bodies and discarded weapons. There was a seed of truth to this idea—the park was a bit of a gang-murder mecca in the '80s and '90s, and that was after the lake was drained in the '70s, revealing hundreds of firearms like so many wads of chewed gum hidden under a used classroom desk. It was safer now, a bit revitalized in recent years. The Metro station was part of that. Still, it wasn't exactly Beverly Hills. Street vendors sat on the sidewalk hawking $5 shoes and flammable toys, and I got one offer for a counterfeit green card on my way across the street, from a tiny, whispering, middle-aged Latino man. I would've been offended, but he offered me a driver's license in the same breath, and I probably looked as foreign as I did underage.

Langer's predated the gang violence by a few decades. It was a Jewish deli with the best pastrami in the States, about as historic a restaurant as you might find in L.A. The violence and recession almost drove it out of business, but the Metro came along to save the day. The deli drew a large lunch crowd, many of them in business casual, stopping in from downtown. It didn't take the Census Bureau to determine that Langer's had the highest concentration of white people in the neighborhood.

Lusig was already waiting when I walked in, tucked into a booth with her back resting against a wall. She raised her hand when she saw me, and I slid in across from her.

"Have you been waiting long?" I asked.

"Sweet freedom," she said. "I've been here for fifteen minutes, just drinking it in."

I nodded with sympathy. Rubina had her on quite the leash—I knew something about that, as part of its apparatus.

"I spent the weekend at her place, thinking it over. It wasn't so bad, I guess. She didn't drive me too crazy."

"I'm glad you said yes."

She shrugged. "I don't see what my other options are. I can't put myself in actual danger, and I don't have the money to hire you myself. It's just one more month. Or maybe this fucker'll come early."

I smiled.

"I don't mean like *tomorrow*," she added quickly. "You know, like two weeks early, when he's still going to be safe."

"Lusig, I'm not here to judge you. I live in a glass house with millimeter panes."

We ordered big sandwiches, hot pastrami on rye with Russian dressing. She got extra pickles and a matzoh ball soup. She asked the waitress to make sure hers was piping hot, and patted her bulging belly in explanation.

"You can't have cold pastrami?" I asked.

"Nope. No cold deli meats."

"That's rough."

"Oh, yeah." She pulled out her phone, fiddled with it a bit, and started reading off her screen. "Also forbidden—sushi, soft cheese, rare meat, hot dogs . . . Technically I can have a beer now and then, but not with Ruby playing goalie in my throat."

"And do you crave all that stuff?"

"When I get rid of this thing, I'm wrapping a steak in salami and raw salmon, then swallowing the whole thing with a pint of whiskey."

"For breakfast, I guess?"

Our food came and Lusig tore into her sandwich, murmuring, "God, this pastrami is saving my life."

I smiled and agreed. "It's legendary."

We ate in blissful silence for a minute, then she showed me her phone. "Look at this."

It was a standard smartphone screen with a background image of Lusig and Nora. They were smiling at the camera with their cheeks nearly touching. Lusig had her hand on Nora's head, pulling her close to her side.

"The picture?" I asked.

"No." She let out an awkward sigh of a laugh. "Right. I have a picture of Nora on there. I meant the apps."

I looked at the colorful icons on the screen, and noticed six of them with the words "baby" and "mommy" in their titles. "Pregnancy apps. Hadn't thought of that."

"These are the best of them. I've probably downloaded more like twenty."

I nodded. "Lot of work, huh?"

"I just feel like I need to convince you or something, that I'm not treating this lightly."

"Sure. Don't worry. I believe you."

"Okay, good. But I also need to find Nora. I am very serious about this. It's why I'm subjecting myself to Ruby's regime."

"Can I ask you something?"

"Go for it."

"Why you? Nora has family, a boyfriend, plenty of friends, it sounds like. Why does this fall on you?"

"Maybe it doesn't," she said. "Maybe it falls on everyone. But I know that my life falls apart without Nora."

"That sounds dramatic."

"It's true, though. I didn't even realize until she was gone, how much she held things together for me. I thought I had lots of friends, but I only had one I counted on, who loved and understood me."

I nodded, and I knew I would go on a rampage if Lori disappeared.

"How long have you been sniffing around?"

"Just a couple weeks. I've been worried sick since she disappeared, but I kept believing she'd turn up, or at least that the police would find her. But then I started to get this feeling, like the momentum was draining away, and I read somewhere that most missing people are found within a short window of disappearing, if they're ever found at all."

"Yeah," I said. "Seventy-two hours. That's supposed to be how long it takes to track down the strong leads."

"It had been a lot longer than that when I started looking."

"What have you turned up?" I asked. "So I don't duplicate your work."

She frowned. "Not very much, to be honest. I haven't wanted to do anything strenuous, so just a lot of Internet stuff."

"I've done a lot of research on her, too," I said. "Her site is fascinating, and it looks like she has a lot of enemies." I had to watch myself to make sure I didn't introduce the past tense.

"Are you talking about those anonymous Internet dickheads?"

"Yeah. Pretty intense."

"Did you see that they found her address?"

"Actually, I've done some legwork since I last saw you."

I caught her up on my meetings with Chris and Hanna.

She listened, chewing slowly, preciously, on her sandwich. When I was done, she asked, "What'd you think of Chris?"

"He was not super happy to talk to me. I caught him off guard." I thought back to our conversation and remembered my mention of Lusig. "Actually, I'm sorry, but I mentioned I was looking for Nora in part because of you."

"It's okay," she said. "I'm not worried about him knowing that. Did he say anything about me?"

"No. But I got the sense that this whole investigation got on his nerves. Offended him in some way. He even seems mad at Nora for disappearing."

"Oh, his princess-in-the-tower shit?"

"What?"

"Chris thinks she would've been safe and happy if only she'd never left her house, at least not without him at her side."

"Yeah, I got that impression. Is he kind of an asshole?"

"Maybe 'asshole' isn't the right word. He means well. He's just . . ." She shrugged and took a big, crunchy bite out of her pickle. "Look, he's an idiot."

"That's a strong word."

"It's the right one. Everyone thinks he's a brain because he went to Penn and has this job. Everyone thinks Nora's an airhead because she wears a lot of eyeliner. No one knows anything, is the moral of that story. I happen to know Chris is as dumb as a rock's ass."

I laughed. "Explain."

"You know how children have no concept of a world they can't see? Chris is myopic like that. He can't see more than one logical connection outside of what affects him. So, of course Nora disappeared because she disobeyed him."

"Do you think he had anything to do with it?"

"I doubt it. He's not savvy enough to keep someone hidden for this long."

"What's your theory, then? You obviously have a head start on me."

"I think she went after her stalker."

"That sounds plausible," I said. "Her last blog post sounded like a declaration of war. Is that what you're going on?"

"Basically." She ran a hand through her short hair, then clamped it over her ear. "I don't have proof or anything, if that's what you're asking."

"Proof would be nice, I guess, but hunches are valuable, too."

"It would be pretty like her, I think, to go on the warpath. She can't stand losing."

I nodded and took a bite out of my sandwich. I thought about what I might've done in Nora's position, and decided a manhunt was reckless but certainly not unprovoked.

"What were you doing in downtown yesterday?" I asked. "Did that have anything to do with her stalker?"

She smiled, a little proudly. "I was trying to go undercover."

"Where?"

"Did you read anything about this lawsuit?"

"A little. She mentioned it on her site, I think. But remind me?"

"Nora's involved in this genocide memorial. It's supposed to go up for the centennial, on April 24."

"Right," I said. "I imagine this is a big deal?"

"Yeah. There are a lot of Armenians in Glendale, and the memorial will be a big statement."

"And what, not everyone is happy with it?"

"Specifically, there's a brand-spanking-new corporation called Europeans and Americans for the Recovery of Truth in History."

"EARTH?" I snorted a little at the acronym. "Sure. What's their deal?"

"They were formed three months ago. Their first action was to sue the city of Glendale to get an injunction against the statue."

"Ah. So what is this, just three angry Turkish dudes?"

"Something like that. But somehow, they managed to hire a super–white shoe firm to represent them."

"Which one?"

"Thayer White."

I could see the name of the firm in crisp letters on the top of a downtown skyscraper. "So you were trying to go undercover there? What's that even mean?"

She shrugged. "Nothing too sophisticated. I just tried to look like I belonged there so I could get in and talk to a few of the lawyers involved."

"You know who's involved?"

"Yeah, it's public somehow. The firm's been getting some bad press for representing straight-up genocide deniers, and a couple of the articles I've seen have listed the names of the lawyers assigned to the case. To shame them, probably."

"Who are they?"

"Two partners, two associates, it looks like."

"Give me their names."

She pulled up an article on her phone and passed it to me, zooming in on the names. Alexander Crenshaw, Robert Moore, Harriett Lehr, Robert Park.

My heart sank at the last one—the name was as Korean as

soju and seaweed soup. I felt an instinctive scorch of shame. Korean-American misdeeds had a sinister way of making me feel bad about myself. I hated that. The average white dude didn't feel compromised by the worst actions of his phenotype. Every white mass murderer was his own shitty island. Then again, no one judged white dudes as a homogeneous group. Minority sins had more of a smearing effect—it wasn't just in our imagination.

I copied down the names and handed the phone back to Lusig. "What made you want to talk to the lawyers?"

"I have this feeling," she said. "The harassment? It got extra bad after Nora went after the lawsuit. She tried really hard to make noise about it, and that's when the threats starting coming to her house. I want to find out more about this EARTH group, and I have no names to go after except the lawyers."

I nodded. I might have taken the same track.

"So, what happened?" I asked. "What was your plan?"

"I knew where the office was, and I decided I wanted to talk to Alexander Crenshaw."

"Why him?"

She shrugged. "First name on the list. Thought he might be the main person on it."

"Did you make an appointment or something?"

"No," she said sheepishly. "I realize now that I wasn't thinking things through."

"What happened? You just walked in and asked to see Alexander Crenshaw?"

"Pretty much."

I shook my head. "He's a partner there, right? Big law partners are very busy, self-important people. I think it's tough to get a walk-in appointment."

"I was hoping I could just get in and find his office, but the receptionist was pretty suspicious. She asked me if I was a reporter."

"Ah," I said. "Right. I'm guessing they don't have a great relationship with the press these days."

"Yeah. And I didn't want to get into a whole scene so I just turned around and left. I was planning to regroup when you followed me to Rubina's."

"Leave this to me. I'll find my way to one of the lawyers. Probably won't go for a partner, though. More likely to have a stake in the case."

"Good point." She smiled. "Are you going for the Korean?"

I nodded. "Have to exploit every angle, right?"

"I get it. Armos are like that, too."

"Like what?"

"You know, we're supposed to help each other out. If I'd seen an Armenian name, I would've thought, 'Pay dirt.'"

"And 'traitor.'"

"Well, yeah."

"I get it, by the way. The historical anger."

"Korea's been bent over a few times over the centuries, right?"

"I've never lived in Korea. Spent two weeks there total, probably. No one there would see me as anything but American. That said, I know what it's like to feel rage in my blood."

"Yeah. I haven't spent any time in Armenia or anything, either."

"My grandparents lived through World War II. My grandma was too young, but her sister was a comfort woman."

"Jesus, really?"

"Yeah, a bona fide sex slave. Or prostitute, depending on who you ask."

"Who says prostitute?"

I shrugged. "The Japanese government, every other year or so."

"Oh shit, and I thought Turkey was special. What's the deal there?"

"They've had enough guilt or something. In any case, they're not really sorry, and they haven't fully apologized without backtracking immediately. Japan did some heinous shit, and there's still tension with Korea because of it. It's been, like, seventy years."

"It's been a full hundred since the Armenian genocide."

"So it's in 'get over it' territory, except no one ever apologized."

"Exactly."

"Yeah, that's what I don't get. If it were easy to 'get over' something like that, like if it weren't a big deal at all, then it should be just as easy to apologize. It's not like the current Japanese prime minister went around raping all of Asia with his own ugly dick."

She laughed. "Sorry, I'm just picturing this old Asian dude fucking a gouged-out globe."

"At least that wouldn't hurt anybody."

"What's the plan of attack, then?"

I shrugged. "It's really easy to get an e-mail to someone. I'll probably try and get in touch with Robert Park, go from there. Seems as good a place to start as any."

"That sounds good. I feel like we see eye to eye, you and me," she said, her tone suddenly careful, self-consciously designating her words as segue.

"Yeah, I guess so," I said, waiting for her to continue.

"Well, I had an idea, actually. I already ran it by Ruby and Van."

"Yeah?"

"You saw how big their house is, right?"

"Yeah, about ten of my apartments, it looked like, stacked two stories high."

"Well there's an empty room next to mine," she said.

I raised an eyebrow. "What are you proposing?"

"I think it would be a lot better for everyone if you moved in for a while," she said. "Until we find Nora. Or at least until the baby comes."

Her expression was expectant and sheepish, like she'd just asked me to the prom. I thought of my apartment, the space that felt vacant without Lori in it. Here was a guarantee of a new companionship, a reprieve from the loneliness I was unprepared to handle.

But it also meant moving into a house of virtual strangers, one of whom I had good reason to believe was a crazy person, at least colloquially speaking.

She saw my hesitation. "There's precedent for it," she said. "I googled it. Private investigators do on-site work all the time. You'd be like a bodyguard, kind of."

"How would that work?"

"You can figure out the details with Ruby. But I think it'd be pretty simple, really. You use the house as your office, home base, basically. That way I can be involved without 'putting myself in harm's way' or whatever." She employed scornful air quotes.

"So I'd have you watching me while Rubina watches you and watches me watching you."

She nodded slowly, untangling the pronouns.

"That doesn't sound like a party I want to go to."

"It might be the only way this works," she said. "I don't know if I can live there without a buffer."

"So this is your idea, not Rubina's."

"Yeah," she said. "Look, I know it sounds like a clusterfuck, but it could actually work out nicely. Ruby doesn't go crazy worrying about me, I don't go crazy with her worry about me, you get paid more, and you get to work the case."

"Is this a condition?" I asked.

"Of what?"

"Of your living with the Gasparians. Of my helming the case."

"What if it is?"

I shrugged. "I'm just curious."

"You seem like one of those obsessive detectives from the movies. Like, if you're into a case, you get *really* into it."

"That might happen once in a while. It just means I'm good at my job."

She leaned in, sensing an advantage. "How often do you get a case this interesting?"

"Once in a long while," I conceded.

"I get this feeling. Call it a woman's intuition, or at least the ability to draw conclusions from the fact that you've interviewed her boyfriend and roommate since I last saw you." She paused and looked at me coyly.

"Uh-huh," I said, waving a hand for her to go on.

"You're going to find Nora," she said with a certainty that was meant, at least in part, to bolster herself. "You've already shown you'd work for free, and I think you'd meet any condition you had to."

I laughed. "Hey, hey, I don't like to be bullied," I said. "For what it's worth, I wouldn't work for free. It's a pretty idea, but this is the only job I have."

She sat back. "I know. And it's not a condition. There are no conditions. I need to find her more badly than you do."

"I will do everything I can to make that happen."

"But, please, will you think about it?" she asked. "My body is weird, my cousin is crazy, and Nora is gone. We could be friends." Her wild eyes took on a fervent glimmer.

"I'll think about it," I said.

"I just really need a friend."

Seven

❧

Lusig drove me to back to the office after lunch.

"Want to come up?" I asked. "See where Rubina bought me?"

"Sure," she said. "I've never been to a PI office before."

The door to Lindley & Flores was open. Chaz was in his office. Arturo was not. I wondered if he was out somewhere, taking video of the poor young bride-to-be.

"Who've you got there, Song?" Chaz called out.

"This is my client Lusig," I said.

He came out of his office, looked at her pregnant belly, and nodded. "Ah, if I'd gotten a good look, I would've figured that out on my own. You're the cousin."

Lusig smiled and put out her hand in a bold, exaggerated motion, a communication of goodwill. "Lusig Hovanian," she said.

"Chaz Lindley. This one taking care of you?" He gestured toward me with his meaty head and winked, though I couldn't tell which of us he was winking at.

"She seems to be doing better than I was."

"Ah, yes, Song tells me you were caught playing amateur sleuth."

She smiled sheepishly, with her teeth lined up.

"Hey, no need to be embarrassed in this company. Song was an amateur. Who knows what she'd be doing now if I hadn't found her."

I rolled my eyes. "Starving, probably. If not dead."

Neither of us mentioned that Chaz had likely saved my life when we first met. He knew it, and he knew I knew it, but it was a fact with enough weight to derail most conversations.

"But it's good that you're not doing that anymore," Chaz said to Lusig, taking a more serious tone. "This job can be dangerous. Turns out people don't like when you ask them questions and follow them around."

"Which is why I'm under house arrest," she said. "Actually, I'm hoping to convince Song to join me."

He laughed. "Under house arrest?"

"She wants me to move in with the whole family until the baby's born." I outlined her proposal.

"What do you think, Mr. Lindley?" she asked. "Is that something she could do?"

"Sure. That sort of thing isn't unheard of, though the exact circumstances may never have happened before. It would really be up to Song, here. If she's up for it, I think it's a fine idea."

She flashed a bright smile at Chaz. "I should get going while I'm ahead." She gave me a hug and trotted out the door, shouting, "Call me!"

Chaz started laughing as soon as she was gone. "You sure pulled a strange one."

"You like her, huh?"

"I do. She's spunky."

"I like her, too. And this case is really interesting."

"It's so interesting you're going to move in with it, huh?"

"I'm thinking it over," I said. "You really think it's a fine idea?"

"It could be a good experience. And God knows you won't be bored."

* * *

Chaz left me in charge of the office to go home early—if I went along with Lusig's scheme, he would have a lot fewer half days. There were no new clients all afternoon, and I set to work finding Robert Park.

It took me a few strokes more than anticipated to find him. When I searched his name on the Thayer White Web site, I got zero results. This was odd, as the firm had a public directory, and I searched the other three lawyers and found their pages. They were all white, the two partners white men who had gone to top law schools.

I knew it was futile to search just his name on Facebook or Google, but I entered it just to see what would come up. It turned out I had mutual friends with three different Robert Parks, and I didn't even have many Facebook friends. Google showed me a sports writer, a TV actor, and a radiologist in Maryland, all within the first page of results. I added "Thayer White" to my search terms and found an article detailing his bio, torn, it appeared, from some now-defunct version on the firm Web site. Robert Park was a third-year associate, a graduate of UCLA Law.

I had a different search term now, and googled "Robert Park" with "UCLA law" and found out he'd participated in the *UCLA Law Review* and served on the APALSA board in his second year. I also found a UCLA e-mail address.

I thought it was unlikely that the address would still be viable years after he graduated, but I thought it might be a good handle to flush him out on Facebook. I searched the address and it took me to one of the three Robert Parks who'd popped up earlier. He was friends with one of my cousins. Of course. They probably went to the same church. Korean-American L.A. was small, despite our large population.

I couldn't see much of his profile—he had his security settings cranked to an intelligent level. I could see a cover photo of the ocean, and a square image of his face, too small to be useful. I could see that he'd gone to UCI for college, and that his high school was also in Orange County. He was two years older than me, judging from his class years.

I couldn't find an e-mail address, so I decided to message him through Facebook. It wasn't ideal as tactics go—unsolicited Facebook messages tended to be weird and creepy. Still, it was worth a shot.

I wrote:

Hey,
Sorry to message you out of the blue here, but I'm trying to locate Nora Mkrtchian, the Armenian-American activist who disappeared recently. I have a couple hunches. One is that you might be able to help me find her, even if you don't know it. The other is that you quit Thayer White when you couldn't deal with their bottomless moral bankruptcy. If I guessed right on that one, I'd really like to talk to you. My e-mail is juniper song@gmail.com. Hope to hear from you soon.

I reread the message a couple of times then hit Send. I hoped I was right about his quitting the firm. If I was wrong, there was no way he'd be willing to talk to me.

I was sitting back down at my computer after a cigarette break when the message popped back up in my Facebook window. It was flashing—Robert Park had replied.

Hi, Juniper. I know who Nora Mkrtchian is, but I've never met her, and am not sure if I'm the right person to help. That said, you're right about me and Thayer. Uncanny guess. Are you police or something? I don't know what I can do for you, but obviously would like to contribute to finding her if you think I have that in me. I will say, though, that if you're a reporter I am not comfortable talking about my old job in the press.
Best,
Rob

It had been about twenty minutes since I'd contacted him, a much better result than I'd expected. He could have been nervous, or just intrigued and unemployed. I had to remind myself that matters of crime and punishment were fascinating to people, not just people of interest.

I wondered why he hadn't e-mailed me when I'd given him my address, then realized I was still online on Facebook. I rarely used the messenger service, and I'd forgotten that it doubled as a chat. There was a green dot next to his name—I could continue this conversation right now.

I started to write a formal response, and deleted it. Instead, I typed one word:

> *Hey.*

His response came immediately.

> *Hi.*
> *Thanks for getting back to me so quickly, I'm not police or press, I'm a private detective.*
> *Like Sherlock Holmes? Philip Marlowe?*
> *Yes, exactly the same. Shoot up coke, solve murder mysteries.*
> *Ha, that's really cool. Where do I sign up?*

I smiled a little. The conversation had taken a friendly tone, one that didn't always come with contacting strangers out of the blue. It felt a little strange to be chatting with someone I'd never met before. I knew it wasn't unusual, but I'd never experimented with chat rooms or the varied online platforms for meet-ups or dating.

I pressed on.

> *I'm helping Nora's best friend, who's really worried about her, and I was hoping we could talk?*

> You mean in person?
> Yeah, I prefer face-to-face. It'd be lazy work if I just sat around chatting with people all day.

I didn't add that in-person interviews gave me a greater interrogative advantage, which I liked to think yielded higher returns of truth.

> At the risk of sounding forward . . . What are you doing right now? Because I'm unemployed and have seen zero people today.

I wondered briefly if he was flirting with me. I knew my profile was locked down pretty tight, so if he was throwing out feelers, it had to be purely speculative. The thumbnail of my profile picture didn't give away much.

> I'm free. I can buy you a drink?
> Where are you?
> Koreatown now, but I live in Echo Park.
> I'm downtown. I can meet you at Mohawk Bend. My dog loves it there. Mind if I bring her?
> Course not.
> By the way, how do you know Nick Jeon?
> He's my cousin. You?
> We went to church together back in the day.

I laughed out loud, but didn't say so.

> Would you believe me if I told you that was my first guess?

We arranged to meet at five thirty at Mohawk Bend on Sunset Boulevard. It was one of the new bars that sprouted in the gentrified soil of my neighborhood, built in an old Vaudeville theater, with craft beers and a patio full of rescue dogs. It was a nice walk from my place, and I stopped home to drop off my Langer's leftovers and avoid dealing with parking. The weather was fine and I thought I could use the movement.

I scanned the patio and spotted an Asian man with a sweet-looking pit bull mix at his feet, sitting alone at a table for two. He looked more or less like a thirty-year-old lawyer—clean-cut, with thick, black, slightly wavy hair, not a grain of stubble on his face; black plastic-framed glasses. He wore a gray sweater under a black fleece jacket. He had his head down, reading something on his phone.

"Hi," I said, tentatively. "Robert Park?"

He looked up with a snap of his neck. "Juniper Song?"

He had a pleasant, nervous face, with long, dark eyes and an expressive lower lip. He didn't smile, but nothing about him read cold. The thought crossed my mind that my mother would love him.

Except that he was currently unemployed, and who knew if he went to church anymore.

"Song," I said, shaking his hand. I sat down in the empty chair. "Sorry, have you been waiting long?"

"Ten minutes, but I was early. I always set aside fifteen minutes for parking."

"That's noble," I said. "I always apologize when I'm fifteen minutes late because I couldn't find parking."

He smiled then, showing a white slice of teeth.

"Boy or girl?" I asked, pointing at his dog, who was staring at me with its tail thumping.

"Girl. Her name's Muriel but you can call her Murry. Like Furry Murry."

"Muriel? How'd you come up with that?"

"My grandma's name."

I laughed. Nowhere in the world was there a Korean grandmother named Muriel. "Bullshit."

"Okay, you got me. The shelter was calling her Cupcake, so I took matters into my own hands. She's named after Muriel Spark."

I smiled. It was hard not to like a guy who named a rescue dog after a female novelist. "When'd you get her?"

"This weekend. I've wanted my own dog since my childhood dog died, but couldn't have one with the firm job."

"Congratulations. Pit and . . . beagle?"

"Good guess. Wow, you really are good at this deduction stuff."

"She's adorable. Can I pet her?"

He assured me she was friendly, and I stroked her soft coat, which was white with brown splotches like the spots on a cow. I was still petting her when a server came and took our drink order. By the time our beers came, I was in good with Murry.

"I looked you up, by the way," he said with no more segue. "I wanted to make sure you weren't a reporter."

I raised an eyebrow. "You stalked me?"

"You're a private eye. I'd be surprised if you didn't stalk me."

I shrugged. "Fair enough."

"What'd you find out?"

"There are a lot of Robert Parks out there, so frankly, not much. What'd the Internet have to say about me?"

"Some interesting stuff, actually. Your name came up in connection with the Joe Tilley case a couple years back. Pretty glamorous."

Joe Tilley wasn't the first dead body that had shown up in my vicinity, but it was the only one people wanted to talk about when the news was no longer news. He was a major movie star, and every dumb blog wanted an angle on the story. My name came up with a hundred others, all dragged in with the season's catch. "Trust me. It was the opposite of glamorous."

"I don't know. I'm into the PI stuff. L.A. noir, all that. Are you?"

"Of course."

"Chandler? Moseley? Ellroy?"

"Yup."

"Robert B. Parker?" He flashed a wide smile.

I didn't mention that my snooping career started as a love for the literature. It seemed like it would sound more frivolous than it was.

We talked about books and movies for a while, and I could feel him sliding into a sort of comfort with my presence. He was reasonably personable, and I got the sense that he found other people more interesting than himself. His manner grew more assured but subtly self-effacing, a combination that rendered him attractive.

"So," I said toward the bottom of my beer. "Why'd you quit your job?"

"I thought you had that all figured out."

"All I said was 'moral bankruptcy.' Could be anything. Was it an oil spill? Mortgage fraud?"

He smiled. "You know perfectly well it was something worse."

"Worse?"

"I guess 'worse' is the wrong word. I'm a litigator, so I've done work for some pretty noxious clients, including a reckless oil company, by the way. In absolute terms, genocide denial might be less harmful than other wrongs I've worked to defend, but it's more . . ."

"Gross?"

"Yeah." He took a sip of beer and looked above him. "The thing is, if a big oil company ruins the ocean, it's entitled to hire lawyers, to mount a defense, yeah, but also to get liability assessments, things that are a bit more neutral. There's nothing behind that but money. No desire to corrupt the world, just an indifference to consequences and a strong adherence to the profit motive. This genocide memorial, though . . . My team was representing the plaintiff—the genocide deniers were suing. So it's a frivolous, unnecessary suit that also happens to be hateful as hell."

"And now your name is associated with it forever, huh?"

He shrugged. "I deserve it, I guess. I should've quit sooner than

I did. It's just hard to get off a track once you've been on it for so long, you know?"

I nodded. "On the bright side, you're one of many Robert Parks in the world."

"Yeah. It's nice not being special."

"What can you tell me about EARTH?"

"Technically? Nothing. Confidentiality and all that."

"But you quit."

"That doesn't mean I'm exempt from the rules."

I held eye contact through a long pause, and I knew that he'd acquiesce. "A woman is missing, Rob Park. I think EARTH might have something to do with it."

He sighed. "Well, I will say I didn't come here expecting to say nothing. This is strictly, uh, off the record?"

I held up my hands. "What record?"

He bent over to pet Murry behind her ears, and when he rose again, he was ready to talk. "EARTH is this brand-new organization, founded by these three Turkish-American men. The purpose of the organization is, supposedly, the discovery and preservation of history, particularly Turkish history."

"A 'let's hear both sides of this terrible story' kind of deal, then."

"Exactly. It has the sheen of fairness and reason, right? Because there are two sides to every story."

"Sure. But sometimes one side is the genociding side." I shook my head. "And, of course, it's just three extreme people hiding behind an acronym."

"There are more than three people involved, but yeah, basically. The organization was formed for this one purpose, and it's small and scrappy."

"How heartwarming. The little hatemongers who could. Did you ever meet any of these clients?"

"Yes, briefly," he said. "Just one guy."

"Who?"

"This man named Enver Kizil. He came in to talk to us once, and I was in the room, though the partner did most of the talking on our end."

"What was he like?"

"Younger than you would think, for this kind of thing. Thirty-five? And maybe I was biased by what I knew about him, but I thought he looked ferociously angry, like if you punctured his skin, rage would flow out of him."

"Do you have a number or e-mail address I can reach him at?"

"Sound like a guy you'd like to get to know?" He smiled and scrolled through his phone. "Here," he said, holding it out to me.

I copied the e-mail address on the screen.

"Did he seem rich, by the way?"

He thought for a second. "Not especially."

"It takes a lot of money to hire a big firm, right?"

"Yeah. I'm not sure how the billing worked, but I doubt Thayer was taking them on pro bono."

"And EARTH is a small operation, you said."

"Yes, but they definitely have money. I think one of the more vocal members is this rich housewife and I wouldn't be surprised if she and her husband were bankrolling."

"Who are they?"

"I never met them, and I don't remember their names," he said. "To be honest, I didn't look into it too deeply. If I'd made a point of knowing all the people I worked for over the years, I might have quit a lot sooner."

"You weren't curious?"

"I was, vaguely." His lips formed a small frown. "You must think I'm a drone."

"No. You're just not an investigator. I'm sure no one at that firm is motivated to put their assignments under a microscope. I wonder, though," I said, leaning forward, "are you motivated now?"

He blinked and gave me a stunned smile. "You want my help?"

"Of course. I take help where I can get it."

"You know how to butter a guy up, huh?"

He was laughing, and I laughed with him. "You seem interested in what I do," I said. "You can join the adventure."

"Down the rabbit hole," he said. "Okay, let's say I am interested. What do I do?"

"Find out who's running EARTH."

"Easier said than done, probably."

"Sure, like anything else. But it's doable. You know people there. Maybe you have some friends who'd help you out, ask around. You could probably even get back in the office if you wanted."

"Yeah, I can think of a few people to talk to."

"Harriett Lehr, for instance."

He laughed. "Sure. I won't ask how you know about Harriett."

"Same way I know about you. It was in the news."

"Right," he said, his face somber. "Poor Harriett. She hates this almost much as I do."

"She's still there, though."

"I can't blame her. She didn't ask for this either."

"Maybe she'll be up for answering a question or two. Off the record."

"What do I ask her?"

"You seem like a smart guy," I said. "There really isn't that much to this shit. You just have to be nosier and more persistent than most people feel comfortable with."

"Okay, I guess I can figure something out."

"Here's a hint, I guess. Someone is paying for this operation. It's never a bad idea to follow the money. That's how they got Al Capone. Maybe it's those rich Turks you mentioned, and all you have to do is get their names."

He saluted, then looked a little embarrassed about it. "I'll do my best." He finished the rest of his beer in a dedicated gulp. "Do you want to stay for another round?"

I'd gotten what I'd come for, but I wasn't in any hurry to get home. I found I was enjoying myself. "Sure."

He signaled for our server and we ordered two more beers. Murry curled up against my leg.

I slipped into bed with my laptop, thinking about Rob, analyzing my unexpected attraction to him. It seemed kind of convenient, I thought, that I'd meet someone interesting just when I was fretting about my personal life.

I remembered talking to my mom about my dad, back when I was a teenager, long after he'd died. I asked her why she'd married him, expecting to hear something wonderful. She'd shrugged and said, "Timing. Everything in life is about timing, and love is no different. We were ready."

I'd thought it was a cold answer at the time, but I knew my parents loved each other. My mom was devastated when he died, and instead of remarrying, she put all her energy into raising me and my sister. She wore her ring to this day.

And she was right. My sister fell in love with her high school teacher, a horrid man who'd preyed on Asian girls under eighteen. If I'd been home instead of at college, if she'd been placed in a different period for history, she might never have seen him. She might still be alive.

Timing may have been a practical consideration, but it wasn't unromantic. It was more like the less glossy, less idealized inner peel of fate. Maybe I would've been more closed off to Rob if I'd met him a month ago. But, maybe not.

Anyway, I wasn't planning our wedding quite yet. For now, I had to deal with my immediate living situation. I had four responses to my Craigslist posting sitting in my in-box, and I had to respond to them. I sent off four e-mails answering questions, offering to show the place. I thought about Lusig's strange proposal and wondered if it would be so bad to immerse myself in this case. I had to admit it was taking up all of my time and head space anyway.

I sent Enver Kizil an e-mail, indicating an interest in hearing EARTH's side of the story with regards to the genocide memorial. I put "genocide" in quotes and felt pretty icky about doing so. I didn't say I was press, but I more or less implied it. I thought that was my best shot at getting an interview.

By the time I'd sent that off, I already had a response from one of the Craigslist prospectives, a woman named Sarah Pitman. She said she was "dying" to see the place, and we arranged to meet at eight the next morning, after her spinning class, before her first meeting of the day. There was a Thoreau quote in her signature: "Success usually comes to those who are too busy to be looking for it."

It was a lot of personality and information for a one-paragraph e-mail. I wondered if she was trying to convey as much of herself as possible, or if she was just kind of insufferable. I decided it'd be best to turn in early.

Eight

✦

I woke up at 7:30 and checked my e-mail. Nothing from Kizil, but another two responses from prospective roommates. Echo Park was a trendy area, had been since before Lori and I moved here two years earlier. It was about a Target away from thorough gentrification, but still attracted hipsters with its east-side edge. My apartment was old and slightly shabby, but its location was prime—the Echo Park Lake was a quick downhill walk away. I could probably subsidize my rent by subletting for a hundred bucks more than what Lori was paying. Not that I would do that.

Sarah Pitman called when I was making coffee, at 7:48. I had meant to spend those last twelve minutes straightening up the common areas, but she was apparently the kind of person who showed up early for an 8:00 A.M. appointment. I put on a bra while she climbed the stairs.

She was a small, fit white girl in her early twenties, showered and fully made up, wearing a skirt suit with black pumps that looked expensive. She carried herself like a wunderkind CEO. I would've been more impressed if she weren't looking to split rent with the likes of me.

We shook hands and exchanged greetings, and in the next second, she was guiding herself through the apartment. She kept her pumps on, ignoring my bare feet and the pile of shoes at the door.

"It's a little dark in here, don't you think?" she asked, somewhat forcefully. "Maybe we could put a lamp in that corner."

I hadn't thought I was very picky, but I couldn't imagine living with this woman, having her rearrange the spaces Lori had occupied with such warmth and consideration. I didn't dislike her, but I thought it unlikely that we'd be friends, or that she'd even tolerate my slovenly habits or irregular hours. Within a minute, I found myself hoping she'd lose interest in the place, so I wouldn't have to ignore her phone calls or e-mails.

She stayed for twenty more minutes, alternately talking about herself and touching things in the apartment while frowning impolitely. She asked several questions about the place, off of a list she had saved on her phone. She never got around to asking me anything personal, like where I was from or what I did for a living.

She gave me a firm but unenthusiastic handshake on her way out the door, and I was fairly certain I'd never see her again.

I went back to my in-box and read the other Craigslist responses, thinking I could arrange a couple more meetings for later in the day.

The first was from a man who called himself Darren. He introduced himself as a sensitive starving-artist type, and said he'd love to take a tour of my place. In lieu of the usual niceties that ended this kind of exchange, he'd attached a picture of his dick.

My fingers curled away from the keyboard in disgust—not at the picture, which was nothing I hadn't seen, but at the reminder of the creeps that lived to troll women, on- and offline. I fantasized about responding to the e-mail, arranging a tour, and taking him to task when he arrived. But I knew it wasn't worth my time to plan even a short con on a guy like Darren. I forwarded the e-mail to Chaz with a warning not to open the attachment, and asked him if he could trace this guy—but only if it wouldn't take longer than five minutes.

I felt better once I sent that off. It might not come to anything, but the guy probably didn't expect a PI on the other end of his dick pic.

I was remarkably tired for 8:30 in the morning. I opened the other Craigslist e-mail. It was from a twenty-four-year-old USC grad student named Emily. She sounded pretty reasonable, in the scheme of things, and I started to draft a reply e-mail.

I got through a standard sunny line of greeting, then I closed the window. I didn't feel like setting up another viewing. I met new people on a regular basis, more often than most, probably—it was part of the job. In a way it was funny that the classic investigator was a misanthrope who drank alone with the shades drawn. There weren't too many jobs that required more human interaction. That a lot of it was adversarial didn't make it any less taxing.

But there was something invigorating about it, too, about narrowing in on answers, rhymes, and reasons. The perverse pleasure of wrested victory—I knew that feeling, how wonderful it could be, even when Pyrrhic, vicious and empty. It made the slog of chasing interviews well worth it. There was no equivalent reward for meeting people about apartments. I could interview a dozen people in a day without collapsing, but personal nuisances drained me quickly. I had very little energy allocated to my private affairs. A psychiatrist might point to my dead dad, my dead sister, my dead best friend, all the demons in my past that might have led me to fear direct dealings with my life. I didn't need to pay a psychiatrist to know that, and it didn't matter anyway.

I checked my e-mail again, but there was nothing in my in-box from Enver Kizil. No word yet from Rob Park either.

I called Lusig to give her an update on my meeting with Rob. She picked up immediately.

"News?" she asked.

"I have an update," I said. "Some progress, at least."

"Can you tell me in person?"

I knew I could give my report on the phone just as easily, but she sounded so eager I decided to humor her. "Sure. Are you at Rubina's?"

"Obviously."

"I can be there in twenty minutes."

"No, don't come here. I'll go to you."

"You sure?"

"This living situation is driving me fucking insane. I need to get out of the house. I'm literally talking to this fetus like a crazy person."

"Sane people talk to fetuses all the time."

"I know, but I'm not, like, playing Mozart for him and telling him he's a sweet baby or whatever. I'm mumbling to him and imagining him rolling his little fetus eyes with me when Ruby isn't looking."

I laughed. "Okay, suit yourself. Drive carefully. Very carefully."

"Ugh. Stop."

She arrived fifteen minutes later and I opened the door when I saw her car parking on the street. I went down to meet her and walk up the staircase with her. There wasn't much I could do to help, but it felt wrong to watch a giant pregnant woman lumber up stairs alone.

"Coffee?" I asked. "Oh, right. Sorry."

"You know what? Sure. My doctor says a cup a day is fine. Ruby is paranoid."

I heated up the pot and poured out two mugs.

"Milk? Sugar?"

"Sure."

I rummaged in the fridge and found the half-empty quart carton Lori had left behind. I flipped up the cap and sniffed. "Actually, I don't have milk."

"That's fine."

I sat down next to her and handed her a cup. She took a grateful sip.

"Can I vent for a minute?"

"Of course."

"It's bad enough that Ruby put a tracker on my car and forced me to move into her house. But she has to FaceTime me every two hours, too? I swear to God I left my phone in my room while I went to take a dump and when I got out there were three missed calls."

I laughed. "That's pretty rough."

"I'm just glad she works."

"What's her husband make of all this?"

"Van? He doesn't love it. He thinks she's being unreasonable. But he won't really intercede for me. She's his wife. I'm his wife's cousin." She rolled her eyes.

"Are you not close?"

"We're close, in our own way," she said. "But obviously not like me and Ruby. It's a little weird living in his house."

"What's he like? I didn't get a good sense of him."

She shrugged. "He's a type-A doctor, a surgeon actually, which, if you know medical stereotypes, is much worse. Too soft-spoken to be cocky, but quietly dominant. Kind of moody, especially lately, with the baby coming and Ruby acting like a psycho. He works a lot, so he isn't home much, even though he doesn't have much of a social life."

"Is he pretty into the whole baby thing?"

"Yeah, but it isn't turning him into, like, a second-act horror movie villain." She dropped her face into her hands with exaggerated exhaustion. "You don't know how good you have it, living without a baby in your stomach and a monkey on your back. You have no idea how controlling she can be."

"I mean, I think I have *some* idea. I am literally getting paid to help her control you," I said. "Do you regret it?"

"Ha! Only every forty seconds."

"If you had the option of turning back time, would you decide not to do it again?"

She slurped at her coffee, looking terribly thoughtful. "It would be tempting," she said. "I'd certainly be less gung ho than I was the first time around. But ultimately, I'd do it all over again, God fucking forbid."

"Why?"

"One, because I love Ruby. I would really do anything for her, as long as I get to complain about it."

I looked appreciatively at her belly. "I guess you've earned the right to say that."

"I also owe her, not that she ever brought that up, or even really thinks so. She basically saved my life when I was sixteen."

"How so?"

"Did I mention my mom died when I was in high school?"

"No, I'm sorry."

"It's okay now, but back then . . . Are both your parents still around?"

"My dad died, but I was really young. I don't remember him much."

"Oh, that sucks. At least I remember my mom. She was pretty great."

"How did she die?"

"Car accident."

"Fuck."

"I was a mess. I was depressed, I didn't eat, didn't want to see anybody. And not just right after she died. This went on and on and on."

"I know what that's like."

"My dad was grieving, too, and besides, he didn't know how to talk to me. The only person I really wanted to talk to was my mom, and I was vicious to everyone else. Said some truly horrible shit to my dad and my aunt, Ruby's mom. To Ruby, too. But she kept checking on me, even though she was busy with residency. She called every day, even when I told her to go fuck herself, and when I started dropping weight and alluding to suicide, she got all the adults together and forced me to get help. Long, long, long story short, I got help. So, yeah, I owe her one."

I nodded. I didn't have a great response. "I guess you couldn't just write her a card?"

She laughed. "There's another reason, too."

"What's that?"

"Ruby and Van need to reproduce. They owe it to the world and the world owes it to them."

"They are pretty fine specimens, I guess. Two good-looking doctors."

"Two good-looking *Armenian* doctors."

"Yeah. Of course."

"We can't let the Kardashian clan be the sole reproducers. You know how there's that memorial going up?"

"Yeah, on the centennial, right?"

"That's right. April 24. Do you know what happened on that date?"

"It was the start date of the genocide, right?"

"Sort of." She smiled, avoiding condescension. "April 24, 1915— there were so many dead Armenians by then, their names could fill a hundred memorials. But April 24 is probably as close as there is to an official start date. It was when all the intellectuals got deported."

"Just deported?"

"Apparently 'deported' is Turkish for 'massacred.'"

"Ah."

"They massacred Armenians for years, but we picked April 24 as the day to memorialize."

"What do you mean by all the intellectuals?"

"They rounded up over two thousand of our community leaders, something like taking the head off the totally innocent beast. They put them in holding centers, eventually deported them. Clergy, teachers, lawyers, politicians." She smirked. "Writers. Obviously the greatest tragedy, in Nora's mind."

"Pretty big blow."

"Yeah. Imagine if that many of the U.S.'s most visible citizens were all murdered in one day. Obama, Angelina Jolie, Toni Morrison, all snuffed, plus a couple thousand more. Imagine what that would do to our culture and morale. And we are much bigger than the Armenian community was even before the genocide."

"But the genocide was recorded. They didn't get all the writers."

"The genocide was recorded, sort of. There were some American and European witnesses, thank God, because without them, what power did we have? The Turks recorded the genocide with their own euphemistic language, and they beat us down bad enough that their story has yet to be bulldozed for all time."

"Were there no Armenian writers left?"

"I wouldn't say that. For one thing, tragedy begets writers. You take a whole population and put them through some shit, a few of them will find a voice. Outrage has a way of getting through, even coarsely."

"Is that what Nora's writing is about? Outrage?"

"Outrage, pride. Two sides of the same coin when you've been victimized. And you know what, it's been a hundred years, but we Armos, we're still defined by our victimhood." She paused and tilted her head, not liking the way that had come out. "Not in a pathetic way or anything, but getting genocided, that's still on our minds all the time. And it means, for one thing, that Van and Ruby have to have some babies."

"But you don't want kids of your own, right? I think Rubina said something like that."

"Me? No. I'm not mommy material."

"You don't owe it to your blood like Van and Rubina do?"

She laughed. "They're smart people. Professionals, you know? I'm just a shithead. This is how I'm doing my part."

"You could change your mind. Maybe you'll meet a nice Armenian dude and pop out a soccer team."

She shrugged. "I'm not saying it could never happen. I know anything's possible. But it's unlikely. Not every woman needs to be a mother, and I'm not so young I have no idea what I want."

"And you don't think you owe the world some babies."

"Don't tell me you think I sound selfish."

I remembered Rubina calling her cousin a classic only child. "No. Have you been told otherwise?"

She rolled her eyes. "Ruby said I was selfish, huh?"

I geared up to deny it or shrug it off, but Lusig stopped me.

"I don't care," she said. "It doesn't bother me any more than her hiring a private detective to follow me around."

"True."

"Anyway, I am selfish sometimes. I know that. No one's perfect, okay? Not even Ruby." She cackled and sighed. "That bitch."

"I haven't seen you acting particularly selfish," I said.

"I am the center of my own universe. I've done things I'm not proud of, probably hurt a few people. But this baby stuff, it doesn't count against me. First of all, really selfish people love nothing more than to force themselves on the world. And if your main goal is to do that, then isn't five of you better than one? The only people hurt by my not reproducing are potential ones, these dumb eggs that don't get a chance to get fertilized. They'll never know any better."

My mind drifted idly back to my donated eggs, treading a path that was becoming worn with use these days.

"Anyway," Lusig said, grabbing me back, "have you thought at all about my proposal?"

I had, in fact, been thinking about it all morning. It seemed less ridiculous after my bright and early encounter with a stranger's erection.

"A little bit, yeah. Let's say I'm interested. How would it work?"

She grinned, like a car salesman laying out the sweetest terms of a done deal. "You'd sublet this place. For a month, or maybe two, until this baby comes. You'd get your own room in that mansion free of charge, and you'd get paid for being on-site."

"Rubina's fine with that? It means her fees go way up."

"I don't know if you've noticed, but anything remotely connected to this baby gets spared no expense."

"All right. And how much mobility would I have?"

"While I'm home, she wants you to stay with me."

"Really? Aren't you always home?"

"Home alone, I mean."

"Jesus. I can recommend her an ankle bracelet if that's easier."

Lusig glared at me. "Please don't."

"Wait, aren't you home alone all the time now?"

"Yeah, but if there's a way to fix that, you know that cuckoo bitch will jump on it."

"So when do I look for Nora?"

"Any office-type work, you can do at the house. Field stuff, whenever Ruby's home. Doctor variation on nights and weekends."

"What, I don't have a social life?"

"Hey, how do you think I feel?"

It occurred to me then that Lusig was as lonely as I was, as lost and bored and restless.

"It would be nice to be able to run things over together," I said, thinking out loud.

"Exactly. I may not be a detective, but I'm not an idiot. I definitely won't get in your way." I didn't say anything, and she pressed on, sensing pliability. "And you'd make more money for more or less the same amount of work. You'd be watching me, but it's not like you'd have to spoonfeed me and take me to potty."

I nodded and pictured this change in lifestyle. It could have been the setup for a twisted sitcom with a feeble laugh track. Still, the proposal had its appeal—it would address my immediate practical concerns, and I'd make money working around the clock as well as from a rent-free living situation; I could immerse myself in the search for Nora, and keep anxiety and loneliness at bay. The only real downside was the profound weirdness of it all, the threat of insanity that came with living with a boss when that boss was Rubina Gas-parian. But unlike Lusig, if I couldn't handle it anymore, I had the option to quit.

"You know what?" I said. "Fuck it, let's give it a shot."

Her face glowed with a happy light that flattered and embarrassed me. "Yes! I could kiss you. No backsies," she said emphatically.

She whipped out her phone, and before I could ask what she was doing, she had a finger in front of her face as a dial tone sung out, just two short rings.

"She's in," Lusig said, sounding positive and triumphant. I must have looked stunned, because she winked at me reassuringly, like I was a child she was tricking without ill intention. "Yeah, might as well, right?" she said, nodding, her eyes on mine, pretending I was a part of the conversation. "Yeah, I think so. See you in a bit."

She hung up and laughed, apparently at me. "Your face," she said. "I didn't want you to change your mind."

"You already said no backsies," I said, sighing. "Rubina's fully on board with this? Inviting a detective into her home?"

"I pointed out that it would help my stress levels."

"So what's the plan, then?"

"What were you going to do today?"

"Wait a few more hours on Kizil, then go track him down if he doesn't respond."

"So not a jam-packed day of dedicated sleuthery."

"Hey, every day is full of dedicated sleuthery," I said. "But sure, my schedule's flexible."

"How about this? Unless you hear from Kizil soon, you take the day off from field stuff."

"And do what?" I asked, watching a grin grow on her face.

"Get settled. Ruby said to ask what you want to do about dinner."

I told Lusig Rubina would fire me if I let her help me pack and sent her back to Glendale, where I promised to meet her later. I called Lori as soon as I was alone. She was at work but stepped out to talk to me.

"Remember that pregnant girl who went off on that waitress?" I asked.

"Obviously."

"I'm about to move in with her."

"Wait, what?"

I caught her up on the arrangement and she listened, laughing.

"This is so weird," she said. "Are you sure it's a good idea?"

"Of course not. But it could be the best idea I have for now."

"You're going to get all tangled up with these people."

"That might not be the worst thing," I said. "I like Lusig, and you're abandoning me."

"*Unni!*"

"Joking," I said, amused by her dismay.

"I didn't even mean it like that. I think it'll be nice for you to be around people, but now you'll be at work around the clock. You're going to drive yourself crazy looking for this girl—and what if you don't find her?"

"I've thought about this."

"And?"

"Chose to ignore it."

She groaned. "Okay, just promise me you'll get out of there if you feel like you can't handle it."

"Sure, if it makes you feel better—I can stop whenever I want."

Lori offered to find subletters for the next month if I could find someone to take over her lease when I moved back in. She said I could crash with her and Isaac if I needed to leave Chez Gasparian for any reason—when Lusig had her baby, or if I started to feel like harming myself or others. I spent the rest of the day packing and cleaning, making the place look presentable. Lori would deal with the rest.

* * *

I showed up at the Gasparian home with two suitcases and a solid sense of foreboding. I'd never done a security detail—most clients preferred the beefier, more masculine Chaz and Arturo, along with whatever off-duty cop friends they might hire. This would be my first live-in job, and I was entering a full and fraught house.

Rubina and Lusig were both at the door to greet me, wearing big grins that said they knew exactly how awkward this was all going to be.

"Welcome!" said Rubina, suddenly peppy as an R.A. meeting freshmen for orientation. "Let me show you where you'll stay."

The house was two stories, and I'd gathered that Rubina and Van slept in a master bedroom upstairs. I was relieved when Rubina led me to a small bedroom on the first floor.

It was a nice space, compact and austere but comfortable enough. There was a desk and a twin bed with a plain gray comforter. It looked a lot like my own bedroom, actually—functional and sparsely decorated, though it lacked a window. I wondered if it would be the nanny's room before deciding the nanny would sleep no less than four feet from Rubina.

"Lusig's right across from you," she said, indicating a slightly larger room across the hall. It was similarly spare—twin bed, futon, dresser, TV. "You will be sharing a bathroom."

"It's like a dormitory," Lusig said. "I even have a PlayStation. You can come over and we can battle. We can discuss deep life things on my futon."

"We can rage with vanilla vodka and Goldschläger."

Rubina gave me a stern look.

"I'm kidding," I said, feeling a sudden need to clarify.

"House rules," she said. "Until the baby is born, Lusig doesn't leave the house without you or me by her side. I can't have her putting herself in danger. It should go without saying that she doesn't drink, and she doesn't inhale secondhand smoke. If you need to smoke, do it outside, as far away as possible. And I have to say, as a doctor, you might want to take this opportunity to quit. I don't know a single doctor who smokes. That should tell you something."

"When is lights out?" Lusig asked, rolling her eyes.

"Promptly at eleven, if you'd like a time. But I doubt you're staying up very late these days anyway."

"Sounds easy enough," I said. "Though I assume I don't have a bedtime?"

"No. You can do as you please, as long as you're in sight of Lusig whenever I'm not home."

"When is she supposed to find Nora, then?"

"At night. On weekends. I didn't get the feeling that your schedule was inflexible."

I raised my hands. "I can work whenever I need to work. You're paying my retainer."

"Good."

"What should I do during the day?" I asked.

"Just spend time with Lusig. You'll be her best friend until the baby comes."

Lusig put her arm around my shoulder, and I slumped down to meet her saddled height. "It'll be one long sleepover, Song. Just like the good old days before the evils of sex and booze. Can we listen to the rap music, Mommy?"

Rubina crossed her arms and looked deep into Lusig's room with an expression that betrayed hurt feelings. "Come on, Lu, you're not being fair. It's not that I'm a prude."

There was a strained silence, and I knew better than to interrupt it. I hadn't even unpacked my bag and here was my first reminder that I was an outsider thrust into one of the weirdest family situations I'd ever seen.

Lusig caught Rubina's tone and bit down on her lip as if she could coax the words back in like a strand of saliva. She stepped over to her cousin and put a hand on her shoulder. "I know, I know. I'm just giving you a hard time."

Rubina held the hand on her shoulder and Lusig squeezed.

"It's just the baby," Lusig went on, her voice sweet and soothing. "I know how important he is to you."

Rubina's eyes sparkled, and she sniffled gently, trying to hide her face by looking at the floor.

"No, no, no," Lusig cooed. "I'm sorry, Ruby. I should stop making fun of you. But really, what's the point of having a surrogate if you're going to be this hormonal, huh?" She poked Rubina in the ribs, a gentle plea for laughter.

The mood passed. Rubina scratched a tear away from one eye like it was a speck of dust and nodded solemnly, pressing Lusig's hand.

"Well, I'll let you settle in, Song. Please let me know if you need anything."

She smiled in the weak way of somebody wounded, and disappeared upstairs.

I looked at Lusig, opened my mouth, then closed it again. I took my suitcase into my new bedroom, sat down on the bed, and took off my shoes. Lusig followed me in.

"Got to hand it to her, huh? That is a woman who knows how to milk a guilt trip. My own mother never got me quite so good."

"She's more delicate than I thought at first."

"Oh. yeah. She acts steely, but sometimes it seems like she's one bad turn away from a complete breakdown."

She sat down heavily on my desk chair with her chin resting over the back. "I'm so glad you're here."

"Yeah." I chuckled. "Sure, me, too."

She dragged a palm across her face. "I feel kind of bad for dragging you into this."

"I was already dragged in. This is my job. There are plenty of worse things I could be doing for a living."

"Like scrubbing toilets at a biker bar?"

"Or like babysitting an actual baby."

"You are my babysitter, huh?"

"Your chaperone, maybe."

"My bodyguard."

The house filled with the sound of a car pulling into the garage. Lusig's ears perked up and she looked out the door. "Van's home," she said.

I stood up. "I guess I should say hi."

The garage door closed with a rumble, and a man's sturdy footsteps sounded down the hall. A jingle of keys, and a shouted, "I'm home."

I followed Lusig out of my room while Rubina pattered down the stairs. All the activity in the house was converging on the entrance of the man.

He looked past his wife and cousin-in-law to where I was standing a couple feet behind them. "Right," he said. "This was happening today."

"We met briefly," I said. "I'm Song."

"I remember. How could I forget?"

There was a note of irritation in his voice that irritated me. It wasn't a great start to a monthlong stint of cohabitation. I had to stop myself from reminding him that this was his wife's idea, that I wasn't just an unwelcome guest crashing for my own benefit.

I couldn't think of anything to say to him instead, so we stood for a strained moment, unsure of how to speak to each other. When the silence had lasted a beat too long, Rubina broke in.

"We'll all go to dinner tonight," she said. "So we can get to know each other."

Lusig clapped her hands together like a wind-up monkey. "Oh, boy!"

Van smiled blankly, having found his footing in the strange scene. "Song, what would you like to eat?"

I shrugged. "I'm easy," I said. "I'll go wherever you guys feel like."

"Have you ever had Armenian food?" Rubina asked.

"Yeah, a few times. I like it."

"Okay, we'll take you somewhere good."

With that, she followed Van upstairs and left me and Lusig tilting our heads.

"Oh my God," Lusig giggled. "This is going to be such a disaster."

"What, dinner?"

"Of course dinner, but also, this whole thing."

"One thing at a time, I guess." I looked at my phone. It was six thirty. "What time for dinner?"

"We eat early here, so probably soon. Everything closes by nine in Glendale."

"That's right. This is suburbia."

"Not that it matters for us. We might as well be on an island. Alcatraz, maybe."

We ate at an Armenian restaurant on San Fernando, a family-owned place done up thick with gold-trimmed moldings and cheesy nature scenes painted directly onto the walls. The staff recognized the Gasparian clan, and eyed me with friendly curiosity. Our waiter addressed both Rubina and Van as Doctor.

Van ordered for all of us and, ten minutes later, the table was spread thick with dishes. The only things I recognized were the usual hummus, stuffed grape leaves, and kebabs, but I ate some of everything and enjoyed it all. We dined family style, and I wondered if Van or Rubina would say something about food bringing people together.

"So, Rubina tells me you went to Yale." This was the first thing Van said to me that had the scent of cordiality. "I went to Princeton myself."

I smiled and nodded, glad to have my mouth full. I chewed on something that tasted like pomegranate.

"How did you end up becoming a private investigator?"

I swallowed and gave a quick, sanitized version of my career trajectory.

He raised his eyebrows and waved his fork back and forth, pointing at Rubina and Lusig. "Have you ever had a case like this before?"

I smiled. I was relieved to see that Van had at least a flickering sense of humor.

"I've had a couple big messes, but this assignment has been pretty unique. Lot of firsts."

"First surrogate?"

"Yes, definitely."

"Surely not your first neurotic client?"

Rubina put down her fork to give Van's biceps a gentle squeeze.

"No," I said, feeling more comfortable. "Certainly not."

"We were hoping for twins, you know. Triplets, even. It's common with IVF."

"Maybe *you* were hoping for triplets," Lusig interrupted, a sour edge to her voice. "I'm having enough of a time with just one."

"Be fruitful and multiply," said Van.

"That's the Armenian mandate. Your priest even said it at your wedding. 'Be fruitful and multiply and dominate the earth.'"

"It isn't just Armenian. It's biblical. Biological."

Lusig turned to me. "Van thinks being angry about the genocide is a waste of time and energy."

Rubina set her fork on the table. It thudded thinly against the tablecloth.

"It was an atrocity, and I get angry each time I think about it," Van said. "But it's been a hundred years. I live here now. I have my own life, my own family. Why do I need to dwell on history? What good does it do me?"

There was no heat in his voice, only a tone too calculated to sound reasonable and dispassionate. Lusig grew visibly impatient as she waited for her turn to speak, each of Van's words stroking her into greater and greater agitation. Rubina, who was seated between them, looked on with her mouth set tight.

"First of all, 'What good does it do me?' Nice, Van. Not at all self-absorbed."

"Lusig, come on," Rubina said sharply.

"Second," Lusig continued, "it would be one thing if our history were set in stone, if it had been dealt with properly. A hundred years ago, fifty years ago, even yesterday. But it hasn't."

"We know what happened," said Van.

"That's not enough."

"Okay, not just us, then. Twenty-two countries and forty-two states have formally recognized the Armenian genocide. Academics are fairly unanimous, too—at least the reputable ones. Why do you care about a bunch of Turks who just want to think well of their forefathers?"

"Because it's still a debate. Which means there's still uncertainty. There's a *lack of solidity* at the core of our identity. Not that we don't believe in ourselves, but as long as we're fighting for something as basic as human recognition, for the world to tell us, 'We know, and it's okay,' there will always be something gooey and unsettled inside of us. And you're not immune to that, Van Gasparian, any more than I am."

He shrugged and popped a nugget of sausage into his mouth. Lusig stared at him, her wild eyes growing furious against his coolness.

"That'll do," Rubina said, putting conciliatory hands on her cousin and husband. "I don't know why you're picking a fight in front of our guest, Lu. And Van, you know you're only egging her on."

"Uncertainty," Van said, elongating the word. His tongue clicked wetly against his teeth and he turned to me, smirking. "Isn't that your trade? Maybe you can solve this for us, too. As long as we have you."

Dinner concluded without further incident, and Van disappeared to his room as soon as we got home. Rubina hung around Lusig, worrying about things, until Lusig finally told her she was going to bed.

I unpacked and washed up and was getting ready to hole up with my computer when Lusig came by to visit.

"Aren't you guys supposed to be sleeping?" I said, wagging my finger at her stomach and head.

"In a minute. I'm just curious what you thought of Van."

"He was pretty polite to me," I said. "You don't like him much, huh?"

"I like him fine," she said defensively.

"You kind of picked a fight with him."

She sat down next to me on the bed without invitation. I smiled and moved over. There was something of the stray pet in this girl, an unconscious disregard for boundaries I found weirdly charming. "Okay," she said, letting her head touch the wall. "I'm not his biggest fan."

"You don't like Chris, either. Bit of a protective streak?"

"Maybe. Maybe a jealous one, even." She smirked and closed her eyes.

Within minutes, she was snoring lightly, a lispy whistle streaming out of her open mouth. I woke her up and she trudged the twenty feet to her room.

Nine

❦

I checked my phone first thing in the morning. No response from Enver Kizil, but I did have a couple texts from Rob Park.

I asked around about EARTH.
Do you have time to talk today?

I asked him to give me a call.

Rubina and Van were at work, which meant I was on Lusig duty. Without anything pressing on her unemployed pregnant agenda, she was still very much asleep by the time I'd showered and dressed for the day. I went outside for a smoke, then sat down at my new bedroom desk with a cup of coffee.

I checked my e-mail again, in case Enver Kizil had decided to reach out in the last hour. No dice. It had only been a day and a half, and I knew it was easy for e-mails to get lost, but I also knew it was likely I wouldn't hear from him at all. He was my best lead, and I couldn't afford to be passive. It was time to look for him on the assumption he didn't want to be found.

I turned on InvestiGate and pulled up a dossier for an Enver Kizil in Los Angeles County, with his e-mail address to verify the match. Google was usually adequate for casual searches, but I wanted a physical address. InvestiGate was a powerful private investigation tool, software for background checks and other purposes of less official interest.

Kizil was thirty-four years old, a high school graduate with some community college on his résumé. He was Turkish by blood, but born and raised in Ridgefield, New Jersey. He'd moved to Los Angeles three years earlier, but his occupation was hard to pin down. He had spare jobs in bars, restaurants, and the occasional hardware store, but he didn't seem to have much in the way of a steady career. He'd also had a couple arrests—for drunk driving and assault. This didn't look like a man with the cash to hire one of the most powerful law firms in Southern California.

I plugged his address into Google Maps and turned on the street view. He lived in what looked like an old house split into apartments, his address ending in 3/4. I wondered if I was looking at his window. I decided to give him the day then pay him a visit.

Lusig woke up just before noon and came into my room, brushing her teeth sluggishly. Her hair shone with grease.

She removed the toothbrush and spoke with her head tilted to keep the paste from dribbling out of her mouth. "Sorry I passed out in your bed," she said. "I haven't been sleeping great, and I guess it just got to me."

"No problem," I said.

She dipped out to rinse out her mouth in the bathroom and came back with her face wet. She walked past me and plopped down on my bed, driving a fist into her lower back. "I have heartburn and crazy gas and my back's been killing me. Sometimes I forget this isn't even the hard part."

"What do you mean?"

"The hard part is when you catch your teenage daughter sneaking back into bed after an all-night rave and she tells you she hates you." She shook her head. "In my defense, I did take it back."

I smiled. "You don't need to defend yourself."

"Do you want kids?"

"I go back and forth. On the one hand, maybe. On the other hand, who needs the stress and heartbreak." I thought of my mother, how losing my sister had destroyed her.

"I think I got a good deal, in a way," she said, drumming her belly. "I get to be a part of this grand project, and I don't have to take care of a shitty kid for eighteen years."

"He could be a good kid."

"Sure. He'll still piss and shit daily, long before that becomes his own problem. He'll still run Ruby and Van's lives like a tiny dictator."

"You're not sticking around to breastfeed and all that?"

She groaned. "Jesus, no. I'd have to sleep in their bed, pretty much. Babies need to feed, like, every two hours when they're breastfed."

"I'm surprised Rubina doesn't insist on it."

"Don't suggest it. I'll seriously kill you."

We laughed and fell into a comfortable silence, Lusig resting her eyes as she lay on my bed.

"I donated eggs a while back," I said, suddenly wanting to talk about it.

She opened her eyes. "You did? That's intense."

"Not more intense than being pregnant with someone else's baby."

"Well it's the opposite, I guess. Somewhere, someone got pregnant with your baby."

"I don't know that that happened."

"Really?" She sat up. "You mean you could have kids out there and you wouldn't know?"

"That's about the size of it."

"Okay, then tell me this: How is it possible that you investigate people for a living, and you've never bothered to find this out? There must be a way."

I felt a thrill as she articulated the forbidden thought that had been lapping at the edges of my consciousness. "I'm sure there is," I said.

"So how would you do it?"

"I'd talk to the adoption agency first. In case they'd give me a break."

"How likely is that?"

"If none of my eggs took, I don't see why they wouldn't tell me."

"And if they did?"

"I think they'd reach out to the parents for me, and it would depend on them."

"I'll bet they'd want to meet you, wouldn't they?"

"Maybe. They could be curious. But it's likely the complications wouldn't be worth it."

"Like, what kind of complications?"

I blinked hard and gave her a quizzical look. "Okay, now you're worrying me a little bit. You have thought through the implications of your arrangement, yeah?"

"Sure. Which is why I'm bowing out as soon as the baby's born."

"As a mother, you mean."

"Yeah. Van and Ruby are the bakers. I'm just the oven."

"Except that you're family, too."

"I'll be the aunt."

"And are you guys going to tell the kid?"

"Of course. That's always been the plan."

"Okay, so he'll know that you acted as his surrogate mother. What happens during his rebellious stage? When he hates his mom and says you're his real mother?"

"That would be ridiculous," she said, shaking her head.

"And what about you? You feel nothing for this kid? You've been carrying him around for months."

"I feel something, definitely. I feel him swimming around in there and I'm really conscious of the fact that he's this whole other life, and that he wouldn't be able to live without me. That's a cool feeling. But when we found out the IVF had worked? That I was pregnant? You should've seen her face. She looked like she'd been rescued from the brink of death. It's one of the only times in my life that I've ever seen Ruby sob."

I tried to picture it and couldn't.

"It wouldn't take a Solomon to pick the real mother here."

I was still thinking of what to say next when my phone buzzed. Rob had responded:

Can we talk in person?

Lusig watched me read the text. "Something about Nora?"

"Maybe," I said. "Rob Park asked around about EARTH."

"What'd he find out?"

"He wants to tell me in person, it sounds like."

"Really?" She stroked her chin. "Why?"

"I asked him to look into some pretty confidential shit. Maybe he did something that could expose him to disciplinary action."

She kept stroking and narrowed her eyes theatrically. "And why would he do that?"

"Because it's the right thing to do, given there's a woman missing?"

"Or maybe he's a young red-blooded Korean-American man, and he noticed that you're clearly single."

"I'm that clearly single?"

"You're, like, the most single person I've ever met."

"Well that can't possibly be a compliment."

She laughed. "It's not an insult. I mean, you seem single like Bond or something."

"All right, I'll let it go," I said. "Do you think it's cool if I have him come over?"

"As long as you don't send me to bed early so you can make out."

I told him to swing by and he offered to pick up lunch. I asked Lusig if she wanted to take him up on it and she said yes immediately, specifying that she wanted a *medianoche* and potato balls from Porto's.

He showed up an hour later, carrying two bags heavy with food.

"I got cheese rolls, too," he said, after I introduced him to Lusig.

"Are you a god?" she asked, her wide eyes shimmering.

I forced him to accept cash for the meal—he only gave in when I pointed out Rubina was paying, and that he was unemployed. We sat in the kitchen and ate our Cuban sandwiches while he told me what he'd uncovered.

"I don't have any slam dunks here," he started.

"That's okay," I said. "Just walk me through what you have."

"I got to look at the engagement letter."

"Nice work. Harriett Lehr?"

"Your instincts were good there," he said. "It didn't take much convincing to get her to talk to me."

"So, whose name was on that engagement letter?"

"Kizil's. Representing EARTH."

"And how much was the bill?"

"Wasn't a fixed amount, but I know what we all billed out for. This is costing someone probably hundreds of thousands, at least."

"And Kizil lives at an address in Torrance that ends in a fraction."

"Right. So I'm thinking he's a mouthpiece."

"Agreed. Either a true believer or well-paid insulation. Actually, I'll bet he's both." I put my sandwich down and leaned into Rob. "Which begs the question: Who for?"

"I asked Harriett what she knew about other EARTH members, specifically that rich housewife I mentioned."

"And?"

"Her name's Deniz Kahraman. Married to multimillionaire Adam Kahraman."

"If they're footing the bill, and their names are already involved with EARTH, then why bother with Kizil?"

"Could be for more insulation, but I have another theory." He smiled like he'd just handed me a velvet jewelry box. "The Kahramans are covering for the Turkish government."

Lusig's fist banged heartily on the table. "Oh, shit," she exclaimed through a mouthful of sandwich. "Of course."

"Hold on. Walk us through it."

"Harriett mentioned, very casually, that the Kahraman kids go to a very small private elementary school, where they play with the daughter of Mustafa Sahin. Do you know that name?"

Lusig and I looked at each other and shook our heads.

"He's the Consul General of Turkey to Los Angeles."

"Interesting," I said, mapping money trails in my head. "So, you think the Consul General tapped the Kahramans at soccer practice to funnel money to fund this lawsuit?"

"It makes sense to me," Lusig jumped in. "The Turkish government always seems to show up when someone wants to talk about the genocide. It's fucking weird. They issue public statements denying every documentary, book, whatever. They even responded to Nora's blog. I should've guessed they were involved in this suit."

"Then why hide behind the Kahramans?" I asked.

"Maybe they don't want to push their luck with the centennial coming," Rob said. "This is all about PR, after all."

"Now I really want to talk to Kizil," I said. "How long until Rubina gets home?"

Rob stayed and hung out for another hour, then left to take Murry for a checkup. Lusig ranted against Turkey and fell asleep, and I spent the afternoon reading up on the Turkish government's ongoing role in genocide denial.

I was surprised by the extent of its involvement—it seemed petty, like a director taking Netflix users to task for one-star ratings. There was a movie involved, too—multiple attempts to film a novel about the genocide called *The Forty Days of Musa Dagh*. The Turkish government shut it down, showing a style since emulated by eminent powers like North Korea.

I thought about Rob's theory, the lines that could lead back to the government. I traced them in my head, tested their strength and elasticity. But what did any of this mean for Nora? How did it bring me closer to finding her?

By the time Rubina came home, I was feeling antsy, ready to find Kizil and learn what he knew. When I heard the garage door open, I was ready. I waved good-bye to Rubina before she could stop me to ask about Lusig.

It took me half an hour to get to Torrance, another city, like Glendale, that I tended to think of as a suburb of L.A. Bordering both Redondo Beach and Manhattan Beach, it felt spiritually distant from the ocean—a sober mix of homes and industry, with more Japanese noodle shops than shark-themed boardwalk bars.

Kizil lived about two miles from the 405, and I drove down wide flat streets as the darkness strengthened around me.

It was amazing, how easy it was to find another person these days. I'd long given up any delusions of privacy, but it was always a little startling to be reminded of how naked we were, how thoroughly exposed, pinned, and labeled. There were the normative walls, the ones that dictated polite behavior, but all it took to breach them was some curiosity and brashness, a little presumption and nerve. I could muster up enough willpower to cross those lines when necessary. I wouldn't have been much of a private eye if I couldn't.

Still, it wasn't too often I went to a strange man's home unannounced at night, especially a strange man with a sketchy connection to a missing girl. I thought about giving him a call—it would've been nice to know whether I would find him at home, for instance. But maybe I didn't want to tip him off, either.

He was home, it looked like. I recognized his license plate number on a Civic parked in front of his building.

I opened my driver's-side mirror and did a quick check of my face. It looked as good as it was going to get, but I ran a hand through my hair to smooth it out. I wasn't molded for the sexy-damsel routine, but it wouldn't hurt to look presentable, especially if he were the type who thought women were purely decorative.

My plan was pretty straightforward—catch him off guard, invite myself in, ask as many questions as possible without making him angry. I'd work out the details as I went along.

I knocked on the door to his apartment. There was a light on beyond the blinds, and the place looked and felt inhabited. When there was no answer, I knocked again, louder. There was a sound of shifting this time, an elongated word flung at the door: "Coming!"

He was a short man, with a dark complexion and dark, droopy eyes. Thick black hair covered his head, his hands, and the top of his chest, a wiry tuft just visible over the neck of a white tank top. He wasn't much to look at.

"Who are you?" he asked, narrowing his eyes into flesh-shrouded slits.

I put out my hand. "Name's Song," I said. "I'd like a word."

He looked me up and down, a few times over, lingering at my chest and hips with a tired absence of lust. "Not interested," he said, and went to close the door.

I wedged myself into the doorway and smiled. "I wanted to talk to you about EARTH."

His face went dark, and for a moment, I felt an arrow of fear slice down my body.

"Who are you?" he asked again. "And I don't care about your name."

I dropped my smile in a dramatic change of expression, to signal that I was conceding to his manly discernment. "I'm a detective," I said. "I'm looking into the disappearance of Nora Mkrtchian."

His stony eyes grew stonier and his mouth stiffened at the edges like he was clamping his teeth on a stick. "I already told you people everything I know."

I allowed myself an interior sigh of relief. This man was nervous, but he was also an idiot who thought I was a cop. I wondered what exactly he'd told the LAPD, and what he'd held back.

"Maybe you wouldn't mind repeating yourself for a minute, then. What's the harm, Mr. Kizil?"

I stepped forward, and he stepped into my track. He was an inch shorter than I was, but he was thick and muscular and I had no doubt he could take eight of me in a fight.

"You can't come in here," he said. "This is my house."

I decided to push my luck. "You're nervous. You have something to hide."

A small tremor ran across his jawline. "I'm not hiding shit," he said. "Now get the fuck out of my face."

I retreated with a smile, one designed to be infuriating. "Fine," I said, raising my hands. "Enjoy the rest of your evening."

I turned around and he called after me. "I hope she *is* dead," he said, almost shouting. "She was a dirty whore."

I'd had the foresight to park under a tree a couple blocks away, where my car wouldn't tip off my quarry, even if I had a pair of binoculars pressed on my face. I looked through them to see if I could catch any views of his apartment, but there was nothing visible past a crack in a shitty pair of curtains. His car was still parked in front—good news for me. I'd worried he'd lam it before I even got to my spying spot.

I'd poked an active nest, and I was curious to see what Enver Kizil would do next. He was jumpy enough that I doubted he'd sit at home and do nothing for the rest of the night.

Half an hour later, he came out of his apartment, dressed in a short-sleeve button-down over his tank top, which still showed over the top with the dark patch of hair. He wore chinos and loafers and looked like a sleazeball trying to look like something else.

I kept a loose tail, as loose as I could manage without losing sight of him altogether. I'd tinted my windows like the creep I was, but there was no reason to take chances with a man with accurate paranoid leanings. I followed him across Torrance, driving down Normandie, one of the long streets that snaked south all the way from Koreatown. The blocks were long and unwalkable, occupied by warehouses bearing names like Sonic Industries, Global Accents.

He pulled into a parking lot behind a bland beige building that looked more or less like a post office. It had a flagpole in front, with two flags flapping over a tired patch of lawn. The top flag was the old red, white, and blue. The bottom one waved the building's emblem—a rhino's head in silhouette.

Apparently, this particular branch of the Spearmint Rhino Gentlemen's Club had taken over some vacated government building. It was a sad sight—at least the slime of neon indicated a measure of effort. This place made me think of sweaty undersexed bureaucrats, mournfully watching porn on their office computers.

Kizil walked in with his hands stuffed into his jacket pockets, with the hunched attitude of a man attending to shameful things. It was only 7:30, still a little early to be visiting a strip club, but I didn't have much experience in that field.

I wondered if my unexpected visit had spurred him into action. I'd seen enough *Sopranos* episodes to imagine a seedy strip club full of underworld characters transacting their business. It seemed more likely, though, that he was going to have a drink and ogle some girls, blow off some steam with some nipples in his face.

It was too bad I couldn't check. Even if I hadn't imprinted my face in his head, there was no way I could follow a man into a strip club without drawing a little suspicion.

But whatever he was doing, there was a pretty good chance it would take him a while. Ten or fifteen minutes, at least.

I drove back to his apartment with a rev in my heart.

I didn't make a habit of breaking and entering, but I'd treated myself to a top-grade lock-picking set for Christmas. I hadn't been able to use it so far—it was a toy, really, that I played with at home, and occasionally at Lori's or Chaz's. Chaz had raised his eyebrows when I first showed him my purchase, but he didn't ask too many questions. He shook his head while I demonstrated its capabilities to his daughters, who screamed with delight as I broke into their make-believe dungeons.

In theory, I would never use it for work. Lock picking was invasive and somewhat illegal. But it didn't hurt to have the right tools in the box. Better to have an umbrella in the sun than a bare head in a storm. I was kidding myself, though. I kept the tools in my trunk, and I was always aware that they sat there.

Enver Kizil was a creep. I knew that. He was a genocide denier at the least, and if he had anything to do with the Turkish men who mobbed Nora, a misogynist, a threatener, and maybe much worse. Creeps had rights, sure, but I wasn't exactly the U.S. government. What happened between me and this creep was between me and this creep, as far as I was concerned. Or so went my rationalizations.

I parked closer this time, just on the side street by the building, and walked up to his unit with my lock-picking kit in my purse. I wouldn't know which pieces I needed until I got a look at the door.

Locks were another one of those thin barriers that seemed naïve from where I was standing. After all, you could pay a locksmith seventy-five bucks to break into your home if you happened to misplace your key. I'd done it once, and the guy who showed up had been a rude red-faced racist who nonetheless got the job done. I had no doubt I could master any skill set he happened to have, and I was right. It cost less than seventy-five bucks to do it, too.

This was the second time today that I was breaching Kizil's faith in the public. I hoped he deserved it.

The lock was uncomplicated, a basic pin tumbler that required one tool and a little feeble jiggling. The door gave in after thirty seconds, and I was back in Kizil's apartment.

The place had a fetid beery smell that I hadn't noticed before. It smelled, more or less, like what I'd expect of a strip club. It was a small place, with old carpet and yellowing walls, a worn fabric couch at the center. There was a laptop open on the coffee table. Its screen was black.

I sat on the most depressed portion of the couch and hit the space bar on the computer. It lit up with an impersonal whir of recognition.

I braced myself for a high security, and was delighted when the screen resolved into an open web browser, with several open tabs. One of these tabs was a Gmail window.

This could be a goldmine. I rubbed my hands together, ready to dive in like Scrooge McDuck.

I went to the search bar and typed in "Thayer." I was surprised when the search yielded no results. "Nora" brought a smattering of hits, but none pertaining to the right Nora. Then I remembered— the e-mail Rob had given me was from a Hotmail account. He used a different server altogether for his anti-Armenian activities. I tried the Hotmail Web site—a URL I hadn't used since high school— but the log-in wasn't saved. I went back to Gmail and tried a few more search terms. "Consul General," "Mustafa Sahin," "Adam Kahraman," and "Deniz Kahraman."

The Kahramans showed up. No mentions of EARTH or Thayer, but two birth announcements, dated five and seven years back, as well as a long chain about a ninetieth birthday party for a family patriarch. I scanned through them and got confirmation for one link in the chain—Kizil and Deniz Kahraman were related.

Energized after my initial disappointment, I opened a new tab and started to enter the URL for *Who Still Talks*. The address auto-filled after I got to the second word.

I felt a surge of adrenaline and opened another tab and started to google Nora Mkrtchian's home address. Another autofill.

He'd known where she lived. He'd looked up her address. Had he harassed her? Had he threatened her? Had he carried out his threats?

I heard the throaty approach of a car engine and got up to peek through the window overlooking the lot.

I checked my phone—he'd been gone less than twenty minutes. I cursed under my breath and darted back to the couch to formulate my exit.

Lock picks, phone, everything I'd brought with me was safely in my bag. I stared at the open laptop, with its alert, manipulated screen. If I took this with me, he'd know I was here, and if there was anything worth finding he would make sure he found me. I cursed again and put the computer to sleep, leaving it more or less as I'd found it.

I couldn't leave the way I'd come without running into him on the stairs. I had to get out some other way, and I had maybe thirty seconds to get out of view of the front door.

I bolted into the bathroom and found a window, but it was too high up to be useful. I tried the bedroom next.

It was a small, messy bedroom, and that's about all I had time to observe before setting my eyes on the little balcony beyond a pair of glass sliding doors. If I'd had more time I could have gone through this space with some proper attention, but Enver Kizil didn't dally at his strip club.

I heard the terrifying sound of keys in a lock and threw open the doors, slipped between them, and closed them behind me in one panicked motion. I didn't hear anything else from the apartment, and I hoped he hadn't noticed the telltale groan of the doors on their rollers.

The balcony was enclosed in a wall of beige stucco, which served to block the apartment from the peering eyes of neighbors. Between me and the bedroom, there was nothing but glass. I hoped he was making himself comfortable on his sofa, but I couldn't afford to be optimistic.

I wondered what I'd do if he found me on the balcony. He'd be within his rights to cause some pain.

There was a tree within reach of the balcony, a leafy tree with a lot of grayish brittle-looking branches. None of them were much thicker than my forearm, and I didn't have too much faith in their ability to support my body for more than a couple seconds.

Luckily, Kizil lived on the second floor, and the building was old and depressing, which meant low ceilings. I looked down and decided it was still a long way to fall, but I could probably land on my feet if I had any kind of stepping stones along the way. I climbed up the balcony wall and got my legs on its outside, balancing myself before reaching out for the thickest available branch. I grabbed onto it with both hands, testing its resistance by applying as much downward pressure as I dared. I didn't have much more time to evaluate—I was better off betting on my agility than I was confronting an angry man as an invader in his home.

I held on to the branch, scooted my ass off the ledge, swung, kicked off the tree trunk, and landed on a knee and a shoe sole. I wasn't exactly a ninja, and my landing raised a fair amount of crash and thud. I got up and scrambled around the building, out of view of the balcony.

I wanted to look back and see if he peeked his head out, but couldn't risk lingering in his field of vision. I could only imagine him throwing open the balcony doors and whipping his head left and right to catch the long tail of my shadow, or the glow of two nervous eyes in the dark. The idea made my heart race.

A sharp laugh escaped from my throat, and I covered my mouth with surprise. I'd broken into a stranger's home and escaped by running down a tree like a clumsy squirrel. I felt exhilarated and entirely ridiculous. I'd fantasized about jumping off balconies before—planning heroic dashes on bad dates, and a couple times, wondering with rock-bottom melancholy if anyone would care if I broke a few bones or died. Here was a new skill to add to my résumé.

I'd crossed a new line, but I didn't feel like a criminal. Enver Kizil was a scumbag, with the address of the missing girl plugged into his computer. The discovery made me feel cold. Whether or not his behavior stopped with stalking, he had waived all claims to decent treatment at my hands. He wasn't decent enough to respect anyone else's walls. It was a waste of feeling to think any more about it.

And besides, I'd done worse things to better people.

I was about to get the hell out of Torrance when my thoughts wandered back to the strip club. Kizil hadn't even stayed long enough to get a drink, let alone catch a decent show. I also happened to know that when he'd left his apartment he'd had some stress to share or relieve. The strip club was open to the public, even if I wasn't quite the target clientele. I was free to walk in to see who I might find.

The lot was full, and I wondered if every driver was inside the Spearmint Rhino. I parked next to a car with a decal of a naked woman in silhouette on the rear windshield, her upturned nipples shaped like spurs. I didn't need to see the man who drove it to know I'd dislike him.

I walked along the side street to get to the entrance on Normandie—there was no sidewalk, just patches of grass and dirt interrupted by driveways. There were no people on the street, but I knew from the traffic and the cars in the lot that the area was reasonably populated. I pictured warehouses packed with people, hidden away from the sun.

I walked into the strip club like I was any old patron, and found myself face-to-face with a man in a polo shirt who asked for my ID.

I handed him my driver's license and he looked it over with a click of his tongue. "Twenty-dollar cover," he said.

"What? Even for girls?"

He gave me a disapproving once-over and said, "Twenty dollars unless you work here, and I don't think you do."

I wasn't sure whether to be offended, so I ignored the comment and forked over the money.

"Want to make any change?" he asked.

"Change?"

"Singles, sweetheart." He smirked. "Not a regular, are you?"

I gave him a ten and he counted out one-dollar bills that had never been creased. They made a satisfying sound as they separated from their stack.

The main room was dim but less dingy than I'd imagined. Instead, it had a tawdry look of aspiring corporate opulence, with chandeliers, gilt picture frames, and a leopard-print carpet. A stripper was dancing to Eric Clapton's "Cocaine." The place was busier than I thought it would be at dinner hour. The clientele was mostly male, but I wasn't the only woman. I wondered what everyone else was doing there. I guessed there were some sad characters in the room, and that I was surely one of them.

There was no telling what time it was in the outside world. The Vegas casino rationale must have applied to strip clubs with equal force: pretend time doesn't exist, and vice finds its window yawns without end.

I walked up to the bar and ordered a Jack and Coke. It seemed like the right thing to do.

The bartender was a tall, busty woman poured into a corset, with tanned skin and long blond hair that was either a bad dye job or a bad wig.

"Is it always this crowded this early?" I asked when I caught her eye.

She shrugged, and her cleavage strained against her neckline. "Tits and booze always sell," she said, not smiling. "That's my motto, anyway."

"That's what my mother always told me."

She gave me a blank stare and turned her attention to a man a few stools down from me. The smile she gave him told me I was taking the wrong approach. She must have taken one look at me and decided I wasn't drooling for her. She was right, but I still resented the outcome.

I addressed her again when she came back my way.

"Are you from here?" I asked, feeling lame. I wondered if the men around the bar had better lines.

"Florida," she said. "But there's no Hollywood in Florida."

I nodded appreciatively. "You act?"

"Sure. Act, model. Whatever needs doing."

"Pretty-girl work."

She smiled now, a bit wryly. "Sure."

"Men must love you," I said, going for a sincere, wistful tone.

"They grab at my ass, if that's what you mean."

"Listen, I'm looking for my fellow," I said, with a girlish play for sympathy. "Have you seen a big Turkish guy in here, in the last half hour or so? Black hair, droopy eyes?"

The bartender raised an eyebrow and shook her head, getting away from my question. The head shake wasn't a negation, more a display of disapproval at my prodding ways. She wandered away and I left a dollar on the bar, a begrudging tip before walking to a vacant table.

I'd never been to a strip club before, and I decided to get the lay of the land before I made any more bumbling inquiries. I sipped slowly at my Jack and Coke and watched the show.

The stage was wide, with three poles and a lot of colored smoke that seemed to leak out of the floor and ceiling. A stripper danced in a black bikini and eight-inch Lucite heels, swiveling around a pole with the slinky grace of a circus performer. She pumped against another pole and slid her top down, tucking the fabric under her breasts. She danced to the rhythm of the music, though the song cut out every fifteen seconds when the DJ's voice came over the PA to remind patrons to tip and to announce lap-dance specials. You could buy two and get one free—a deal that seemed to highlight how many of these men were here alone.

When the song ended, she pulled her swimsuit back into place and ceded the spotlight to the next performer. The smoke changed color, and the new girl started dancing while the old one collected her tips from the floor. I felt a pang of vicarious embarrassment until I recognized the thoughtless, nonchalant look on her face. She could have been picking up photocopies, staring at a spreadsheet—this was just her job.

I was nearing the end of my drink when a stripper came to my table. She was thin with big implants that stuck out from her body like a couple of softballs. I couldn't tell her age or ethnicity—she could've been anywhere between twenty-five and forty, and was either Latina or Asian, possibly mixed. She was wearing a burgundy bra and matching panties, with a garter belt holding up fishnet stockings. Her shoes were enormous and silver.

"Are you having a good time?" she asked, standing over me.

"Yeah," I said, floating an uncomfortable smile.

"Is this your first time here?"

I nodded and took another sip of my drink.

"You have to get a dance, then." She touched her top lip with the tip of her tongue.

"Maybe later," I said. "I just got here"

"Okay," she said, winking and fluttering one hand. "I'm Melody, if you want to find me later."

I sat still through a few more songs, but no more strippers came to offer me a lap dance, though there were at least six on the floor, working the room. They were more diverse than I thought they'd be—ethnically, sure, but in body type, too. The girls were all tall in their towering heels, but some were still taller than others. Most of them were thin, but some had guts and cellulite that they carried with as much unself-consciousness as they did their topless breasts. There was variation in these, too—Melody hoisted one of the only pairs of obvious implants, and the natural ones ranged from small and perky to ponderous and baggy. If I'd come wearing lingerie and a lot more mascara, there was no reason I would've stood out, as long as I didn't try dancing.

I'd never really known a stripper, and I wondered who these women were, where they'd come from. The only ones I ever heard from were the blogger types, whose essays on the sex industry sometimes made it onto my newsfeeds. They were all white and middle class, stripping to pay for law school, or to supplement their freelance writing careers. There was one girl in the room who looked like she might write feminist think pieces in her free time—she was white and skinny with her unenhanced breasts tied in a simple blue bikini.

The voice came back over the PA to announce that private rooms were available for purchase in half-hour and hour-long slots. Spearmint Rhino seemed too corporate to be an actual bordello, but I had to wonder what exactly went on in a private room between stripper and patron for a whole hour.

Then it occurred to me, I could use some privacy with one of the girls.

I was here for information, and any number of people in the room might have been able to help me, but I knew that not all of them would. I wondered who I should approach, given what I wanted. I could probably win some sympathy from an NPR-listening sex-positive stripper. But if bribery was part of the plan, I knew my money would talk louder to a girl who wasn't taking her clothes off as part of some adventure.

I waited for Melody's turn onstage, then I left my seat for one of the ringside chairs. There were about twenty of these seats, and only two others were occupied, on the other side of the stage. Melody was dancing in front of the men who occupied them. She knelt on the stage and bounced her tits, pulling them toward her neck. Then she licked one of her nipples, a feat that I would've guessed physically impossible, like tickling yourself, or biting your elbow. One of the men flung a single dollar at her knees and she eyed it slyly, her expression bold and flirtatious. But underneath her fluttering lids and vixen's smile, I thought I saw a flicker of contempt for the men who came to leer and drink and part grudgingly with their singles. I had a feeling a few bills would go a long way with her.

She noticed me as soon as she was back on her feet. She gave me a huge smile then got down again on her hands and knees. She crawled toward me across the stage with her back arched, her ass in the air.

"You came," she said happily, as if I were a school friend who'd shown up to see her band play at a bar.

"I did," I said, trying and failing to match the breadth of her smile.

She leaned off the stage and dipped herself over me, trapping my head and her breasts in a smothering fort walled by her long hair. When she got up again, she stared down at me and giggled.

"Are you a lezzie?" she asked playfully, displaying a tongue stud with her languid "L."

"Not really. Are you?"

"Sometimes." She smiled, pleased that I'd asked. "I like when girls come in here," she said, speaking just loud enough that I could hear her over the PA system. "Usually better than the guys."

"Do girls ever take you to the private rooms?"

"Sometimes."

"How much does that cost anyway?"

"Half hour or hour?" She tried to keep her voice sexy, but I could sense her counting cash in her head.

"Half hour, let's say."

"For you?" She winked. "A hundred bucks."

That was more than I liked to pay for an interview, but I didn't think I'd get much out of Melody while she was onstage. I guessed I could get a lap dance instead, but the averted awkwardness would be worth the extra cost in Rubina's money.

"What if I just want to talk?" I asked, already resigned.

She stopped moving for a second. "There's no discount," she said. "And if you want me to talk you off, that'll definitely cost extra."

I leaned back with my hands up. "I promise it'll be easier than that."

"I'll get you after my dance," she said, winking again. I threw five singles on the stage and she moved back to the other side, where the men stared at her hungrily. I finished my drink and ordered another while she danced the rest of her song.

She came to get me as promised, and led me through a hallway that glowed with red-and-amber light and shadow. She opened the door to a private room, and I followed her in with the expectant obedience of a john.

The VIP room had the same cheesy aesthetic of the rest of the club, with both walls and sofas decked out in faux tufted leather. Mirrors paneled the walls, reflecting us back to each other from every angle.

She closed the door behind her and started dancing to a loud, fast-paced song. The room was hardly less frenetic than the main area.

"Melody, I'm Song," I said, trying to interrupt her before she pushed me down and landed in my lap.

A mirthful smile splashed across her face. "Like two peas in a pod," she said, winking.

"I was wondering if you could help me out with something." I tried my best to match her flirty carriage, not quite in amplitude but with a friendly tone.

"That's what I'm here for, Song." She made a sound with her tongue like she was snapping gum and put her hands on my waist.

"It's kind of a straight-girl problem," I said. "You can just sit down if you want. Those shoes look like they hurt."

"They're not so bad." Still, she sat down, maintaining a posture that pushed out her chest. "But thanks."

"I'm here about a guy, actually. You may have seen him around here." I stayed standing and watched the pep drain out of her as she relaxed out of her sex-kitten persona.

"Oh, I can't talk about other customers," she said. Then added, "Are you a cop?"

I shook my head but resented that she was smarter than she let on. I sat next to her, trying to abandon any airs of authority. I swiped nervously at my nose. "He's someone I've sort of been seeing."

"I can't rat out customers to their girlfriends either, babe."

"Just humor me for a minute, please? We have half an hour, and I must be cuter than most of the guys who come here." I gave her a pleading smile and touched her wrist, lightly.

"You can tell me about your boy," she said.

"His name's Enver Kizil," I said. Then I paused and stopped myself from describing him like a perp. "I call him 'Envy,' actually, because I'm the envy of every other girl in town." I didn't have to will myself to blush. I was ashamed of that one.

She laughed. "That's cute."

"Honestly, he's not that much to look at. He's really hairy, kind of paunchy, and he has eyes like this." I pulled down on my cheeks to mimic Kizil. "And he's short, too. I can't wear heels when I'm with him. Definitely not like yours."

"You're tall, though."

"I guess. He's probably about my height, but he might even be an inch shorter."

She narrowed her eyes, picturing the man I described. "Does he have black hair?" she asked.

I perked up and let it show. "Yeah, he does."

"And he's like, Armenian or something?"

"Turkish. So you have seen him, huh?"

She wrinkled her nose and snorted a little as she giggled. "Yeah, I think so. If he's who I'm thinking of, you can totally do better," she said.

I agreed but frowned instead. "He's a good guy."

"Oh, no offense," she added, though without particular concern.

"Anyway, things are getting kind of serious, but I don't know if I should trust him, or trust myself with him. This might sound lame, but I've just been burned before, you know?" Melody looked like she probably would know.

She tilted her head and gazed down at me with hard sympathy. "This might sound funny coming from me, but it could be that you date guys who are straight-up regulars at strip clubs."

I tightened my face into a mask of misery. "Is he a straight-up regular? I was afraid of that."

"I've seen him around, definitely."

"Like today, for example?"

She thought about it for a second, then conceded with a nod.

"Have you spent any time with him?"

"I guess I might have given him a lap dance, but I can't be sure." There was a note of guarded apology in her voice, and I decided that would work to my advantage.

"Does he just come here to look at girls? Like alone?"

"Let me think." She leaned back on her elbows in a pose that required too much flexibility to be comfortable. "I see him alone sometimes, I'm pretty sure. Almost everyone here seems to come alone at least sometimes. But I've also seen him with another customer a few times."

My senses sharpened in a way that told me I was getting somewhere. "A friend?"

"Sort of. Maybe a business associate."

"What makes you say that? Have you heard them talking to each other?"

She bit her lip. "Yeah, a couple times."

"Are you a good eavesdropper?"

"I don't have to be. Men don't lower their voices around me. I'm just furniture with tits and a nice ass."

My mind raced ahead of me to vast revelations, conspiracies caught whole in Melody's consciousness, waiting to be plucked free.

"What kinds of things do they talk about?" I asked, keeping my voice curious but calm.

"Like money stuff, I guess."

My heart sank at the shrug in her voice.

"Have you heard them mention a lawsuit? Or a girl named Nora?"

She narrowed her eyes and thought for a few seconds, nodding in the end. "That sounds right."

So much for perfect recall. I switched my line of inquiry. "This guy, is he like Enver's boss or something?"

"Yeah, I think so," she said, sounding slightly more sure of herself. "It seems like he's the one in charge. He always pays, too."

"Do you know his name?"

She shook her head. "He doesn't really talk to us girls."

"Was he here with him earlier?"

"Yeah, I think so."

"What's he look like? I'd love to say hi."

"Like, short and kind of busted. Not even sure his mother would call it handsome."

The door swung inward with a sound that rose over the steady thump of music. We both started and looked up, and I felt more exposed than I might have with Melody in my lap. It didn't help that she looked petrified.

A man stood sneering in the doorway. He was short with an average build and a creepy set to his facial features. He wasn't hideous, exactly, but his eyes bulged, the better to see you with, and his white teeth glinted, the better to scare you with in a dark, dark room.

"You can't be in here," Melody said gamely. I knew we were both wondering the same thing—whether this man had been listening at the door, catching every word despite the music and noise of the club.

"You're mistaken," he said, advancing into the room as the door closed heavily behind him. "I'm the highest paying customer here. I can come and go as I please."

He walked over and stood between us, looking down. Everything about him was a little bit unctuous, from his thick cologne to his flashy suit to the precious wet-tongued way he delivered his accented English. He looked at me like I was naked under his boot.

He turned to Melody and bent down to hook a thick finger into her bikini top at her sternum, the back of his hand mashed carelessly against her breasts. "Melody, yes?"

She received the insult of his touch with a steadiness I had to admire. I knew she wasn't unaccustomed to strange men's hands, but I doubted her average customer was this overtly threatening. Her well-used smile grew stiff on her face. "That's my name," she said. "What about it?"

"You'd better check in with Mr. Olson," he said. "This is your last day here."

She snapped up to stand next to him, stumbling on one of her heels. "What are you talking about?"

"He's been informed that you've been giving out information about customers."

"To me?" I asked, as innocently as I could. "She hasn't told me anything."

"That's right," she said, indignant.

"Go plead your case," he said. He reopened the door and waved her out. She glanced at me with a mix of nerves and anger she didn't have time to process, then left.

He sat down right next to me as the door closed us in together. His cologne seemed to grow more aggressive, engulfing me in a con-

centrated musk that smelled, more than anything, like an oncoming
headache. I had an urge to place my palm over the top of my drink.

"Come here often?" he asked without a trace of humor.

"I don't know why that's any of your business," I said, as calmly
as I could manage. I was alone in a room with a man who scared me,
and who was fully aware of his advantage. I had meant to find and
talk to him before he entered the room, but this conversation was
not happening on my terms, and I struggled to maintain some sem-
blance of authority.

"You're not here to see the dancing whores," he said. "I believe
you're here to see me."

"What gives you that idea?"

"Because Enver Kizil told me 'some Chinese cunt' came to his
home and gave him trouble. And then I see you talking up the girls,
not an hour later. I hope you will not take it as a compliment when
I tell you you stand out in this place like a severed thumb."

His words knifed their way under my skin, and my nerves were
reacting more than I was willing to show. "And who are you?"

He held a hand out with a terrible smile, and I pretended I didn't
see it. After a second, he grabbed me by the wrist. I gasped.

"Relax," he said. "You wanted to talk, we talk. Come with me."

His fingers were disproportionately large and sturdy, and they
clamped around half of my forearm, digging in with insistent pressure, his thick thumb burrowing between my bones. I thought about
the Taser I'd left in my car, and knew I couldn't reach for it even if
it were in my purse. He kept his eyes on mine, and I saw that I wasn't
hiding the terror in my face.

The scream rising inside of me was about to spill out when he let
go. He tilted his head and a curious smile curled on his face. He had
the look of a child scientist watching the snail he's just sprinkled
with salt.

"Or," he said, with a cool, reasoning air, "you are free to leave. It
is your choice. I am indifferent."

"Who are you?" I asked again, lamely.

He shook his head. "We can have that conversation in a different place, under different rules."

I felt the phantom of his grip glowing red against my skin, and I lost my will to fight. It had been a long time since I'd had a glimpse of a man's capacity for violence, and the view drained my ready store of power.

I knew what he meant to tell me. Without even raising his voice, he'd communicated what mattered—that he was a man, and that I was a woman, and that he had no problem crossing boundaries if I continued to pretend that I wasn't weak where he was strong. And once the promise of transgression entered my consciousness, a million images and stories flashed through me, of women tortured, beaten, raped, and dismembered, in a million brutal, creative ways. The images and stories available to every woman and every man.

Later, I fantasized about the ways this scene might have played out. I thought about the information he was holding, the ingenious ways I might have pried it from him without revealing an inch of myself. I'd just come from breaking into a burly man's apartment, bubbling over with the thrill of my narrow escape. I had no doubt that this man had underestimated me. He was probably bluffing, a cheap trick to scare the little girl away. I was smarter than him, and worst-case scenario, I knew where his balls were.

In the moment, fantasy lost to fear. I left the strip club without another word, and it took all my remaining energy and pride to prevent myself from running to the door. If I'd been calm, I might have stuck around near the parking lot and tried to track this man to his next destination. But I needed to get the fuck out of there. I got in my car and called Chaz. He was home, and I invited myself over, then drove straight to Van Nuys.

It was almost ten when I got there, and Chaz and his family were watching TV after dinner. Molly gave me a kiss on the cheek and the girls jumped off the couch to greet me like puppies, wrapping themselves around my waist and knees.

I'd spent a lot of time with the Lindleys over the last couple of years, eating their food and helping Opal and Ruby with their homework. Chaz and Molly assured me I was always welcome, and I took frequent advantage of their hospitality, repaying them with babysitting on the rare nights the two of them wanted to leave the house. The girls loved me for some reason. Opal even told Chaz she wanted to be a private investigator when she grew up, "just like Auntie Song," causing her father to shed a single tear. I laughed and imagined telling her this story when she was an adult—that is, if I still happened to be in the picture. I saw the appeal of domesticity when I visited, the promise of lasting warmth in mandated bonds. The Lindleys were the most functional nuclear family I'd ever seen up close.

Chaz took one look at me and knew I needed to talk to him. He excused us from the living room and I followed him into the office, which held his computer as well as all of his daughters' toys.

"Well, well, well," he said, when we were alone, settling into a swivel chair. "One day away from the office, and you need my help already. I'm going to have to tell Opal about this."

"Still not over that, huh?"

He chuckled. "So what's going on, Girl Detective?"

"Did you find anything out for me? About those commenters?"

"You came all the way here to ask me about that? I could have told you on the phone. Or waited until morning." There was no annoyance in his voice, but I knew I'd brought work into his treasured time with family.

"Sorry, Chaz. I've had an eventful evening. Came here on momentum."

"What happened?"

"You go first."

He raised an eyebrow, then filled me in. "All right, I'll start with the bad news: It doesn't look like we can get any definite IDs for these commenters. No jackpot open IP address, no traceable e-mails. Nothing you could take to a jury, nothing solid enough to get you far with police even."

"But the good news?"

"Assuming this is just for you? To help you piece together your story?"

"Yeah, that's all I need," I said, almost licking my lips.

"I didn't do anything fancy. You want to know what I did?"

"What?"

"I read all those disgusting comments. Every single last one."

"Wow," I said. "I lost my stomach for it after a few posts' worth."

"I didn't enjoy it, either, trust me. The thought of anyone talking to my daughters like that, or Molly, or you—just makes me sick."

"Or you. No one should talk to anyone like that."

"No one calls men those filthy things."

"What was the payoff?"

He smiled proudly. "You said you were interested in one stalker in particular, so that got me thinking. There were clearly multiple people attacking this girl, but a big chunk of the anonymous comments could've come from the same person. Now I'm no language analyst or anything like that, but certain things stand out to anyone who's looking careful enough."

"Like back in the day, when people used distinctive typewriters."

"Exactly. In this case, there was some wonky capitalization, and a few consistent misspellings. The key here?" He dropped his voice to a whisper. "'Dirty hore,' without the 'w.'"

I heard the words in Kizil's voice and was sure that he'd said them at his door. I could feel the case tightening around him, click by click. "You found him?"

"That exact phrase popped up in three comments, all anonymous, posted on different days. Like I said, I can't prove they all came from the same person. I also can't prove that this same person has a You-Tube account under the handle 'KiZillion79,' from which he comments on Armenian genocide documentaries and Taylor Swift videos—Taylor Swift being a 'dirty hore' in his opinion."

"A YouTube account? I assume those can be anonymous. There are too many trolls on that site for that not to be true."

"Yeah. But 'KiZillion79' is a step up from 'Anonymous,' and I found an Instagram account under that same handle. This one has a real name attached."

"Enver Kizil."

His head jerked back, giving him two chins and a look of surprise that relaxed into a grin. "Enver Kizil, that's right," he said. "Which means you found him, too. Which means we both got the right guy."

"I'm impressed, Chaz."

"You found him anyway—this was just another channel. But what the hell, I'll savor the teaching moment. You thought I'd get here with fancy computer tricks, but the fanciest computer"—he paused to point at my head—"is your brain."

I laughed. "Okay, thanks for that, Sensei."

"All right, how about you fill me in now?"

"Well, for starters, I think I just met someone dangerous." I thrust out my arm. In the half hour it took to drive from Torrance, the skin had started to bruise.

He started in his chair and gawked at my forearm. "What happened? Are you okay?"

I told him about my trip to Torrance, from my brief interview with Kizil to my encounter at the Spearmint Rhino. He listened and pinched the flesh between his eyebrows.

"Hold on, hold on. How did you get into Kizil's apartment?"

I'd held back that little detail, as well as my escape out his window. "You don't need to know that," I said.

He shook his head. "Do you need a lecture?"

"Some other time, maybe. But, to your knowledge, I've done nothing wrong."

"Or illegal."

"Come on, that's not what I came to you to talk about. I'm freaked out, Chaz. This man, I don't even know his name, and he was ready to kill me."

"You did good to leave," he said with a sigh. "Sometimes I think you don't know where to stop, and I applaud you for stopping somewhere."

"But I got nothing from him. I went after him on what turned out to be a pretty good hunch, and I have shit to show for it."

He nodded and tapped at his keyboard to wake up his computer screen. "Not 'shit,'" he said. "You saw him, didn't you? What was the name of that genocide truther group?"

"EARTH. European and American something or other, Truth in History." I stood up and walked behind him so I could see his computer screen.

EARTH had a rudimentary Web site, in English and Turkish, showing banners of vaguely patriotic propagandistic nature scenery against a parchment-colored background. There was a mission statement full of horrible lies and bald self-pity, lamenting the maligned reputation of the Ottoman Empire, a particular concern for preservation of national pride. A few linked pages offered further details about the organization. Chaz clicked on the personnel page, and my heart beat hard until the page loaded with neither pictures nor names.

"Not a single contact?" I said, annoyed.

"Maybe on some level, they recognize this is shameful."

"They probably recognize other people might think it's shameful. They probably feel pretty persecuted."

He snorted and clicked onto another page. "Well how about this?"

I scanned the page. It relayed information for an event Friday at seven, at a community center in Glendale—a discussion and strategy meeting regarding the erection of the genocide memorial. It was open to "all people interested in discussing the nuances of our history." Snacks and soft drinks would be provided.

"You think I should go to this?" I asked.

He shrugged. "I'd be happy if you never saw that man again, but if you want to get more information out of him, you can and should do it safely, when he doesn't see you coming. This seems low risk, and if you want, you can take a buddy. I just so happen to be free Friday evening."

"Thanks, Chaz. I think I can handle it on my own, but I'll let you know if I get nervous." I smiled. "I thought you might try to lock me in a tower and protect me from the world."

He reached an arm behind him to pat my shoulder. "You're all grown up now, Songbird. You just let me know if you need back-up."

Ten

❧

I left the valley after Molly fed me dinner—reheated penne, at her insistence—while Ruby and Opal braided my hair. I missed the 134 Interchange and was almost at Echo Park when I realized I had to trek back to Glendale. It was strange going home to someone else's house.

As I drove up the hill, I noticed a pair of headlights following me through every turn, a path that grew more and more specific as I neared the Gasparian house. When I pulled over and pretended to park, the car passed me and I let go of my fear—it was Van, going home.

I got to the house right behind him, and he kept the garage door open when he saw me come up the driveway.

"Late night at work?" I asked.

"It's how it goes," he responded, sounding tired.

I caught a whiff of a familiar scent. "Korean barbecue?"

He raised an eyebrow. "What?"

"You must have had *kalbi* for dinner. I'd know that smell anywhere."

He pulled his sweater to his nose and gave me a wry smile. "I guess I'll have to wash this."

I smiled back at him and was about to go in the house when he stopped me with a touch to the elbow. I turned. "Are you coming in?"

"Can I buy you a beer?" he asked.

I looked at him curiously. There was nothing suggestive about his demeanor, or even his touch—only the casual friendliness of a bored coworker. Still, I wondered if it was appropriate to go out drinking with my client's husband.

He caught my hesitation. "Ruby asked me to talk to you, by the way. I was going to wait until tomorrow, but why not now?"

I thought about my night, about how much I deserved a nightcap. "I could use a beer," I said, knowing there was none in the house.

He drove us downhill to a dive bar in a strip mall with painted mermaids peeling quietly on the walls. College football played on an old TV, but there weren't many patrons getting into the game. Two grizzled men played pool at a well-worn table, and two more sat several stools apart at the bar. We grabbed a Guinness and a club soda with lime, then sat in one of the many empty booths.

"I thought you wanted a beer," I said, taking a sip of mine.

"I said I wanted to buy you a beer. It was a social proposal." He lifted his glass to meet mine. "I thought it'd be appropriate to get to know you, seeing as you live in my house. I just don't happen to drink."

"Fair enough," I said.

"Are you wondering why?"

"It's not because Rubina forbids it?"

"Not exactly." He chuckled. "It's that I'm an alcoholic."

"Recovered?"

"Never recovered. In remission."

"How long?"

"Two years. Ruby didn't tell you about this, huh?"

"Why would she have?"

"Because it's why we couldn't conceive," he said. "One of the reasons, anyway."

I sat back, struck by his sudden display of vulnerability. "I didn't know alcohol prevented pregnancy, Doctor," I said, keeping my tone light. "That's a useful thing to know."

"An indirect reason, I should say. I wasn't one of those movie alcoholics. I didn't beat my wife, or lose my job, or brawl with strangers in bars. But in ways that were both subtle and not, alcohol was the central force in my life, and I felt like the other stuff was out of my control. It was all I could do to go to work and be home once in a while. I couldn't start a family the way I was, and I refused to try, even when Ruby begged me. By the time I was ready, IVF was the only way to go." He spoke calmly, without any intimations of self-pity or regret.

"Out of curiosity, why are you telling me this?"

He squeezed the wedge of lime into his glass. "I want you to sympathize with Ruby," he said. "Everyone is always hard on her, but she's been through a lot."

"She is my client," I said. "I'm paid to sympathize with her. You don't have to worry."

"I understand you and Lusig are getting along."

"Thank God we are, given the circumstances."

"Of course, and that's fine. Lusig is a charismatic girl, and I understand that Ruby, in contrast, can come off as somewhat unreasonable. I just want to remind you that you're not paid to sympathize with Lusig."

I nodded, caught off guard, and took a sip of beer. "Okay."

He smiled. "Don't get stiff on me. I just want you to like my wife. We all have our burdens. Ruby only ever does the very best she can."

Rubina was gone when I woke up the next day, and I decided I was glad to have missed her. I didn't like that she'd sent her husband to talk to me, but I knew there was no reason to confront her. I also couldn't blame her too much—despite their love for each other, Rubina and Lusig were positioned as antagonists, and I was more Team Lusig by temperament.

In my defense, though, the housing arrangement also threw us together. We were spending all our time getting to know each other, working toward a shared obsession. If we were partners in a cop novel, we would have been sleeping together by now. Rubina, meanwhile, showed a general lack of interest in anything but Lusig's pregnancy. I updated her on Nora as a courtesy, but she wasn't concerned about the details.

Lusig, on the other hand, listened in rapt fascination as I told her about my adventures of the previous night. I was taking her through Chaz's work, following the links that pinned down Kizil, when an ad popped up on the side of my screen.

"What the fuck?" I said, turning it to her.

The ad showed a woman's T-shirt with the words FIND NORA written in block letters across the front. I could buy it for $14.99.

Lusig laughed. "Oh, this is your first time seeing that?"

"What is it?"

"A fan must've made it when her disappearance was in the news more often. It's through one of those custom T-shirt places. There are bumper stickers and posters, too."

I remembered the sticker on the subway car window. "I've seen them around."

"Creepy, isn't it?"

By disappearing, Nora had filled the city. She was nowhere, and so she was everywhere, her remnants blown apart like a handful of ashes scattered in sympathetic winds. Her face was on streetlamps; she wedged herself between pages of books. Her name sprawled across the face of the Internet, its letters black, dead, unmistakable.

"She'd be happy to see all this," said Lusig. "I hope she comes back and gets to enjoy it. She always fantasized about being remembered when she was gone."

"Don't we all do that? I mean we all know we're going to die one day, and I think dreaming of our legacy goes with that territory."

"You know what I've been thinking?" Lusig asked.

"What?"

"After I have the baby and we find Nora, I think we should find out what happened to your eggs."

I laughed uncomfortably. I'd flirted with the same idea, but was unprepared to commit to it. "I'll think about it."

"We have to," she said.

"What's this 'we'?"

"I'll help you, like you're helping me. It's not like I'll have anything better to do."

"There are literally a billion things that are better to do than tracking down children from closed donations. For example, we could do nothing."

"Well, the offer's on the table." She winked. "Sorry for egging you on."

I spent the rest of the afternoon trying to focus on my actual case, scouring the Internet for additional appearances by Kizil, looking for any signs of confederates. I found no trace of the man at the Spearmint Rhino, but it felt good to immerse myself in the case. When Rubina came home, I left to meet Veronica Sanchez for dinner, at a Korean restaurant on Olympic.

Veronica had a thing for Korean food, and she liked having a Korean around to tell her what she was really eating. It was to her credit that she never joked about dog meat, but then again she was a Mexican-American lesbian so maybe she knew a thing or two about not being a jackass, of that kind, anyway.

We weren't friends exactly, but we met up now and then for a beer or a meal. I could tell that she liked me in her begrudging, sarcastic way, and I had a fair amount of respect for her. It was also endlessly useful to know an active policewoman, and she knew she might see me when I grew greedy for information. I'd stored up some goodwill over the last year by using my access sparingly, and I was about to cash all of it in.

She was waiting for me outside the restaurant, wearing a polo shirt and khaki chinos, her casual weekend gear. She was a tall, thickset woman with short spiked hair and a broad face that was friendly in spite of frequent efforts at scowling toughness. She looked up as I approached her and shook my hand.

We made small talk and ordered a large spread of food, and within minutes our table was covered in dishes of varying size.

"So, who's this girlfriend?" I asked.

She twisted her lips to limit the brilliant stretch of a beaming smile. "Who wants to know?"

"Oh, now you're all coy?" I smiled back at her. "You don't have to tell me. I'm just being friendly."

"Not jealous?"

"Would it break your heart if I said no?"

"Her name's Mary. She teaches special-needs kids, a real sweetheart. Plus she's beautiful. Filipina, brown like me, yellow like you."

"Sounds like a catch. No wonder you look so damn happy."

She waved away the compliment. "How come you're such a bachelor, Juniper Song?"

I shrugged. "Takes a lot of work not to be, and I guess it's not my top priority."

"It isn't weak to like the company of others, J.S."

"I know, V.S." I grinned. "Good grief, you've had a girlfriend for five minutes and now you're a guru."

She laughed. "Not a guru, but I think we have a few things in common. We're both stubborn women who value our independence. We're nearly unlovable."

"That's some regressive shit, lady."

"Oh, can it. It's not because independence is unlovable. Just no one wants a closed-off partner."

"I have an ooey gooey center. Everyone knows that."

She rolled her eyes. "Yeah, it's practically oozing out of you."

"I did meet someone I could get to like recently," I said. "Nothing's happened but I have a good feeling, for once."

"Good for you. Who is he?"

I let her quiz me about Rob, and I asked more about Mary in turn. I was happy Veronica found my personal life interesting—discussing crushes and significant others felt like a sign of friendship, as much as it had in middle school. It was also a trade of confidence I hoped would repeat itself when I needed more serious dirt.

"So, do you think you'll marry your Mary?"

"We're lesbians, not fucking morons. So too soon to say, but I do like her."

"Do you want kids?"

"If I can have them without being pregnant, sure."

"Hard to do as a woman, though there are ways." I thought about my conversation with Lusig, then recognized a good segue to the business at hand. "Did I tell you about my clients?"

"The missing girl's friends."

"Yeah, more specifically though, it's a tag team of expecting moms. Two cousins. The biological mom and the surrogate. Surrogate's so full of baby you can practically see the thing swimming."

"I did talk to some people for you," she said with a yielding sigh.

I showed her my teeth in an eager mock grin. "So what do you have for me? Full copy of the case file?"

She rolled her eyes. "I'd like to believe you have a little respect for me."

"I do, I do. I was joking." I threw up my hands. "Though, just so you know, if you were to breach protocol for my benefit, I wouldn't hold it against you."

"You're a sweetheart, really, a goddamn peach. Unfortunately, I don't have much to offer. If we had more on our end, your girl would've surfaced by now."

"I'll take whatever I can get."

"The case has stalled a bit, nothing really new over the last month."

"Are people still on it?"

"Yeah, of course, but if you want to know whether our best officers are working night and day on this case and this case only, well, I can assure you that that's not happening. Our city's too big for that."

"Which is why my clients hired me."

"Now, I will say that this case hasn't been ignored. We've poured a lot of resources into finding this girl."

"I can imagine there's a lot of pressure when a pretty woman disappears. I know it made the news."

"Yeah, the media acted like she was blond or something," she said drily. "Like a real white girl."

"Armenians are white, aren't they? I mean, it doesn't get more Caucasian than the Caucasus."

She chuckled. "I was mostly joking, but you know what I mean. Middle Easterners are all white, too, and, incidentally, about half of the Mexican population. My family splits for the census, not because we're all different, but because we get to choose. Maybe if I weren't so damn brown I'd be tempted to pass, too."

"You really think you get to choose?"

"We all get to choose how people see us, to an extent, right? My cousin Elena, she's a pale girl, married to a dude named Stephenson. She works for a startup and drives a Prius, listens to podcasts on her commute to Santa Monica. People are always surprised she's Chicana. Bet that wouldn't be the case if she'd pursued different stereotypes."

"You think Armenians code switch in the same way?"

"Not exactly, but they can do things to play their whiteness up or down. I'd say disappearing while beautiful plays it up."

"Do you think if Nora had been blond, there would've been more pressure? That you would've had to find her?"

"No, J.S. This is a high-profile case and it's gotten its fair share of attention." She leaned forward, fingers drumming the tabletop. "I'm not saying you won't crack it wide open in your lonely little thinking chair, but I don't think we missed any of the obvious angles."

"I'm not saying I'm smarter than a roomful of policeman, but you could be wrong even so. You've been doing this long enough that you must know that, right? Sometimes the light has to fall just the right way, through just the right crevice, and you don't need genius to see it, but you do need to be around to catch that glimpse. I plan to be around." I scratched an itch behind my ear and gave her a supplicating smile. "If you know some of those angles, maybe I can ask you a few questions?"

"You can ask me anything you want." There was a playful condescension in her tone. "Just like you can write Justin Bieber a fan letter. Whether I answer—well, okay, I'll answer if I can."

"Did you guys know she was being harassed on her blog?"

She rolled her eyes. "Juniper Song, come on. You probably figured that out within half an hour of googling her. Do you actually think the LAPD is run by monkeys?"

"Fair enough," I said, feeling a warmth rising in my cheeks. "And I assume, then, that you guys looked into this EARTH group? The genocide denial group she lambasted on her site?"

"Yes, brain-dead as they are, my colleagues investigated the missing girl's known enemies."

"Right," I said, remembering Kizil's hostile greeting. He'd been interviewed in some capacity. "How much attention was paid to Enver Kizil?"

She frowned, both annoyed and thinking. "You're throwing names at me now? I'm not even on the case. I'm going from memory of secondhand reports."

"He must be the L.A. liaison for EARTH. He's the guy who meets the lawyers, that kind of thing, but probably not the heart of the operation. Too poor."

She laughed. "You need money to be a public nuisance?"

"No, but you need money to hire an international law firm billing out at, like, $800 an hour. I doubt his rent is much higher than that for a whole month."

"We cleared a person of interest who might be your Kizil guy."

"You did? Based on what?"

"Like I said, I didn't download the file directly into my brain. But going on a hunch? Maybe I remember something about a strong alibi."

"That's not enough. There isn't even a strict time of disappearance," I said. "You guys should bring him in again."

"Based on what?"

I chewed my lip and remembered swinging from a tree branch off Kizil's balcony. "I paid him a visit."

"And?"

"I saw some things that led me to believe that he was stalking Nora. Not just on the Net. I mean, he had her address, went to her house. I'm sure your colleagues heard someone was doing that."

"What things?"

"Will you just trust me? I don't want to get into it."

She scowled. "I don't like this. If you can't tell me where it came from, I have to assume what you're giving me is tainted in one way or another."

"I'm not handing you tainted evidence or anything. I'm just asking you to send your people to this place to find the evidence yourselves."

I watched her with a sense of unease. I didn't need her to believe I met the most stringent of her cop standards, but I did need her on my side. She had to believe I was one of the good guys.

"I'll mention it, okay?" She stuck her chopsticks into a sliver of seafood pancake, using them like a two-pronged fork. "Got anything else?"

I walked her through my work so far, and she nodded along, eating vigorously and smiling from time to time, fitting my statements into her view of the case. I could tell from the way she listened that she had a better grip on it than she'd led on.

When I finished, she crossed her arms on the tabletop and looked at me, grinning.

"What?" I asked, feeling defensive.

"What about the boy toy?"

"Oganian?" As the name left my mouth, I knew it was wrong.

"That's the boyfriend. Has it not crossed your mind that this girl could've been screwing someone else?"

I saw her stream of selfies, their unabashed sexual potency. "She could have been, if she felt like it." I bit. "Was she, or is this boy toy just hypothetical?"

"Look at this smug smile," she said, forming an impressively smug smile. "What do you think?"

"Who is he?" I resisted the urge to point out that I'd had less time to piece the case together than the LAPD.

"All right, I'll throw you a bone," she said. "You'll like this."

I waited, but Veronica savored the pause. "Yeah?"

"In the weeks before her disappearance, she was fucking her very own young Turk."

I tilted my head slowly, weighing the likely veracity of this new information. I had wondered how Nora could have a serious lover without her best friend being any the wiser. If he were Turkish, maybe that was something to hide. Still, I asked, reflexively, "Are you sure?"

She nodded. "I don't gossip about this stuff. It's serious."

"What can you tell me about him?"

"Not much, but he was interviewed, and he was cleared of suspicion."

"Name?"

"Taner Kaymak," she said. "Spelled like 'tanner' with one 'n,' 'kayak' with an 'm.'"

I texted the name to myself. "What about Oganian, then? I'm assuming someone talked to him?"

She rolled her eyes. "Are you kidding? Of course. Cheating girl-friend disappears, you think you're the only one who can spin a theory from that one?"

"Hey, I said I assumed."

Veronica bought me a drink after dinner, so it was past eleven when I got back to Glendale. The house was asleep, and I decided to postpone updating Lusig until morning. I was fairly certain she didn't know about Nora's extracurricular romance, in which case the news was bound to disturb her.

I opened up my laptop instead. It turned out Taner Kaymak was an easy find. He was an assistant professor at USC, with a full faculty page, and an active presence on every social media plat-form I knew by name. He was a historian with a hefty pedigree, Harvard undergrad, Berkeley Ph.D., tenure track. I didn't know too much about academia, but I understood enough to recog-nize a big shot when I saw one. His scholarship focused on the Ottoman Empire, and he'd published extensively on the Arme-nian genocide.

I saw the contours of a Romeo and Juliet romance. Young, beau-tiful daughter of Armenia. Brooding Turkish scholar seeking atone-ment in work and forgiveness in love. Fucking tragic.

I decided to talk to Lusig before I tried to contact him. I got ready for bed and was already under the covers when my phone buzzed with a text from Robert Park.

What're you up to tomorrow night?

I felt myself smiling. I realized I'd been waiting to hear from him again. I typed:

I have plans,
But maybe you could tag along.
Ah, I guess it is a Friday night. What kind of plans?

A community meeting in protest of that genocide memorial.
Ha ha, okay, not what I was expecting.
Want to go?
Sure. Sounds romantic.

There it was—a sign of unambiguous interest.

I'd managed to stumble through most of my adult life without many flares of romance. My one good relationship had happened early, in college, and I'd ended it when the happiness of a whole other person became too much for me to handle. It turned out that the events in my life that formed me into a good detective had also hardened the softer parts of my person, the parts that could start to trust and adore in a way that overwhelmed suspicion. I felt like one of those TV clichés, the lonely hero who finds truths and changes fortunes, and ends the day in a quiet home with a drinking problem for company. Of course, those heroes were men almost by definition.

Marlowe was always a cold customer when it came to matters of romance. He'd kiss a dame here and there, but his heart never fluttered, his palms never sweat. He certainly never kept his eye out for text messages. I had to concede I was more human than that. Rob Park had shown up to remind me.

It's in Glendale. We can follow it up with a candlelit dinner at the
Outback Steakhouse.
We can share a Bloomin' Onion.
Sounds like a dream.

An ellipsis showed up in the text window to let me know he was typing. I watched it appear and disappear.

About a minute later, he sent me a picture of Murry curled up on a dog bed, with an Outback Steakhouse cap perched on her head.

I laughed.

You just had that lying around?
I'm from Irvine. That's chain country. Bloomin' Onion was my favorite food in high school.
How's that explain the early 2000s trucker hat?
Birthday gift from the early 2000s.
From who?

We talked about Outback Steakhouse for another ten lines before the conversation shifted to high school, and stretched back between past and present as we grabbed for shareable anecdotes, offbeat details, pieces of insight and personality broken off in attempts to amuse each other. It wasn't terribly personal, but it was exciting in a light, flirtatious way. I went to bed ready to see him again, a desire forming for something more.

Lusig slept in until one in the afternoon, around the time I started to wonder whether I should drag her out of bed. She was still in her pajamas when she stuck her head in my room, resting her body against the doorway.

"So, how was dinner?" she asked, her voice croaky with sleep. "I wanted to wait up but I wiped out."

"I thought about waking you up."

Her eyes widened, instantly alert. "Did your cop friend come through?"

There was no way around it—assuming Lusig wasn't withholding key information from me, Nora had kept a big secret from her best friend. It was her right to do so, but I knew what it was like to learn a life secret about someone you love through other channels. I couldn't strip this news of all taint of betrayal.

"Sort of," I said. "I learned something new that we should talk about."

Her eyes grew wide and attentive. "Is it serious?"

"It's another piece of the puzzle." I rolled my desk chair toward the bed and patted the mattress, summoning her as a dentist does a child. "Come on, sit."

She moved cautiously to the bed and climbed in, digging her feet under the covers. "They didn't find her or anything like that? It's not that kind of news?"

"No," I said quickly.

Her face relaxed in a way that showed relief and disappointment in equal measure. "Okay, what is it?"

"I'm sure the cops asked you about Nora's personal life. Her love life, I mean."

"Yeah. I told them about Chris, but they didn't seem that interested."

"Did they ask you about anyone else?"

"Why do you ask?" She pulled the covers up so they covered her knees. "Because they did, and I thought it was really weird. I said she didn't have anyone else."

"Were you telling the truth?"

"Of course I was," she snapped. "Look, I can tell you have something to tell me, so just say it. I'm already feeling like an idiot. Don't make it worse."

"The police seem to think she was seeing someone else."

Her face twisted with a look of disgust. "Really."

"You don't seem that surprised, actually."

"So that was her secret. I should've known, that silly bitch."

"You knew she was hiding something?"

She leaned forward, clasping her hands around her knees like she might spring apart if she let go. It was another minute before she started talking again.

"I didn't tell you this because I don't like to think about it. But we weren't on great terms when she disappeared."

"How so?"

"She was being really shady. She flaked on me a few times like it was nothing, then didn't bother to explain. Then when I did see her she just acted . . . She was fucking annoying, that's how she acted. She told me, like, a month before she disappeared, that she had something she wanted to tell me. And then she got coy, and refused to go on. I was curious, but I dropped it, like a considerate friend. And of course she brought it up every time I saw her." She laughed bitterly, and hot bright tears welled up in her eyes. "I miss her so much I almost forgot," she continued. "She was a real bitch sometimes."

"No one's perfect."

"Nora is *far* from perfect. She lives every day like it's her fucking birthday and everyone else is just there for her party. I wonder sometimes if we'd be friends if we met today."

"But you are friends."

"Yeah, I love her and I'm going to find her and tell her all this to her face." She took a deep breath, swallowing a sob.

I rolled my chair closer to the bed and patted her shoulder. We sat like that for a minute while Lusig collected herself.

"So," she said, blinking and swiping at her nose. "Who is this asshole?"

I retrieved my laptop from the desk and opened up the faculty profile. "He's an SC professor. Taner Kaymak. Do you know him?"

She grabbed it from me and pulled it close to her face, her forehead almost pressed against the screen. "He's Turkish?" There was naked disbelief in her voice.

"Yeah. He's a history scholar," I said. "For what it's worth, he appears to know there was a genocide. I wouldn't be surprised if he met Nora through her site."

Lusig shook her head. "I assumed he wasn't a genocide denier."

"Still shocking?"

"Just kind of surprising," she said. "I have to say, I know not every Turkish guy is an asshole, but I've never gone out of my way to be attracted to one. Is that terribly narrow-minded of me?"

"I'm guessing your family wouldn't like it if you brought one home."

"Yeah. I can pretty much guarantee my dad would disown me. I think even Ruby and Van would be scandalized."

I remembered an old conversation with my dead father's sister when I was in my early teens. In her stammering hybrid of slow Korean and broken English, she explained what kind of men I should and should not date. Korean men were on top, followed by Chinese, who were, apparently, easily dominated and kind to their wives. Educated white men ("American" men, in my aunt's coded shorthand) made up the last acceptable tier. At the very bottom, below the Mexicans and blacks, were Japanese men, even Japanese-American men named Tom, Dick, and Harry, born in L.A. in the 1980s. Blood grudges ran deep.

"So even a liberal Turkish-American dedicating his life to the study of genocide . . . no?"

"The best-case scenario but, still, a scandal next to an Armenian finance guy like Chris," Lusig said. She shook her head. "I'm surprised she was cheating on him, but I'm not at all surprised she didn't love him."

"You don't know she didn't love him," I pointed out gently. "People cheat for all kinds of reasons."

"Okay, maybe I'm projecting," Lusig said. "I never liked him, and I never thought they were quite right for each other."

"It does sound like she treated him poorly."

"He treated her poorly. I don't blame her one bit."

I was almost touched by how quickly she accepted her friend's behavior. "About Chris," I said. "Is he the jealous type?"

The conversation had picked up some of the excited pace of gossip, but my question stopped it dead. I was introducing murderers everywhere.

"Yeah, definitely," Lusig said after a pause. "But I don't know if I'd say abnormally jealous."

"When you had dinner with him at that deli—wasn't that to get information out of him?"

"Yeah, but not—I just wanted to see if he knew where she was. I thought he might know more than I did."

"And why would he know more than you if he weren't responsible for her disappearing?"

"I don't think he killed her," she said quietly. "I don't like Chris, but if that's what happened to her, I'd put my money on someone else. This other guy—do you think he's suspicious?"

"I don't know," I said. "I haven't reached out to him yet. I figured I'd see if you knew him first."

She blew out a sigh through pouting lips. "Isn't it strange that when a woman disappears, we automatically list all the men who might have loved her?"

I smirked. "It would be strange if it weren't so logical. Can't argue with the stats."

"I know the stats, but it still seems illogical. I would never consciously hurt someone I loved."

"Makes sense, in a way. When a man kills his wife or whatever, it's often a crime of passion. Passion doesn't go with indifference. And, well, men hurt women every day."

"I feel like a traitor, talking about her like she's dead."

"Don't," I said. "We won't get anywhere with our heads in the sand."

While Lusig went to numb her worries with television, I went ahead and reached out to Kaymak. His e-mail was public, and I sent him a disingenuous note, expressing interest in his scholarship. I tracked down one of his publicly available articles, a slim piece of writing on *Slate*, and I went to town kissing his ass. I ended by asking him if he had a minute to spare for a coffee.

His response came almost immediately:

Dear Miss Song,
Under normal circumstances, I'd be delighted to meet for coffee, but I am taking some time off from work due to personal calamity. (My life is falling apart.)
Best,
T.

I read the short e-mail three times and wondered how many like it he'd sent in the last month. It sounded like Nora's professor was having a calm but pervasive meltdown.

I wandered over to the living room to update Lusig. She was sitting on the couch with the decimated remains of a Chinese take-out lunch spread out on the table in front of her.

"I feel for him," she said, shaking her head. "But if he feels that strongly about her, he'll help. You should just tell him what we're up to."

"That might be the right approach."

I drafted another e-mail reintroducing myself, with Lusig looking over my shoulder. I sent it off. There was no immediate response this time.

Lusig sighed and sank down in the couch. "I feel so useless," she said. "All I do is wait around, for this baby, for you. And now I'm watching you wait while I wait. I could explode."

"It's part of the job, Lusig. Don't worry. We're getting places."

"If you say so. What else is on the agenda for today?"

"We're going to that EARTH meeting I told you about. In protest of the memorial."

She looked up in surprise and pointed at her chest. "We?"

"No, don't be silly. I'm hunting for criminals," I said. "I'm going with Rob."

She laughed. "Wow. You might be even worse at romance than I am."

"Thanks." I picked up a fortune cookie from the table and tossed it at her. "No eligible suitors in your life?"

"They were circling the block before I got knocked up."

"But no one in particular?"

"I was seeing this one dude, but it wasn't serious. Nothing that could take this kind of weight." She patted her stomach. "Once this baby's out, it's open season."

Rubina relieved me at six, and Rob came at 6:30, as scheduled. I met him outside to prevent delay. The community center was less than two miles away, but I didn't want to be late—as two Asians in a room full of Turks, I figured we'd stand out enough without drawing attention to ourselves.

"You know, by the way, that this errand is for work, right?" I asked as we got in my car.

"I figured you didn't hang out with genocide deniers for your usual weekend fun."

"I should probably have mentioned this earlier," I said. "But work has gotten pretty fucked up lately. I think we'll be safe, but I don't want you saying I didn't warn you if something weird happens."

"This is all very enticing," he said, opening the passenger door with exaggerated slowness.

I told him about getting threatened at the Spearmint Rhino. "He wasn't any Deniz Kahraman. Not her husband, either, unless I found the wrong millionaire Adam Kahraman on the Internet. He's a new player, but also likely involved in EARTH. Kizil never showed up with a stocky Turkish guy, or had one waiting for him in the elevator bank? Bug eyes, heavy cologne, fingers thick as ropes?"

"Doesn't ring a bell, but I can't say I notice fingers on everyone I meet."

"I wasn't checking for a wedding ring." I held out my wrist, where the bruise had faded to a faint oxidized stain. "This is four days old."

"He did this to you?"

"Yeah. And I'm hoping to see him again tonight. I didn't get to ask him much the first time around."

"You sure he'll be there?"

"No, but more likely there than elsewhere."

"Kizil could be there."

I nodded. "Yeah, he could. But I'm not scared of him."

"Why not? He could be a murderer."

"First, I know more about him than he does about me. Second, he'll never get me alone."

"All right, then, boss. Let's do this."

The community center was off Brand in a part of Glendale riddled with strip malls. The walls were peeling beige, the carpet worn down to its last threads. There were about twenty people when we arrived, arranged in stackable chairs with metal legs and thin cushions.

As expected, we were the only Asians in the room, and we drew a few stares as soon as we walked in. I led the way to the refreshment table, where we filled paper plates with cube cheese and baby carrots.

"Some party," Rob whispered.

"We should've thought to bring a flask."

We took two seats toward the back of the room, and I scanned the faces for the ones I might know. Neither Kizil nor the anonymous Turk were there when the meeting started, around 7:15, and I wondered if this was a waste of time. Then a thin, dark-haired, fox-faced woman positioned herself behind a wooden podium and cleared her throat, shushing the pockets of chatter around the room. It only took me a few seconds to place her.

"Hello," she said. "Thank you all for coming. My name is Deniz Kahraman. I am here on behalf of the Europeans and Americans for the Recovery of Truth in History. Welcome."

The crowd was too sparse to generate actual applause, but a few pairs of hands splashed together.

"We are here to discuss a very grave matter, one that concerns the continued slander of our homeland and our blood." She cleared her throat again. "As most of you surely know, the city of Glendale has elected to raise a memorial for the centennial of what they are calling, in so many words, the Armenian genocide. This action is invasive and unjustified, not to mention a sinful expenditure of taxpayer money. We at EARTH believe we have a moral duty to oppose this atrocity."

I had to stop myself from visibly wincing at that word. An atrocity—the erection of a memorial for a million victims of slaughter.

She continued in this vein before laying out the basic threads of a legal argument, boiled down for delivery to a civilian crowd. It all sounded pretty bogus, but I sat and listened carefully. I could feel Rob next to me doing the same.

When she finished her opening speech, Deniz Kahraman opened the floor to questions. There was a pause as it became clear the crowd was too small to generate lines at a microphone. A small elderly woman in the front row asked a general question about what she could do, and Deniz answered it gratefully, paraphrasing a sizable chunk of her prepared speech. When she was finished, a man in the second row raised his hand.

"I'm a Turkish-American," he said, trying to find his voice. He paused, and when he spoke again, he was louder. "And I'm ashamed of what is happening here today."

"That is not a question," Deniz noted drily. A quiver of anger passed across her face. "But I will answer it, regardless. Shame is what they want us to feel," she said. "We are supposed to be ashamed of our blood, of our history, of things that were in contention a hundred years ago. How is this fair?"

"I didn't say I was ashamed of the genocide. I said I'm ashamed of this, right now. This attempt to deny history."

"We are looking for truth. We are looking for history. We are the thinkers, the only ones who are not content to accept the sourest version of Turkey's past. In America, it is almost a crime to say that there are two sides to every story."

"But that's because there aren't two sides to every story. Sometimes there is one truth. This is one of those times. EARTH isn't looking to tell a second truthful side—it's trying to obscure the truth in favor of whitewashing history. It's examining what happened under the guise of objectivity, but no one's fooling anyone here. There's an obvious agenda."

"Everyone has an agenda. You clearly came with one of your own."

"What I want is what every proud person of Turkish blood should want. I want to move on, and do it correctly." When she didn't interrupt him, he started again with more fervor. "No one hates Germany anymore. Not for their part in the Holocaust. They owned up to their guilt, and they were able to move on."

"The Germans?" she shouted in disgust. "You would compare us to the Germans? No, that is your first mistake. We are nothing like the Germans."

"You're right, of course, and that is what I'm saying. The Germans did right by history. They acknowledged their sins, and the shame of their nation was absorbed by their people generations ago. When I see a young German I feel sick with jealousy."

"In the first place," Deniz continued, ignoring the dissenter, "the Germans committed *genocide*. As I have already discussed, what happened between us and the Armenians was *war*."

He laughed. "War? What war? Let me ask you—when a husband beats his wife, is that a fight?"

"I don't see how this is relevant."

"Because this argument is classic victim blaming. The wrong was so great, that the only way to make it not a wrong is to villainize the dead. That is pure cowardice, an unwillingness to engage with guilt in a thoughtful, responsible way."

"We Turks are the only ones with any interest in examining the intricacies of this past."

"With what evidence?" He let out a single bark of a laugh, cutting off his own question. "No, forget that. I have a better question—why do you care?" He turned around and took in the whole room with a beseeching gaze. "Why did you all show up here tonight? To fight? For what? To maintain a lie a hundred years old?"

"I might ask the same of you," said Deniz Kahraman, who was growing pink in the ears. "You are the one crashing our meeting."

"*Your* meeting? I am a Turk. I care about truth in history."

"You came here to demonize our ancestors—your own ancestors."

"Who are dead! Why victimize the descendants of their victims? Why does this memorial offend you?"

"The lie is an outrage to the blood."

"'The blood'?" he asked, employing scornful air quotes. "Okay, how about this? Why does it matter to *you personally*, Ms. Deniz Kahraman. Did your mother not hug you enough? Does your husband find you sexually uninteresting?"

He stood up pointing, with a wobble in his knees, and at that moment I knew two things. That this man was stinking drunk, and that he was Assistant Professor Taner Kaymak, Nora Mkrtchian's sidepiece.

"You should all be ashamed!" he shouted. "As a Turk, as a man, as a citizen of this earth, I am ashamed of you!"

There was a long silence. Kaymak had crossed a line, and he was acting erratic enough to ignore, like a screaming paranoiac or a subway evangelist. I could feel the relief in the room as the genocide deniers decided he wasn't worth their time.

He stood looking for a few beats, then nodded as if he'd confirmed something within himself. Without being asked, he started toward the door.

Eleven

❧

I weighed my options. I could stay through the meeting and talk to Deniz, or I could chase after Kaymak. Deniz had ties to the Consul General, and she might be the key to understanding the EARTH scheme. She knew, in all likelihood, where the money came from, and if I leaned on her, I could find out whether she acted on behalf of the Turkish government. But Kaymak was Nora's secret boyfriend, and he was, from the looks of it, a volatile kind of guy.

Deniz could wait. I tapped Rob's knee and whispered, "We're following him out."

Sometime before we caught up with him, Kaymak had found a bush to puke in. He was bent over its trimmed edge, grabbing his knees and hurling.

I walked to his side and lowered my head to speak close to his ear. "Didn't your mother ever tell you not to engage with crazies?"

He stumbled and swerved to look at me. "Who're you?"

"I'm Juniper Song," I said. "I e-mailed you earlier, Professor Taner Kaymak. This is my friend Robert Park. Pleasure to meet you."

He stared at me with his jaw slack. "How did you—"

"I didn't come here to find you. I came here to find Nora Mkrtchian."

"Nora—my Nora? You know where she is?"

I had to admire the guy—he'd held out pretty well with the speech making considering he was too toasted to keep reasoning ahead of emotion.

"No, I wish I did. I'm looking for her on behalf of Lusig Hovanian."

He perked up. "Lusig? She knew about me?"

"No. The police told me about you."

"The police?" His eyes widened and then narrowed to slits. "Well next time you talk to them, tell them they know where to find me. I have nothing to hide." He spat into his puke bush. "Those incompetent bastards. They can't find her, so they come knocking on my door. I tell them everything I know, and they still can't find her. And now what, they want more of me? Now *that* is a waste of taxpayer money."

"Relax, they're not breaking down your door anytime soon. Though I'd watch out for the CHP if you're going home like this."

He sat down on the curb. "I'm responsible," he said. "I took a cab."

"You got wasted and decided to crash this community meeting? What the hell for?"

"To give these fuckers a piece of my mind."

"You were doing okay for a while there. For what it's worth, I'm on your side."

"Logic and justice and goddamn human decency are on my side. Scholarship is on my side. The only people not on my side are blind hateful scum like the people in that room."

"Not just politically. I'm looking for Nora. You and I—we want the same thing."

He cleared his throat noisily and spat again. "Do we?" he demanded, taking a step toward me. "Do you want her back so you can caress her again? So you can hear her sleepy voice in the morning?"

Rob and I glanced at each other and raised our eyebrows in unison. I turned back to Kaymak. "You got me there, I guess. I'm not sexually invested in her return."

He grimaced, somewhat smugly, before recognizing the sarcasm in my voice.

"All I'm saying is we're on the same side. I want to find Nora. There is really no reason to antagonize me."

He hung his head, looking more drunk than chastised.

"I'd like to talk. Maybe we can get some food in you." I looked at Rob. "Maybe he'd eat a Bloomin' Onion?"

Kaymak's head snapped up and he narrowed his eyes again before nodding. "I would eat a Bloomin' Onion."

We walked to my car and piled in. Ten minutes later, we were seated in a booth in an Outback Steakhouse.

"I thought this was going to be *our* thing," Rob whispered in my ear with mock petulance.

"We can always come back to the Outback."

"Is that from a commercial?"

"No, you think I could sell it to them?"

Kaymak watched us gloomily and I decided this was not the best time to flirt with Rob.

"So," I said, turning my attention back to Kaymak. "Self-hating Turk, huh?"

"Please don't."

"I'm kidding. But Deniz Kahraman seemed to think so."

"A lot of Turks would call me self-hating. Worse than that, too. A traitor." He wiped his lips and leaned forward, growing more animated. "Do you know that my own mother wouldn't speak to me for days when I first used the phrase 'Armenian genocide' in her presence?"

"Just the phrase?"

"The phrase is everything."

"I guess 'genocide' is a loaded word."

"I'm an academic, you know? Language matters to me, and this is something I've always known. But the fact is, language matters to everyone, all the time. And when it comes to defining anything sensitive? Language is everything. The vocabulary matters. Its provenance matters. This word—'genocide'—it was coined by Raphael Lemkin in 1943, to describe what had happened to the Armenians of the Ottoman Empire. It's fascinating that there's a question today about whether this term defines the phenomenon it was conceived to define. But there is a question. It's been forced on the Armenians, to prove that the death of a million people was genocide, not war. No one asks whether a million died."

He was interrupted by a cheery waiter in a red polo shirt who came to take our order. By the time he went away, Kaymak was itching to get back to his subject.

"Obama," he exclaimed, as soon as our menus were taken away. "Before he was elected, he publicly acknowledged the Armenian genocide, and he promised to formally recognize it as such when he was campaigning. As soon as he became president, he changed the way he talked about it, to the extent he's talked about it at all. Turkey has too much power, believe it or not. They're an American ally, and the U.S. is afraid of pissing them off."

"What do you mean, changed the way he talked about it?"

He smirked. "He's said that his opinion on Armenia has not changed, has literally referred people back to a prior time, when he was free to express himself. Which is something. We know he believes it happened. But it's not the same as having the leader of the free world come out and proclaim himself. Do you know who the Armenian community's favorite president is?"

"Who?"

"Reagan. Democrats and Republicans, all across the board. Because Reagan was a fierce advocate for recognition."

"And Obama is not."

"To his credit, he has given commemorative speeches on April 24."

"That's awkward. How's he refer to the genocide without referring to the genocide?"

"Metz Eghern."

"Mets what?"

"It's the Armenian synonym. It means 'Great Crime.' But spoken by the American president, it becomes a euphemism. A dog whistle, even."

"The vocabulary matters."

"The vocabulary matters. Turkey's decided that the word 'genocide' is a slap to the national face. I'm not ashamed of being Turkish, but I am ashamed of Turkey."

"Are you alone in this feeling?"

"What do you mean?"

"You've aligned your sympathies with the Armenians. But you can't be the only one. How about other Turkish-Americans your age?"

"Some of them agree with me. More and more every day, it seems like. There are a lot of us who stand for truth and recognition, who are just tired of being tied to the embarrassing stance of the Turkish government. But not all of us. I'm not friends with any overt genocide deniers, but some of my Turkish friends don't like to talk about it at all."

"They must be aware of your views? What you study?"

"Yeah, it's strange. I have a handful of educated, liberal, Turkish-American friends who will talk your ear off about racial justice, feminism, you name it. But they don't want to talk about the genocide. It's too close to home. It makes the blood shriek."

"What do they say?"

"They mumble, they say no one knows what happened. They speak in probabilities, allowing that atrocities 'might' have occurred.

But they hedge, and they introduce the usual arguments, sheepishly. The things they heard from their parents when they were too naïve to know what not to ask." He sighed heavily, his head lolling down before snapping back up. "It's a legacy, is what it is, your classic inheritance of guilt. It's terrible to say so, but I envy the Armenians."

"Have you tried that one on your Armenian friends?"

"Oh, yeah, and of course it doesn't go over well. But what would it matter to my life to have ancestors who died before their time? I would rather have an inheritance of steely pride and outrage than one of heartless criminality, one that can only be worn with shame."

"You said you envied the Germans, too."

"I do. But you know, they were no better. It's just that they lost the war. They weren't allowed to write history as they pleased. They didn't have that kind of power. But the result was that the guilty generation absorbed the brunt of that legacy. The right people atoned, and their descendants here can sit in American classrooms and learn about the Holocaust without feeling personally blamed."

"Japan lost, too," Rob offered. He was reaching for the Bloomin' Onion with one hand, which had apparently been set on the table while Kaymak talked. "Not all losers do it right."

"But winners always do it wrong," Kaymak continued. "What we have is a poisoned lie that's been passed down from generation to generation, and to call it what it is is not only to spit on our ancestor's graves, but on our own grandparents'. It's to spit in the faces of our parents."

I nodded and he sat back in his chair, done with his rant. He snapped off a piece of Bloomin' Onion and chewed it morosely, looking a hundred times drunker than he had a minute earlier. It was time to start asking harder questions.

"What do you know about Deniz Kahraman?"

"I know she's married to Adam Kahraman, and that the two of them spend their time and money with this EARTH garbage."

"Did you know their kids go to school with the Turkish Consul General's?"

He stopped chewing. "What?"

"Do you think it's possible EARTH is a civilian cover for the Turkish government?"

He laughed, loud and bitter, opening his mouth wide to a view of mashed batter and onion. "Of course," he said. "Of course of course of course! It's like the Turkish government has a Google alert for the phrase 'Armenian genocide.' And whenever it pings, they get their people ready."

"But you have no actual knowledge in this case, I guess."

"Look, have you ever heard of someone named Hrant Dink?"

"Sounds familiar," I said, reviewing all the new names I'd processed since taking this case.

Rob piped up. "He was the Turkish-Armenian journalist who was assassinated in 2007, right?"

I looked at him and smiled. "You've been doing homework, too?"

"Just a few long nights alone with Wikipedia."

"He was a newspaper editor. He wrote about Armenian issues, including the genocide, and he was prosecuted for 'denigrating Turkishness,'" said Kaymak. "Then he was murdered. They caught the gunman—a seventeen-year-old nationalist. But the whole story never came out."

"You mean there was a second gunman," I said.

He scowled. "This is not some Turkish JFK conspiracy theory. There was almost certainly a government cover-up. Evidence was destroyed on the grounds that it constituted state secrets. There's widespread belief that the Turkish Gendarmerie was involved, particularly the JITEM, the intelligence wing."

"So let's say the government is behind EARTH, and that Nora went after them. Do you think that might explain her disappearance?"

He shuddered, and I felt Rob wince next to me. I was asking Kaymak if he thought his girlfriend had been murdered by his parents' homeland.

"I don't know," he said. "It sounds way too plausible, but I don't know."

He shook his head violently, then collapsed in on himself, cramming his face in his hands. This line of questioning was going nowhere—he didn't know any more about EARTH than I did.

I pointed to his glass of water. "Drink that, maybe. Get your head clear."

"My head is clear. It's my heart that's hurting."

"I'm sorry about Nora. I'm sure it's been terrible for you."

"I haven't had a good night's sleep since she disappeared. She wakes me up every hour, alternately blaming and begging for help. I don't believe in ghosts, but she haunts me so systematically that I've started to believe in her death."

"The two of you were serious, I take it?" I decided to try out the past tense and see how he responded.

"Yes, very."

"How did you meet?"

He swallowed. His Adam's apple was thick with a raw look, and it bobbed in his throat.

"She messaged me. Online."

"Like on a dating site?"

"No. She read a piece I wrote on my Turkish heritage and sent me an e-mail. She thanked me. She said I made her cry."

"I get the sense there aren't a lot of Turks in her circle."

"I'm the first Turkish person she was ever friends with. And honestly, we were just friends at first. It was very innocent. We e-mailed about Turkish-Armenian issues and politics in general, and at some point we showed up in each other's Gchat lists."

"I hate that, don't you?" I turned to Rob.

He smiled. "There's a woman who interviewed me for a job I didn't get whose name shows up in my list every day."

"Well it worked out for me," said Kaymak. "Our e-mails were getting longer and longer, with more and more bits to respond to. Then one day, I was waiting for her to write when she just chatted me. I guess it was around then that I realized how much she was starting to mean to me."

"So you were AOL chat-room buddies or whatever. When did you decide to meet up IRL?"

"Last April."

"Almost a year ago?"

"April 24, actually."

I whistled. "Was that supposed to be romantic?"

"Not consciously. We were both going to a memorial event, and we decided to go together."

"What about Chris?"

He bristled at the first mention of Nora's boyfriend. "Chris doesn't care enough about history to spend his afternoons at events." He hesitated before adding, "And he was working that day."

"Ah. So you met up at this event, and what, love at first sight?"

"I think we were already in love by then. We just needed to be near each other once to know it."

"So you fell into each other's arms. How sweet. But you knew she had a boyfriend?" I tried to keep my voice free of disapproval.

"Yes. But she didn't love him anymore."

"Then why didn't she just leave him?"

"It was complicated. He was completely dependent on her, to the point where she thought it would be kinder to stay with him than leave. And she couldn't leave him to take up with a Turkish man without upsetting her family, friends, and fans."

"Did Chris ever find out about you?"

"Not before Nora disappeared. But he must know about me now. The police asked me about him. I'm sure they asked him about me."

Chris hadn't mentioned Kaymak when I'd cornered him, but

maybe that wasn't the kind of thing you shared with a total stranger.

"Is Chris a jealous man?"

"Yes. I'd even say very jealous."

"What makes you say that?"

"Nora was always wary of me texting or even e-mailing her sometimes because she suspected Chris of going through her phone."

"Was he ever violent with her?"

"No. I wouldn't have let that stand."

"Do you think he had anything to do with her disappearance?"

He took a long, contemplative breath and let it back out. "The police asked me the same thing."

"What did you tell them?"

"I told them what I know about Chris, anything they asked, but when it came to my opinion, which I don't think they gave a flying fuck about anyway, I said I didn't know."

Rob raised his hand, like I was the TA in the world's weirdest seminar.

"Go ahead," I said, tempted to laugh.

He nodded. "Narratively, it makes a certain kind of sense. The jealous long-suffering boyfriend discovers the love of his life has a different love of her life. Even if he never touched her before, he might lash out in the heat of passion."

I patted him on the back. "Very good, my dear Watson."

He made a short bow and broke off a piece of Bloomin' Onion.

"We have to assume the police have pursued this theory, and that the reverse theory has also been explored."

"Which is?" Rob asked.

"That Professor Kaymak here was having second thoughts about an affair that could smear him with scandal at the start of his career. That maybe he was frightened by the intensity of things. Maybe she was pregnant. There's no body. We don't know."

Kaymak was turning a dark, ugly shade of red.

"You said she haunted you. You said she blamed you." I stared at him across the table. "What aren't you telling me, Kaymak?"

He closed his eyes, and his eyelids twitched like he was having a bad dream. "I didn't hurt her," he said. "I would never have hurt her."

"Then why do you feel guilty?" A minute passed, and I pressed him again, raising my voice. "What are you hiding?"

"I was the last person to see her," he blurted miserably. "At least as far as anyone knows."

"You saw her after Hanna Bloom?"

"Yes," he said.

"On the sixteenth or after?"

"The night of the sixteenth."

"And you didn't tell the police?"

"I was scared. They were looking to hang something on me, and I didn't do anything."

"Tell me," I said. "If you really didn't hurt her I won't say a word to the police. Tell me what happened."

He took a long time to start.

"She came over," he said finally, "and I could tell right away she was riled up. Her eyes were red, and I thought she'd been crying."

"Was this about her stalker?"

He nodded. "He'd been ramping up his assaults and she was scared, scared and angry. She said she wanted to kill him."

"She said something like that in her blog, too."

"I told her I wanted to kill him, too, that if I ever found out who he was, I'd wring his neck with my bare hands." He looked at his hands as if assessing their power, then looked up at me. "She got real quiet for a while. Then she said, 'What if I know who he is and where he lives? What if I could tell you?'"

Veronica was wrong—the police hadn't gotten everything. Not even close. "What did you say?"

"I backed down. I said I was speaking figuratively." He hung his head and his mouth opened in a dry sob. "That was the last time I saw her."

We dropped Kaymak off at an apartment in Pasadena. I noted the address in case I needed to find him again.

Given the intensity of the interview, we had failed to order steaks, and the Bloomin' Onion had gone half uneaten. I made it up to Rob by taking us to an In-N-Out, which he declared outranked even Outback in the Irvine kid chain-restaurant hierarchy. We ate cheeseburgers sitting in my car.

"I think he's innocent, by the way," he said.

I laughed. "Yeah, me, too. Though he should probably have told the police about that last encounter."

"Yeah. I get why he didn't, though. And it's good news for you—it means you know more than they do. Maybe you'll crack this thing after all."

"That's the hope." I took a bite of my burger.

"You lead an exciting existence," he said.

"Beats being a lawyer, maybe," I said, my mouth full.

"Are you hiring?"

"Maybe. Do you like your money in tiny amounts?"

"I stormed out of big law, didn't I?"

"True. Do you like feeling like a night creature, creeping into strangers' lives to dissect and occasionally ruin them?"

"Well, now that you put it that way." He smiled and shook his head before pausing and looking into my eyes. "Wait, do you?"

I shrugged. "It's an acquired taste, I guess, but yeah. I enjoy the job."

"Why?"

"Have you ever been into puzzles? Like jigsaw puzzles?"

"Yeah, sure, on a rainy day, when I was ten."

"But do you know the feeling? That singular drive to finish something just because you started it?"

"You mean obsession?"

I laughed. "Maybe. It might be obsession. I also happen to be pretty good at puzzles. Why did you go into law?"

"Wanted to help people?" He made a sarcastic snorting sound.

"Hey, genocide deniers are people, too."

"True, and so are corporations. But you know what I mean," he said. "Poor people, oppressed people, more victim-side litigation, you know? People hate lawyers, but we really aren't all bad."

"I know. I've known some lawyers in my time. A mix of types, like anywhere else."

"Some of us are assholes, I know that. But none of us went into law school thinking we'd like to help oil companies avoid liability for murdering seals when we grew up."

"So, at Thayer, you didn't just sit in a circle twirling your mustaches and counting your money?"

"Actually, it's considered pretty gauche to do both of those things at the same time."

I laughed again. "So how'd you end up at Thayer?"

"Paid the bills, I guess. Mostly of the loan repayment kind."

"Fair enough. So are you fucked now?"

He shut one eye. "I wouldn't go that far, but I'll need to line something else up eventually. Sooner the better."

"Any regrets?"

"No," he said. "This whole thing has been so eye-opening. In law school I never forgot that there were people in the world doing crazy things—horrible things, sometimes marvelous things—that were completely foreign to my experience. We were always reading cases, which are really stories about people that become so big they can't handle them anymore without an actual professional judge. Immigration and malpractice nightmares, obviously the whole range of criminality. I used to be able to see myself as a character in these stories, a hero, maybe, at least a sidekick. I thought I could help people, change lives, change institutions, change the world. And then I started working, and gradually, without my realizing it, my field of vision shrank. Within a year I saw nothing but the cases I was on, and these weren't stories."

"Sure they were. Everything's a story."

"Not in the same way. These were maybe news stories, industry-level stuff. I did some pro bono. Thayer paid lip service to helping the community, and I thought, going in, that I could do more. It was 'unlimited' after all. But in practice, it was clear I'd be fired if I did as much pro bono work as I wanted."

"That's the job. You have to bill and bill."

"Exactly, and I had to bill so much I didn't have time to sit back and mull over every little thing I was doing, or even the subtleties of the larger purposes I was billing to serve. I was miserable there, but for the wrong reasons only. Selfish reasons. Like, I wanted weekends off, and I wanted to sleep. I wasn't thinking about the soulless nature of the work."

"Until you started drafting memos in defense of genocide denial."

"There's only so much you can ignore, I think, and retain a strong sense of yourself. I started looking for legal arguments that fit the goals of this case, and I found a case that could help us and got excited. I caught myself halfway to pumping my fist, and all of a sudden I saw what I was doing. I'd let myself get lost in the neutrality of details, and the big picture came up and knocked the wind out of me."

"Is that when you quit?"

"It was the beginning of the end. I had to call my mom and go through a big existential crisis first. It's not easy walking away from a six-figure job when you're six figures in debt."

"You're six figures in debt?" An incredulous laugh sneaked its way into the question.

He smiled at me, a crooked smile showing a dimple and a sliver of teeth. "Whoops. I guess I should've kept that one in my pocket."

There was something unbearably wonderful about him just then, something tender and thin and irresistible, like the bubbled surface of a topped-off glass, quivering on the edge of overflow. I reached for his hand, addressing this spark of longing—not sexual, exactly, but analogous at least, a fierce desire for contact, fusion. I hooked my index finger around his and held it tightly, as if I were holding him suspended at a great height. I didn't have to wait long for the answering pressure, knuckle pushed back against knuckle. I leaned into him and he mirrored my body until our foreheads were almost touching. When we kissed it felt inevitable. My nerves flooded with relief.

We came up for breath, and he spoke with my face cupped in his hand, his words crossing into my mouth between parted lips. "Never thought student debt would be a selling point."

"I'm a sucker for martyrs," I said. "I've never been good enough to be one."

Our burgers were cold by the time we separated. I felt flushed and silly, making out with a boy in an In-N-Out parking lot like I was in high school. We joked around while we finished our burgers, then I drove us back to the Gasparians'.

"I'd invite you in," I said, "but I live with my clients."

He grinned. "Next time."

I watched him drive off, then started up the stairs to the front door. A large hand on my shoulder stopped me cold. It was followed by a blast of cologne and an oily voice, saying, "Don't scream."

His hand kept me facing forward, but I didn't need to see him to recognize the thick-fingered Turk.

A chill ran through my body, followed by a deepening heat, my nervous system sounding the alarm. I'd gone looking for this man in a public place, and here he had me alone, in still suburban darkness, outside my clients' home.

"I didn't think I'd see you again."

He spoke quietly, but his voice sliced into me and lodged itself so his words seemed to reverberate in my own throat.

My wrist ached where he'd grabbed me, in fearful anticipation. I tried to find my voice, but I didn't know what to say.

"I understand you're looking for Nora Mkrtchian," he said, speaking into my ear. "That is why you were following Kizil."

I didn't move or answer, and he went on.

"I never liked how he went on about that girl. He was too inflamed by her. I should have known he might bring trouble."

I ventured a question. "You knew he was stalking her?"

"I knew he had taken too much interest in her."

I swallowed. "Did he kill her?"

"He did nothing to her with my pardon," he said, his tone genteel. "But regardless, Kizil was my man. He was my burden. Not yours."

I felt my face slacken as I processed what he was trying to tell me. "Kizil was your problem. And you fixed him."

"No," he said. "Now you put words in my mouth. But it is true that the problem is fixed. There is no further need to pick at this wound. It has scabbed over. The scab has fallen off. There is no point in it bleeding out all over again."

"Is that what you came here to tell me?"

"Yes. Your work is done. Further prying would embarrass us all. It would upset me."

I remembered the power of his hand on my wrist, the cool way he looked into my eyes as he crushed me beneath his gaze. He had seemed so calm and unruffled, as if I'd barely qualified as an annoyance. I did not want to see him upset.

"If Kizil killed Nora, then where is her body?" I listened in horror as the question slipped out of my mouth.

His grip tightened on my shoulder.

"If she's dead I need a body. I can't just tell the people who love her, 'This scary man says she's dead and don't worry about the details.'"

"That is not my problem," he said. "That sounds very much like your problem. It is not the biggest problem you can have."

"You can't produce a body, can you?" I whispered. "You're bluffing. You don't know anything at all."

"I know what I need to know. The rest is not your business."

"But it *is* my business. It's exactly my business."

"I didn't come here to argue with you. I came to relay my message, and I have told you everything that, in fairness, I believe you ought to know." He let go of my shoulder.

I turned around and watched him walk down the street, rounding the corner out of my sight. I had no idea where he'd come from.

Lusig called my name when she heard me come into the house. I went to her room and found her in bed with a book. She put it down when she saw my face.

"You look like you've just seen a ghost," she said. "Sit."

My legs went limp and I sat down on her futon.

"I guess now is a good time to give you an update."

I recapped the evening's adventures, ending with the encounter on the Gasparians' front steps. I left out one thing only—my suspicion that Kizil was dead. It seemed like too upsetting a prospect to introduce if it might not be true.

"You can't tell Ruby all this," she said, seriously.

"I brought a dangerous man to the house, Lusig. It may be the kind of thing I have to report."

"No, you can't do that. She'll fire you."

I thought about that. "Yeah, that seems likely."

"So you can't do it. You can't do that to me." She swung her legs over the side of the bed and clasped her hands together. "I need you on my side. Please."

Twelve

✦

Rubina and Lusig had gone to a doctor's appointment when I woke up the next morning, and I put off thinking about the man at the Gasparians' doorstep. Instead I spent my Saturday morning debating whether to call Veronica. She called me first, just before noon.

I felt my pulse spike at the caller ID. I knew why she was calling— she'd found Kizil, probably dead. It wasn't entirely impossible that she'd found Nora along with him, in whatever state she was in. I'd given her a solid lead after all.

"Hey, what's up?" I asked, speaking too quickly.

Instead of talking, she took a deep breath and released a heavy, exaggerated sigh that took five whole seconds to complete.

"What? What is it?"

"J.S." she said.

"V.S."

"You fucking troublemaker."

"Just get to it, will you? You're making me nervous."

"I got a new case today, thanks to you."

There it was—Veronica was a homicide detective. She was crediting me for landing her a murder.

"Not Nora, I hope."

"No," she said. "Your missing girl is still your missing girl."

"Then, who?"

"Your friend Enver Kizil."

The confirmation still came as a shock. My shoulders slumped, and I sank into my chair. I didn't like Kizil, thought he was a scumbag, maybe worse, but I was never happy to hear tidings of murder. I'd already come across more dead bodies than likely as a civilian, and I'd entered this case hoping I'd exit without seeing any more.

"We checked out his apartment yesterday. We searched the place, but he wasn't there. Turns out, he was out getting murdered."

"When? Where?"

"He was found a few hours ago in Redondo Beach, at the pier. Dead at least a day."

"How was he killed?"

"Classic execution. Three shots to the back of the head." She sighed. "Look, Juniper Song, we're going to have to meet and talk about this in person."

"Sure," I said. "When are you free?"

She laughed huskily. "Free? This is work. You come into the office. Formal interview, the whole thing. As soon as possible is best."

"Shit," I said before I could stop myself. "Of course."

"Relax. I don't think you did it."

"You sure?" I tried to sound light, but my voice came out clunky. She ignored me. "When can you come in?"

Veronica worked at the station downtown, a place with bad associations for me and probably everyone else who went in without police colors. She met me outside and led me into a sparse interrogation room.

"Aw," I said, going for levity. "This is where we first met, isn't it?"

"Yup. You were a nightmare to interview."

"You were poking around about my client."

"I'm hoping you'll be more forthcoming this time around."

"Sure." I thought about the shadowy Turk, the ominous smell of his cologne. "I have no loyalty to Kizil."

"Do you want coffee or anything?"

I shook my head. "I'm good. Where's What's-his-face, your quiet partner man? Are you interviewing me solo?"

"Redding's around. We decided we'd keep this friendly. I told him I knew you."

"Sure, friendly." I smiled. "Meanwhile you're trying to assess whether I might have emptied three shots into the back of someone's head."

"Hey, hey, hey. No need to get smart," she said, waving her hands as if to disperse a fart. "But we are going to have to talk about Kizil."

I was nervous, and she could tell. I didn't want to talk about my visit to that apartment. I didn't want to be one of the last people to have seen him alive. I didn't want to implicate a scary man I didn't even know by name.

"When did you last see him? Tell me the exact time."

I steeled myself and answered. "It must've been about nine P.M. Wednesday."

She asked me about Kizil's movements that day, and I told her about his trip to the strip club.

"Was he meeting anyone?"

I hesitated. "I can only be vague," I said.

She scowled. "This isn't PI playtime, J.S. It's serious."

"I know. I mean I only know enough to be vague. But I'm pretty sure I've met the person who did this."

I told her about my encounters with the man who'd claimed Kizil as his burden.

"I know nothing about him," I said. "Not a name, not an occupation. I can't even say he lives in L.A. My guess is he's a Turkish national, and if so, he's probably back home, out of reach by now."

"You don't know nothing. You have a theory. Let's hear it."

"Don't laugh at me," I said. "I think he's Turkish intelligence. JITEM."

I saw her stop herself from laughing. "What? Explain."

I told her about EARTH and the Kahraman connection, about the speckled history of Turkey and their Gendarmerie.

"Okay, hold on," she said. "Assuming any of this is true, why would Turkish intelligence kill Kizil if they hired him in the first place?"

"Because when they picked him, they didn't figure him for a pervert. They didn't count on him getting obsessed with a blogger, then stalking and killing her."

"You don't know that he killed Nora."

"No, I don't. But it looks that way, doesn't it? It must look that way to the people he works for, and they can't afford to have their PR tank even further."

"How do you even know he was stalking her? You said you knew he had her address, but we didn't find anything."

"I had access to his computer. He opened the door for me, and he used the restroom."

Individually, all these statements were true. Somehow, knowing this made it easier to lie. "Nora's Web site and home address auto-completed in his web browser."

She shifted in a way that brought her whole figure into sharper focus. "You're sure about that."

"I didn't hallucinate. Why?"

"Because we pulled his laptop. The browser history was wiped. I checked personally."

"Of course," I said, thinking this over. "Of course it was. This guy, Kizil's handler—he must've wiped it. They knew what I was sniffing around about, and they must've come to the same conclusion I did. But they didn't kill Kizil to solve a murder for us. They killed him so they could cover one up."

"You're sounding pretty paranoid with your 'theys' and your government conspiracies."

"These theories are all I can manage now," I groaned. "Kizil died without admitting anything. He was my best lead."

She stood up and patted me on the back. To my relief, the interrogation was over, at least for now. "It happens," she said. "Sometimes all the answers get buried with the dead."

I called a meeting when I got home. Van was out, so Rubina, Lusig, and I sat in the kitchen like we had on my first day in the house. It felt like a long time had passed since then.

I told them about my visit to the station, along with everything I knew about Kizil's murder. They listened, rapt and gaping.

"Shit," said Lusig, when I was done. "Holy shit."

"Yeah, that's about what I said."

The cousins sat in a mournful silence, processing the news of death. I remembered that most people were pretty unacquainted with the business of murder and wondered if I was callous—Kizil's death had surprised me, but I didn't think the world would miss him on balance.

Lusig's face was white when she spoke again. "And if *he's* dead," she whispered, "what does that mean for Nora?"

I'd been running the same question through my head since I heard what happened to Kizil. Murder had been lurking at the edges of the picture this whole time, but now it revealed its true position, front and center. Even if Kizil hadn't killed her, the possibility that she was dead rather than missing seemed more compelling now that there was another body.

"I don't know," I said. "Look, we all know nothing good happened to Nora, right?"

"We don't know," Rubina said, with a tone of rebuke.

"We can hope for the best, but the fact is she's been missing a long time. We all know she could be dead. If she's being held somewhere against her will, that is literally one of the best outcomes we can hope for. No one believes that she just ran away. We would be taking different tactics if we thought that were really possible."

Lusig started crying silently, holding her face in her hands. Rubina rubbed her back and whispered in her ear.

"I'm going to lay out what I think is going on here, and then we'll have to decide how to move forward," I said.

Rubina nodded over Lusig's shoulder.

"Here's how I see it: Kizil was murdered by the people behind EARTH. They killed him because they knew about his obsession with Nora, and came to the conclusion I've been trying to verify— that he was responsible for Nora's disappearance."

Lusig sniffled. "You mean that he murdered her."

I nodded. "It would've been bad news for them to have Kizil arrested, for him to be conclusively tied to her death. It would've made the anti-genocide cause look even more ridiculous, and if I'm right and the Turkish government is running EARTH, it might have been an international scandal."

"I don't see that he's been exonerated by his own murder," said Rubina, stroking Lusig's back.

"He's not exonerated, but he'll never be charged, and he'll certainly never talk. If there had been evidence that he killed her, it would've been found by now. We know that he stalked her, but that isn't conclusive. The question is—is it good enough for the two of you?"

Lusig looked up with an expression of panic. "You mean, this is it?"

"I'm asking you guys," I said. "Because if Kizil killed her, we may never know with one-hundred-percent certainty. And we can look for alternate theories, but obviously, if he did kill her, that's the only answer out there. We'll never find anything else."

"But we have to know," she said. "We can't give up. There isn't even a body. How can we say we've done what we can if we don't even know if she's dead or alive?"

I felt her protests run through me like the gritting of my own teeth. Because after all this, where was Nora? And if the answer was not in this world, then where was the body? I could feel the madness around this uncertainty. The tension entered our speech, our thoughts, and every moment we hoped and grieved, hoped and grieved, picking up her traces and wondering what they were meant to be—just things, the ordinary markings of a woman on the world, or remainders to be cherished, revered, enshrined. If her body surfaced, it would destroy the people who loved her, and yet it must bring with it a measure of relief, from the mental agony of toggling between gears, modes of thought, modes of living. I found it exhausting, and I'd never met the girl—here were all these people who loved her.

"We may never know," Rubina said gently. "We may have to accept that possibility."

"No," said Lusig. "*We* don't have to do anything. There is no *we* here. *I* am the only one here who cares about her, and *I* won't give up, even if you do."

"There's something else I have to mention." I looked at Lusig, then lowered my eyes in apology.

"No," she said. "No, don't."

"I have to," I said. I could feel the sharpness of Rubina's attention as sure as an ant feels light through a magnifying glass.

"Please," Lusig mouthed, her face twisting into a look of agony.

I averted my eyes from her and addressed Rubina. "I have to tell you that looking for Nora could be dangerous. And I mean more so than we thought."

"What do you mean?" she asked.

"The man responsible for Kizil's murder came to warn me off." When she didn't jump out of her seat, I added, "He came here."

"Here? To this house?"

I nodded.

She scooted her chair away from Lusig. "And you were hoping to hide this from me?"

Hot tears spilled out of Lusig's eyes.

"No. This is too much," said Rubina. "This is over, do you understand? I want Nora found, but this child comes first."

Lusig moaned. "No, no. It can't be over. I won't let it be over."

Rubina rose, her whole body alive with fury. She started shouting. "If you want to martyr yourself, go right ahead. But not until you can leave my child out of it!" Her words resolved into a sudden loaded silence that filled the whole room, with Lusig at its center, no longer speaking or crying, her face pained and tense. Then, as we watched, she doubled over, breathing hard.

Rubina knelt in front of her and grabbed her face. "What's wrong?" she shouted.

I got up and put a hand on Lusig's back. It came away wet with sweat.

She grabbed at Rubina's shoulders and told her, wheezing with effort: "He's coming."

Rubina shook her head. "No. It's impossible. This would be three weeks early. You're bluffing. You're trying to punish me."

"Get me to the hospital," Lusig said. "He's *here*."

As it turned out, Lusig was not bluffing. Rubina's fear had come true—Lusig's stress had impacted her pregnancy, causing her water to break during her thirty-fifth week.

And like that, the concerns of death gave way to the urgent, gushing demands of life. Rubina and I loaded Lusig into my backseat, and I drove us to Kaiser Permanente, Lusig roaring at every stoplight.

Alex Gasparian was born seventeen hours later, on the morning of March 22, healthy and weighing six pounds and one ounce.

Lusig stayed in the hospital for two days, and though Rubina told me I was welcome to stay as long as I needed, I moved quietly out of the Gasparian house.

Instead of subletting the apartment, Lori had offered it up for short-term rentals, collecting hotel rates without locking in tenants for the entire month. I was grateful; there were two sets of visitors lined up for the next week, but I wouldn't be stranded for longer than that. Rob and I went on a date that didn't involve genocide denial, as a result of which we got to know each other better. He offered to let me crash until I could move back into my place, and I split my time between him and Lori. I didn't like the feeling of floating between homes, but this, at least, felt like a shift back toward my own life.

Thirteen

❖

When I walked into the office that Monday, Chaz and Arturo both peeked out of their offices, expecting to see a prospective client.

Chaz gave me a sympathetic smirk. "Don't tell me," he said. "They killed each other."

I shook my head.

"You got fired," guessed Arturo.

"Neither. She had the baby early," I said, before the guesses could get more insulting. "If you guys have time, I'll update you. It's a pretty long story."

We gathered in Chaz's office and I told them the whole thing, top to bottom.

"I haven't heard shit from Lusig since she had the baby," I said. "And as far as Rubina's concerned, my job is done."

Arturo got up from his chair and patted me on the back. "You did good. It was a tough job," he said. "I'll leave the counseling to Chaz."

He closed the door on his way out.

"I don't know," I said, grateful to Arturo. "It doesn't feel right."

Chaz chuckled. "Of course it doesn't. Kizil didn't record a confession for you before he died."

"I'm not at all positive that's even the right story," I said. "I feel like I did all this work, figured all this shit out, and for what? An educated guess?"

"Some cases aren't solvable," he said. "It doesn't mean you didn't do the best you could."

"Lusig thinks I failed her."

"Then let her see if she can do any better. She's got her body back."

"I don't know, Chaz. I feel terrible."

He sighed. "If you can't handle uncertainty, you're in the wrong business, I can tell you that."

I landed an easy case that afternoon, and by Friday, I moved back into my apartment in Echo Park, feeling the old rhythms, when I got a call from Lusig.

"What're you doing tonight?" she asked by way of greeting.

"I'm supposed to watch a movie with Rob. How have you been?"

"Cancel," she said, ignoring my question. "Let's go out tonight. I want to get wasted." She paused, then added, "You owe me that much."

We arranged to meet at my place at ten and pre-game before cabbing to a club downtown. Lusig showed up wearing a blousy black dress that cut off mid-thigh and a black leather jacket on top.

"You look good," I said.

"I know. This is the best I've looked in, like, a year. What're you wearing?"

"I don't know. Want to help?"

I gave her free rein to rummage through my drawers and brought two beers from the kitchen. She took a thirsty sip, and smacked her lips with an appreciative sound.

"Take it easy," I said. "You're probably a lightweight now. Did you eat a good dinner?"

"I've been eating nothing but salami and sushi since I got out." She spoke of pregnancy like ex-cons spoke of prison. "Cheers."

"I thought you were pissed at me," I said clinking my bottle against hers. "I was glad to hear from you."

"I was pissed. But I also kind of missed you." She blushed and took a swig of beer to cover it.

"I'm sorry about that day," I said. "I know you felt like I abandoned you, but I really didn't have any choice."

"It's okay. I get it."

"Are you going to look for her?"

"Yup."

"I'll help," I said. "I can't do it 24/7 anymore, but I'll do what I can."

"It's okay. I think I've got your method down anyway."

"Yeah? What's that?"

"You just ask questions and hope no one tries to kill you."

I laughed, though I wasn't sure she was joking. "So how've you been? Did you move out of that house?"

"Yup. Out of my cousin's, back into my dad's. I should probably look for employment at some point."

"Have you been seeing Rubina at all?"

"Yeah, I gave in and said I'd pump milk for her, so she picks it up and takes it to the hospital. She acts like it's the least I can do, and she's probably right. I've been by to see Alex, too."

"How is he?"

"He's still in the hospital, which is standard for preemies. He's healthy, despite everything."

"And how's Rubina?"

"She's neurotically watchful, can't help herself, but mostly she's just smitten to pieces in love. My great nightmare is pretty much over." She went back to rifling through my clothes, dismissing almost everything with a flap of her hand. "Where's your slutty stuff?"

I smiled. "I don't know, in my early twenties?"

"You didn't keep any of it?"

"Your dress isn't slutty."

"I still have preggo body. And anyway, sure it is. It's not tight, but if you look close you can almost see where the baby came out." She flicked her hem and gave me a flash of underwear.

I laughed. "Okay, I guess that's convincing."

She pulled out a tight black dress with a fake leather panel down the front. "Oh, hey, you did keep one."

I got dressed and put on makeup while Lusig chugged beer and chanted "more eyeliner" over my shoulder. I called a cab and we got through another round of beer while we waited.

"Let's fill your flask before we go."

"How do you know I have a flask?"

She shrugged. "You've spent your life perfecting this old-school gumshoe shtick. I'm almost positive you have a flask. You were probably born with one glued to your naked baby hip."

I found my flask in a kitchen drawer. "I don't use it as much as I thought I would, though. It's a pain in the ass to clean. Rye okay?"

"Whatever you feel like, you fucking alcoholic."

The cab came after I topped off the flask, and we went down to meet it. The driver was a middle-aged Korean man, and Lusig made multiple attempts to engage him in conversation. He smiled and responded politely in hesitant English, and seemed relieved when we made it to the club downtown. We paid the fare and stumbled out of the cab, Lusig clutching on to my arm.

The Mayan was an old theater that served as a nightclub on weekends. Downtown had gentrified with enormous speed in the last several years, but The Mayan was at the outermost edge, still a little bit dicey after dark. Last I'd heard anyone talk of The Mayan, it was because someone had been stabbed right outside. There was a metal detector on the way in, and we had the privilege of walking through it after forking over a $20 cover.

The detector beeped angrily when I tried to pass, and I groaned as I remembered the flask.

"Please don't take it from her," Lusig pleaded. "It belonged to her dead grandmother."

I pictured my maternal grandmother watching her Korean period dramas on VHS with a flask in her hand. I had to stifle a laugh. Miraculously, we were let through.

The club was loud and crowded, the dance floor crammed with bodies. Lusig dragged me to the bar, where she ordered two blue drinks that smelled like nail polish.

"I am too old for this shit," I said, wrinkling my nose at my plastic glass. "I think it's actually glittering."

"Oh shut up, Song," she said, slinging an arm around my neck. "You're not above this."

"Fine," I said, taking a long, horrible gulp. I knew she was right.

We downed them quickly and ordered another round. She drank with determination, and I could see her loosening with every sip. Her tolerance must have taken a big hit during her months of patrolled abstinence.

"Rob didn't mind you canceling?" she asked.

"No. It was fine. We've been seeing each other plenty."

"So, things are going well?"

"Yeah, I like him."

"He's a cutie. Is he good in bed?"

I laughed and took a sip of my blue drink, which was tasting more tolerable by the minute.

She pointed at my chest with exaggerated force. "Answer my question! I command you!"

"I wouldn't know."

She gasped. "You're lying."

I laughed, and the bubbly sound of it told me I was well on my way to drunk. "Yeah, I'm lying. He's good. A+, would bang again."

"Do trumpets play? Does the earth move?"

"No," I said. "You're thinking of the apocalypse."

She led me to the dance floor, where lights strobed blue and gold across hundreds of sweat-dampened faces. We finished our drinks and held the glasses loose in our hands.

"Van's kind of hot, isn't he?" she shouted.

"I know what you mean. He's not movie-star hot, but he has a look. Strong arms, dark eyes, a little stern."

"Yeah, like he's a *man*, you know?" She flexed her forearms and crunched hard on the word. "He has that lantern jaw. And, actually, it's not even the arms, it's the hands. He has these compelling hands."

"Sure," I said, turning my head at her. "Compelling."

"You'd fuck him, wouldn't you?"

I laughed. "Jesus, we're having this conversation?"

"Fuck, marry, or kill?"

"That's not how that game works."

"Fuck! Marry! Or kill!" She flung her fists up and down as she danced.

"Okay, given those options? Fuck."

"I knew it!" She squealed triumphantly, throwing her head back. Then she stopped dancing, standing still in the writhing crowd, and looked at me with sudden purpose. Her lips moved. She'd said something at normal volume.

"What?" I asked.

She shouted in my ear, vying against the music: "He's mine."

I felt her words fly at me with the velocity and danger of a penny free-falling off a skyscraper. They landed with a vicious ping in the middle of my head.

"What are you talking about?" I asked, but I already knew.

She bit her lip and watched my eyes, and when I returned her gaze with the intensity of understanding, she nodded back at me slowly, like a teacher encouraging a child on the right path.

I wasn't dancing anymore, and neither was she. Without a word, we left The Mayan and stood on the sidewalk outside. It was still busy with people coming in and out of the club, but I could tell right away that my ears had been plugged from the music and noise inside. The newer quiet rang between them.

I lit a cigarette and offered one to Lusig. She took it with gratitude.

"Lusig," I said, after a long drag. "Are you telling me Alex is your child?"

She covered her face in both hands and swayed, the tip of her cigarette sending a ribbon of smoke tracing above her head. "God, I must be drunk."

"No shit, you're drunk. What did you think would happen if you mixed every alcohol after nine months off?"

She groaned.

"Lusig, did you invite me out tonight so you could get this off your chest?"

She opened her fingers like blinds and peeked at me with a caught expression in her eyes. "Maybe," she said. "I don't know."

"You're not still sleeping with him," I said, exploring.

"No, God no."

"Why did you sleep with him in the first place?"

She took a greedy drag on her cigarette. "To get pregnant. To let Van and Ruby have their baby."

"Isn't that what the IVF was for?"

She nodded then shook her head, nodded then shook her head. The motion set her off balance. I grabbed her arm so she wouldn't tip over. "It was insurance," she said.

"What do you mean, insurance?"

"IVF has an iffy success rate. Less than fifty percent."

"So, what, you guys decided to open another avenue of attack?"

She nodded.

I held my head, trying to get a grasp on that logic. It was too much for me in my present state. "Why?"

"Ruby would've been devastated if it didn't take."

"But she knew, right? She knew it might not work?"

"Yeah, she knew."

"So failure was always a possible outcome, even a likely one, for the first try at least, right? And I'm guessing money wasn't really an object?"

She kept nodding. "It's expensive, but you're right. They were prepared to do it more than once."

"So, what happened? I assume Rubina wasn't in on this back-up strategy."

She shook her head. "Van and I decided on our own."

"What do you mean 'decided'? Was this a strategic e-mail chain?"

She looked at me with a trace of misery, and I wondered if she regretted telling me.

I softened. Lusig was my friend and she was trying to confide in me. "Just tell me how it happened."

"Van and I were never close before this whole surrogacy arrangement. To be honest, when Ruby got engaged to him, I didn't like him at all. I thought he was stodgy and stern. Too smart, kind of arrogant, not weird enough, just this somberly handsome doctor, you know?"

I reviewed my initial reaction to Van and decided it had lined up with this image. "And then?"

"We were thrown together by this baby madness. You get it. You lived in that disaster zone, too. It was crazy, and it was uncomfortable, but it was also intensely intimate. We were talking about cycles, eggs, the nitty-gritty of human reproduction, at a real TMI level. But it wasn't just that, either. Ruby already knew me, but Van and I had to fall into each other. Ruby encouraged this, obviously, because we were going to be in each other's lives now. I was going to play this huge role in their marriage, in their child's life. Van had to know me. He had to study me. And the whole time, I could feel it. The way he was learning me, like no one else had really bothered before."

"You fell in love with him."

"Not exactly, no. But I did fantasize about him. I felt so close to him, and we'd never so much as hugged in a nonfamilial way. I started to wonder about his body, what he kissed like, how he moved in the dark."

It had been a while since I'd nursed a fixation. I'd spent most of my adult life getting laid when I felt like it, whenever convenience and desire aligned. I hadn't suffered an infatuation since high school, not the kind that smoldered with no way to quench or snuff it out. But I sympathized with Lusig, I recognized the truth and aching in what she'd said. It was a curiosity that demanded satisfaction, that could only be addressed with knowledge.

"I swear I wasn't planning anything. I didn't try to seduce him," she said. "One day, Van got off work before Ruby, and he asked what I was doing. My dad was out, so I told him I was bored at home, and he said he'd stop by."

"Had that ever happened before?"

"Him coming over alone?"

"Yeah."

"No, it hadn't."

"Then did you know right away what was going to happen?"

She shook her head vehemently and I reached out a hand to stop her from tipping into the street. "I swear on my life, I didn't."

"Really?"

"It felt so natural. We were close, you know? And we had Rubina in common, and the baby soon, so why would it be weird for us to be in a room together?"

"Oh, I don't know, because you wanted to sleep with him?"

"Okay, I may have overstated that."

"You didn't fantasize about fucking him?"

"I did, but that was just part of the big picture. Also, I'm telling you I was attracted to him *now*, in retrospect. But before anything happened it all felt very unreal and far away."

"So, when did it turn into a romantic encounter?"

She bit her lip, thinking. I could see muddled thoughts crossing slowly, haphazardly across her forehead and eyes. "Not right away, but quickly. He came in, and we hung out in the living room. I remember he was wearing a jacket, and he took it off and hung it on the back of a chair. Like this." She mimed placing a wide-shouldered jacket on the back of a chair with great care. "That's when my heartbeat picked up on the possibilities."

"Why? Because he was peeling his clothes off?"

She laughed. "No. This is stupid, okay?"

"Sure. I mean you're telling me about the time you fucked your cousin's husband."

"Fair enough." She squeezed her eyes shut and winced. "But the jacket. It was this nice jacket. Like, nice wool, not a wrinkle in it, neat lapels, whatever. And look, I've had some guys over at my house, okay? It's not like I'd never seen a man in a jacket before. But the way he hung it was so precious, like he wouldn't want to dirty my floor with his shit. Like he cared enough, or respected me enough, and I thought, What would it be like to live with a man like that?"

"Did you consider that maybe he's just fastidious?"

"That's not the point. It was visceral, okay?"

"Sure. So what happened? He took off his jacket and you jumped on him?"

"No, we sat on the couch and chatted for a while. We had a beer, nothing crazy. And then he told me how stressed he was about the IVF, and how Ruby had been just a crazy neurotic mess."

"Ah, the crazy neurotic wife. Maybe who didn't understand him?"

She looked at me with a touch of misery. "No, it wasn't like that. Obviously, Van knows I love Ruby. He wasn't trying to seduce me by pitting me against her."

"Oh," I said. "Jesus, that's brilliant. He convinced you that a brief, functional affair might help Rubina."

"Don't you see how that might have been true?"

I tilted my head and gave her a gentle, skeptical look. "I don't think that argument passes muster, and I'm a more lenient judge of these things when drunk."

"Maybe sober, you'd see the logic more clearly."

"No, Lusig. Come on."

She sighed. "I know, I know. But at the time, we convinced each other. We crossed a line, but at least part of my motive was pure."

"Lusig." I laughed all of a sudden, the ridiculousness of her confession catching up to me. "Come on. You must know how insane this sounds."

She giggled reactively, and we fell into a call-and-response of weird laughter, getting louder and louder until club patrons started looking at us.

"You're right," she said, wiping a tear from one eye. "It was insane. I don't know what I was thinking."

"Come on, let's get some tacos or something. We're at a nightclub with a metal detector, and people are staring at *us*."

We walked over to a stand called Tacos Mexico. It was five minutes away, on Broadway by the renovated Ace Hotel. The street was littered and a homeless man shouted at us as we walked by, his face distorted by anger that had little to do with us. Broadway was gentrifying in strange, random heaves, but it wasn't the prettiest part of downtown to walk in at night. It wasn't the safest part either, but I'd dealt with worse demons than the poor and schizophrenic.

The taco stand was well lit and crowded, with a dozen drunk hungry twentysomethings lined up around the counter. I recognized two Asian girls from The Mayan—they'd been the only other ones. They looked at us, and I could tell they recognized me, too. One of them even gave me a quick nod.

We ordered a mess of tacos, chopped pork and beef parts piled into hot tortillas. We received them with gratitude and loaded up on salsa, and after we paid we got lucky—one of the little tables opened up, and we sat down with our feast.

She bit into her third taco and made a face. "What the fuck is this one?"

I held a hand out and she passed it to me. I took a bite. "Oh, this must be the buche."

"What is that, a body part?"

"It's pork stomach, I think? Or intestine?"

She stuck her tongue out and wiped at it, then picked up a carne asada taco. "You know we live in a country where you can just walk into a grocery store and buy bacon, right?"

I shrugged and took a bite of her reject. "And we live in a city where you can eat buche tacos at two in the morning. Maybe you didn't know this, but Koreans love innards. They're one of our top-ten categories of drunk food."

"There are more than ten categories of drunk food?"

"Most Korean food works as drunk food. The rest is hangover food."

She laughed. "Do you have anything left in that flask?" She pointed at my purse with the hand that wasn't holding half a taco.

"What, are you serious? You're going to puke."

She shrugged. "Then I puke."

I shook the flask. It was mostly full. We'd only managed a few pulls in the cab on our way to The Mayan. I unscrewed the cap and took a sip. It wasn't expensive whiskey, but it tasted like nectar compared to the drinks in the club.

She held out her hands, cupped together like I might pour it directly into her palms. I passed her the flask and watched as she took a long gulp.

"How do you know the IVF didn't work?" I asked.

She swallowed. "I may have stated that too strongly. I don't know that the kid's mine."

"But you think it's likely?"

"Given IVF success rates, yeah."

"So I take it you guys fucked more than that one time."

She nodded. "After that first time, pretty much all the way until I was pregnant."

"And then?"

She drank from the flask again. "And then I was pregnant. That was that."

I remembered Lusig's hostility toward Van, Van's admonition against getting too close to Lusig. "That was that, huh?"

"What could we do? I was never supposed to be the mother, and neither of us wanted to hurt Ruby."

"So," I said. "What's your plan? You and Van, both of you, are going to keep this a secret, from Rubina and Alex, for the rest of everyone's lives?"

"When you phrase it that way, I guess it sounds naïve."

"I won't patronize you. You've held on to this secret for almost a year. You must have some idea of what a secret like that weighs." I thought of the skeletons in my own closet, what I wouldn't do to get rid of them. I knew the way guilt could gnaw at you, claim skin and soul, make you different from the inside.

"It's terrible. And I know I shouldn't even have told you. I just . . ." She started to cry. "I haven't had anyone else I could talk to since Nora disappeared. I miss her so fucking much."

Something tingled in my head, a missed train of thought, an alcoholic blip. I grasped for words, but I didn't know how to comfort her.

"I feel like I'm being punished, you know?" she went on. "I did something horrible to someone I love, and so the universe took Nora."

"I don't think it works like that," I said.

She took another pull from the flask. "Please don't tell her," she said.

Rubina was my client, and I knew that I owed her a duty of truth and loyalty. Still, I answered immediately. "I won't."

Fourteen

❧

Lusig's confession stayed with me like a hangover that refused to dissipate. I felt undeniably closer to her, bonded by the implied intimacy of her confidence. That feeling stayed with me even as I processed my sympathy for Rubina, my disgust at the facts of the affair. But that wasn't all. The night's revelations unsettled me completely, and I went back to them again and again, whenever my brain found time to be idle.

I didn't buy that Nora's disappearance was cosmic punishment for Lusig and Van's affair, but the more I thought about it, the more I became convinced that they were somehow connected. They were two enormously important events in the same small circle—I couldn't believe that they had nothing to do with each other.

As soon as my head cleared, it struck me that Nora must have known about the affair. That was an easy connection to draw, and it seemed like it must be meaningful. But it wasn't sufficient. I thought about who else knew that secret—Van, Lusig, Nora, and now me. Did Rubina? And if she did, would she have wanted to punish Lusig?

I was becoming less and less satisfied with Kizil as Nora's killer. There were pieces of this story I could still uncover. I could feel the answers breathing near me, tantalizingly out of reach.

When Rubina walked into the office days later, I felt like I'd conjured her with my renewed sense of mission.

I stood up to greet her and she shook my hand.

"It's good to see you," I said. "How's Alex? Is he out of the hospital yet?"

"Next week," she said. "He's in good condition, thank God. Would you like to see a picture?"

She handed me her phone, open to a picture of a tiny, dark-eyed newborn in a blue cloth hat. I wondered if Rubina questioned his maternity, then noticed her watching me look at her son. I scrolled to the next picture and the next, and saw her nod her head with each swipe, tracking my attention with unconscious approval. Whether this child was Lusig's or not, he definitely belonged to Rubina.

"He's lovely," I said. "I'm glad he's doing well."

There was a long pause as I waited for Rubina to tell me why she'd come. I doubted I was on the top of her list for visiting with baby pictures.

"What can I do for you?" I finally asked.

She bit her lip and I wondered what could make a woman like her hesitate.

"It's my husband," she said.

My heart leapt. "What about Van?"

"I have reason to believe he's been lying to me."

I kept my face neutral. "About what?"

"I don't know," she said.

I started bargaining in my head. If she asked me point-blank about an affair, I would deny knowledge, but I wouldn't pretend to look into it for her. If she didn't, I knew I would never recuse myself.

"Then why do you think he's been lying?"

"There's some activity in our joint account that looks suspicious."

This took me by surprise—I'd expected lust and betrayal, but not money.

"I'm not a financial expert, but what kind of activity?"

"You don't need to be a financial expert," she said. "I'm not either. I hadn't even looked closely at our statement for over a month."

"The activity started in the last month?"

"Yes. Regular withdrawals of large amounts of cash. Five hundred here, a thousand there. About once a week."

"You're sure Van's the one making them, and not a thief with your pin number?"

"I'm fairly sure. All the withdrawals come from the same ATM in Van's hospital. Also, Van is much more attentive to our finances than I am. There is no way he wouldn't have noticed if this were fraud."

"What do you think is going on?"

"I don't want to speculate," she said.

"But you're worried."

"Yes. I am. We have a child now. If Van's developed a *very expensive hobby*, I need to know."

She was alluding to infidelity, but I didn't think he was withdrawing large sums of money to give to Lusig. I decided not to press the question.

"What would you like me to do?" I asked.

"Monitor him," she said. "He comes home late very often. Sometimes he stays out all night. It's possible that he's always at the hospital, and if that's the case, tell me so, and I'll confront him myself. If it isn't, please let me know."

"When do I start?"

"Tonight, if you can. He has an overnight shift. I'm using the same GPS tracker I used for Lusig."

Van worked at the County hospital in Boyle Heights, and according to this tracker, he was at work when I left my place at six o'clock.

I made camp at a nearby Mexican restaurant. I ate dinner and drank two micheladas before settling in with a book while I waited for movement. I was starting to think he was really on an overnight shift when he left the hospital at eleven o'clock.

I tracked down Van's black BMW 5 Series and followed it west from Boyle Heights, riding the 101 and the 110 to the bending dark of Olympic. I maintained a good distance between us, keeping my eye on the slick shark fin of the back antenna.

He drove to Westlake, just outside downtown, and pulled into a parking lot off Olympic, lit dully by a glowing sign that announced Seoul Tokyo BBQ. I pulled to the curb and parked my car a half block up.

I remembered the Korean barbecue smell that seemed to hang perpetually on Van's clothes and considered the penchant some Korean business owners had for casually illicit activity—I'd seen the after-hours bars and indoor-smoking zones firsthand without really trying. Despite the mixed provenance of the name, I had no doubt that Seoul Tokyo BBQ was 100-percent Korean.

I waited for a minute then drove around the block. The restaurant looked closed. There was no light coming through the windows, and if I hadn't seen Van pull into the lot I might have thought it was empty. Then as I rolled past, I caught a telling glance of the parking lot—within a few spots of each other were a bright yellow Bentley and a red Ferrari.

I couldn't follow Van inside without being recognized, but I had to find out what was happening in Seoul Tokyo BBQ. I knew this much—if a Bentley, a Ferrari, and a lying doctor walked into a Korean restaurant after eleven on a Tuesday night, it probably wasn't a Korean restaurant.

I weighed the possibilities on my drive home, and decided it was either a brothel or a gambling operation, but that I'd put my money on gambling. I doubted anyone would shell out to get laid on a table, and gambling fit what I already knew about Van.

I called Rob.

"How would you like to go to work with me tomorrow?" I asked him.

"I'm inclined to say yes, but what's the plan?"

"I need to check out an illegal casino."

"Yes," he said, with great enthusiasm. "I am all-in for this plan."

"Good. Are you okay with a little role-playing?"

"Of course."

"You'll be going as stereotypical Asian male with gambling problem, a perennial casino favorite."

"And you?"

"I'll be fluttering my eyelashes as arm candy."

"You'll be very convincing."

I laughed. "We'll have to be."

"Should I bring money?"

"Yeah," I said. "Bring lots of money. Stuff a clip full of ones if you have to. I want you looking like a jackpot."

"I can see this turning out badly."

"Don't worry. Hopefully we won't have to spend much, and I can reimburse you for what we do spend."

"Okay. Anything else?"

"Yeah. I think maybe we should smell like booze."

I asked Lusig to lunch the next day, and we met up for ramen at a place in Little Tokyo. I hadn't seen her since the night at The Mayan—she'd passed out drunk at my place, but left before I woke up. I wondered if she regretted telling me about Van, though I suspected she'd meant to ever since Kizil's murder. I wondered if it started to bother her, too, a stone with the look of irrelevance, but too large to leave unturned.

She showed up fifteen minutes late, looking unwashed and gloomy. Her face turned red when she saw me at the counter, and she walked over to me with her head tilted down, her greasy hair catching the light. She sat down next to me without giving me straight eye contact.

She continued to act sheepish and weird through a half-muttered stream of small talk that filled the gaps when we weren't slurping noodles.

"So," I said, when we were nearing the bottoms of our bowls.

She noted the shift in my tone and her body tensed, waiting.

"Do you regret telling me about—"

She put up a hand. "Please, don't even say it."

"I'll take that as a yes."

She took a long sip of soup, her eyes intent on it. "Yes and no," she said, looking straight ahead. "I wanted to tell you. If I hadn't told you then, I'd be gearing up to do it now. So, yes, I regret it, but only because I'm ashamed and I worry what you think of me."

"Don't worry. I have no desire to scorn you," I said. "But I have been thinking about what you told me."

She looked at me then. "What about it?"

"Well, for one thing, why did you tell me?"

"I told you. I just needed to talk to someone."

"Are you sure that's all? It has nothing to do with the fact that you told Nora, and then she disappeared?"

She sucked in her breath. "What are you saying?"

"No, I'm not suggesting it's your fault. But you did tell Nora, didn't you?"

"Yeah," she said, cautiously. "I told her probably three or four months ago."

"Who else have you told?"

"Just you."

I nodded. "It's a big secret for a missing woman to have in her pocket through coincidence."

She didn't respond for a while, but her expression grew thoughtful and agitated, like that of a poker player warming up to a big call.

"I know," she said finally. "If I'm being honest, yeah, it's been bothering me for a while. I didn't feel right letting you walk away without telling you."

"Why didn't you tell me earlier?"

"Because it didn't seem connected to me. It still doesn't. Sure, it's a big secret, but it isn't Nora's secret. I just don't know why it would endanger her."

"Maybe she was looking to tell."

"No. Never."

"But can we just pretend, for a second, that she was? Who would've wanted to shut her up?"

Her chair squeaked against the floor as she pushed away from the counter. "This is dumb," she said. "I should leave."

"Do what you want, but if you refuse to even ask questions, you'll never learn anything about anything."

"What're you getting at, that Van—?"

"Not necessarily," I said. "But I get the sense that there's something going on with him. Have you noticed anything off about his behavior?"

"You mean recently?"

"Recently, or even when you were sleeping together."

She shook her head. "I don't know. I can't think of anything. But honestly, I could have missed something. I don't think I've been objective about him for a long time."

"He has a lot riding on your secret staying a secret," I said.

"I just don't see him murdering Nora to keep it. He barely even knew her."

"Is there anyone else who'd want to keep this quiet?"

"I don't think anyone else knows in the first place."

"What about Rubina?"

She froze. "Ruby doesn't know. That's the whole point."

"Van and Rubina are married. You don't think it's possible that he broke down and told her at some point?"

"But she would've talked to me. She would've let me have it."

"What if she had good reason not to do that?"

"Like what?"

"Like maybe she'd rather not introduce a question of maternity." I pictured Rubina the day I met her, cool and commanding in her kitten heels. I remembered her reluctance to engage in the search for Nora, then her eagerness to have me live under her roof. And now, she was siccing me on her husband. "And maybe," I continued, "she wants you to suffer."

Lusig blanched. "No, not Ruby. You can't possibly think . . ."

She trailed off, and I spoke before she could finish the sentence. "I'm just exploring, here," I said. "I still think it's likely that Kizil killed Nora. But if you want to put everything on the table, Van and Rubina might have had motive."

"None of this ever occurred to me," she said dreamily.

"Maybe not consciously," I said. "What if I find out what happened to Nora? Do you want to know no matter what that is?"

She only hesitated for a second before giving a firm nod. "It's too late to get off this train now."

I went straight to Rob's with makeup and a change of clothes in an overnight bag. He lived in an apartment at Sixth and Main, on the edge of Skid Row, where the addicted, ill, and homeless put up tents every night. His place was a handsome loft, new construction, with hardwood floors and an enviable view—what a difference a block made in this city.

I'd agreed to spend the day with him before our evening mission—in case things turned dangerous and we were cheated of our lives together. We hung out at his apartment, and I helped chop vegetables and turn fires on and off while he made an early dinner. We dressed up for a night on the town—he put on slacks and a sport coat; I wore a black pencil skirt and a tight blouse, and spent an extra fifteen minutes on my makeup. We left the apartment to get drinks at a trendy speakeasy across the street, one of the places built on nostalgia for a time when Japanese internment and the L.A. riots were things California still had to look forward to. We drank stiff cocktails and smelled each other's breath for whiskey. We both reeked sufficiently after one round.

Rob drove to Westlake while I double-checked Van's location. He was safe at home tonight, and we were free to enter Seoul Tokyo as strangers. I reapplied lipstick in the vanity mirror. I liked vamping it up once in a while, particularly on the job—cinematic dragon ladies notwithstanding, no one suspected a dolled-up Asian girl of anything. All I had to do was giggle with one hand over my mouth, and my disguise would be foolproof. It made me feel like a spy.

We parked on Olympic to avoid subjecting Rob's car to scrutiny, then walked up to the front door of Seoul Tokyo BBQ. I put my ear to the door and heard sounds of life that weren't audible from the street. No raging music, but plenty of conversation.

"You knock," I said to Rob.

"Okay, what do I say?"

"Just say we're here to play, but be kind of tentative and respectful about it. How good is your Korean?"

"It's okay. My accent's decent."

"Okay. If a Korean opens the door, you bust out your best good-boy Korean."

"I can do that. Anything else?"

"Just remember: You have pockets full of money that you're itching to give away." I ruffled his hair and undid the top button of his shirt. "Okay, now knock."

Twenty seconds later, a beefy Korean man opened the door. He was in his forties, with dark glasses and the build of a wrestler; short, but powerful. He wore a black suit that was too small around his chest. His shirt buttons strained.

"May I help you?" he asked in clipped, impatient Korean. The interior sounds followed him out, a mix of K-Pop and mild chatter, though I heard one victorious shout that I'd never heard more than twenty feet from a blackjack table.

"We heard we could play here. . . ." Rob's voice was meek, but searching. I stood behind him and smiled as daintily as I could manage.

The bouncer looked at us skeptically. "This is a private birthday party," he said after a stern pause. "We open for lunch tomorrow at eleven thirty."

He started to close the door again.

"*Ahjusshi*, wait!" Rob called, slurring the address. "I have money."

The door paused long enough for me to step forward and get a hold on it. The bouncer's face came back into the opening. We waited for him to say something, until it was clear he was waiting on us.

Rob peeled out a respectable wad of bills—it must've been all he brought with him, but he made it look like there was more where it came from. He licked his thumb and made a show of separating out five twenties, each bill slapping against his fingers. He proffered the hundred dollars, which the bouncer took in one oversized hand and slipped into his jacket pocket.

We waited for the door to open wider. It didn't. The bouncer didn't move after he put the money away, not a pixel. His eyes were blacked out by his ridiculous indoor sunglasses, but he had to be staring at us. The effect was unnerving. Rob shook his head and started counting out more bills.

"The Armenian doctor," I chimed in. "He told us to come here."

The bouncer's face lost its frozen quality, his eyebrows lifting into an expression of surprise. He was reevaluating us—mentioning Van had upgraded us in his perception.

If I'd spoken up a few seconds earlier, I might have saved us some money. Rob had been too dramatic with his counting. The bouncer looked pointedly at Rob's hands, waiting for him to finish.

But he pocketed the second hundred dollars with less coolness than before, even an air of casual gratitude, like he was a valet and we'd just tipped him a little extra. "IDs," he said, suddenly a professional.

We handed him our driver's licenses, and he pocketed them without even pretending to look them over.

"Arms out," he said to Rob.

Rob complied, and the bouncer patted him down. "I feel like we're getting on a plane," Rob said, his tone jokey but mildly exasperated. "Should I take off my shoes and belt?"

When the bouncer was done, he looked me up and down, detached as a metal detector. I started to put my arms out when he shook his head. "You're fine." He pointed to my purse. "Bag."

I opened my purse and he scanned it quickly. He didn't need to pat me down because there wasn't room between me and my clothing for weapons. I wondered what kind of Korean barbecue joint needed to watch out for guns.

He opened the door and the familiar smell blasted out at us—meat, soy sauce, sugar, smoke. More smoke on top, from a roomful of lit cigarettes.

We stepped past the bouncer, and a young Korean woman greeted us with a bright toothy smile that didn't quite reach her eyes. She led us into the main room of the restaurant, though there wasn't much leading necessary.

It was a Korean barbecue joint like the many I'd seen before, with a couple dozen tables topped with grills and grill fans. No one was seated at these tables. The noise came from the rooms around the main room, private dining spaces for families and large parties. I'd been in several of these rooms growing up, thrown together with cousins and family friends for interminable birthday dinners without any cake.

"Are you here for anything in particular?" asked the hostess.

"No," I said. "This is our first time. Do you know Van Gasparian? The Armenian surgeon?"

Her smile went taut at the name for a fraction of a second. It cost me some effort to pretend not to notice.

"He's his friend," I said cheerily, latching on to Rob's arm.

"We go to Commerce together sometimes, but he said this was more fun," Rob said, taking his cue. "More central, cuter girls."

"What are you looking to play?" she asked.

"I thought I'd take a look and go with my gut. Live dangerously," he said with a flirtatious lilt.

She re-upped her empty smile and turned to me. "Do you play, too?"

"I'm just here to watch and drink," I said with a giggle. "Maybe I'll keep you company."

"I'll take you to our main floor," she said, ignoring my idea.

We looked around at the empty tables topped with cold grills.

She pointed to a stairwell to our left. "Follow me."

The stairwell was lit, and as we ascended, the noise from the upper level gathered around us. We followed her down a hallway of closed doors to the one at the end, which opened onto a giant room set with multiple round tables, each one occupied by a white-shirted dealer and a number of gambling men, most of them Asian. I'd been in analogous rooms in other restaurants many times before—they were logical venues for the big Korean gatherings I remembered from my childhood, celebrating baby's first birthdays, or eating cold noodles and battered fish fillets in funeral clothes. And now here was a banquet of an entirely different kind, without the festivity of a true casino to mask the aura of sweaty desperation.

We walked around, watching the action, and Rob selected a poker table where he could sit on the sidelines without bleeding too much money. When I turned to look for her, I saw that the hostess was no longer in the room.

"I'm going to find her. I think she might know something I don't," I whispered in Rob's ear. "Good luck."

He squeezed my hand. "You, too."

I stumbled around the restaurant, playing the lush, giggling and whoopsying as I burst through closed doors. She wasn't anywhere, and I knew better than to ask after her. Instead, I went outside, where a Korean hostess might take a cigarette break—or in this case, to get away from smoke and trouble for a breath of fresh air.

I found her standing at the edge of the parking lot, shivering and smoking with great concentration. I walked up next to her and lit my own.

"What's your name?" I asked, dropping the ditz act and hoping she wouldn't leave.

"Ara," she said. "And you're Juniper."

I raised an eyebrow, then remembered the bouncer had taken our IDs. "Song," I said, holding out a hand.

She took it politely. "You're a private investigator."

I nodded and showed her my license.

We stood smoking in silence, and I waited for her to speak. She'd figured out I was a private eye because I'd asked about Van. Yet here she was, standing next to me, neither objecting nor walking away. Something told me that if I stood still and listened, she would give me what I wanted.

"The Armenian doctor," she said after another cigarette. "Why were you asking about him?"

I inched closer to her. "I've been hired to see what he does in his free time. I followed him here."

I crushed my cigarette and looked at her straight on. There was something twitchy about her demeanor, her body held tense and ready to spring. The corners of her red-painted mouth were slightly upturned, but not in a smile.

"Someone else came looking for him," she said.

"Was it an Armenian woman?"

She nodded, and I pictured Rubina following her husband in the dark, finding out everything she'd hired me to find out.

"Dark hair?" I continued, my mind racing, trying to parse her motivations. "Short and thin, in her late thirties?"

"No. She was younger." She shook her head, shutting her eyes closed tight against what she was about to say. "It was the Armenian girl. The one who went missing."

I nearly lost my footing. "Nora?" I asked. I pulled out my phone, where I had her picture open in a web browser. "This girl? Nora Mkrtchian?"

Ara nodded and looked over her shoulder toward the door.

"When was this?" I pressed on.

"She came twice. In February."

"February what?"

"The first time was the night before Valentine's Day. The second was two nights after. The sixteenth."

"Are you sure about that?"

She nodded. "I saw her on the news after she disappeared. It was less than a week later. I recognized her right away."

"What time on the sixteenth?"

"Midnight, at least."

It was later than anyone had seen her that I knew of—after she left Kaymak's.

"Why don't the police know about this?"

She started to scrunch up her face in a display of tortured conscience. "I—"

I cut her off. "Right. This place. It isn't on the books. You would've lost your job."

She nodded, and I could see that her eyes were welling. The sight made me push an advantage.

"I mean, not that you couldn't have found another job. You're a pretty Korean girl in Koreatown. You could've gotten a hostess job anywhere. But I guess the average barbecue joint doesn't pay illegal casino money." I lit another cigarette, stuck it in my mouth, took a long drag while I looked at her with concentrated contempt. "This girl's been missing for months. If she's alive, she's not having fun, and you might've helped her as soon as she was reported missing. If she's dead, you've held back what could be vital information in a murder investigation." I shook my head. "I hope you get some great fucking benefits."

She was tearing up. "I have a daughter," she said. "Please, don't torture me. I'm trying to do what's right now."

I was moved in spite of myself, but I didn't show it. She looked about twenty-two, and I did feel sorry for her. In any case, it looked like my guilt trip had done its job.

"What did she want?"

"The first time, she came by herself and charmed her way in. She drank and joked around with the other customers, even the old Korean men who barely spoke English. I swear I don't remember anything she said. But the second time, she talked to me." She stopped talking and bit her lip. "She asked if I'd seen the doctor."

"Did she ask anyone else?"

"I don't know. I told her where he was gambling."

"But at the very least, several people must have seen her."

"Yes, but no one ever mentions it. Sometimes I think I imagined her."

I thought about what Nora might have wanted with Van, a man she only knew as her best friend's cousin-in-law and sometime paramour. I was still figuring it out, trying to visualize the connections as I talked to Ara. The only thing I knew was that there could be no coincidence this massive, this hidden, this potentially harmful.

"No. I'm sure you didn't," I told her. "Did she find him?"

"I don't know," she said.

"So when her face came on the news, did anyone talk about it?"

"No one."

"Did you tell anyone?"

"Yes. I told my manager."

"Who is he?"

"Please." She sniffled loudly. "Don't tell anyone I talked to you."

I dropped it. I knew what I had to do next, anyway. "Okay. What did your manager say?"

She bit down on her lip again and it trembled. "He said I must have been mistaken, but that to be safe, I should keep my theories to myself."

Fifteen

✤

A ra gave me our IDs and went to fix her makeup while I collected
Rob from the poker table. He was almost sorry to leave—he
was about two hundred dollars richer than when he'd started. I explained what I'd found out on our drive back downtown.

"So if Nora found Van, he might have been the last person to
see her alive," he said, gripping the steering wheel.

"And I think she must have found him."

"But what for?"

"I'm trying to figure that out." My mind was frothing with ideas,
but all of them hinged on knowledge that wasn't mine to share—
about Lusig and Rubina and Alex. Instead I said, as authoritatively as
I could, "I have to talk to Van."

"The man you think is a murderer?"

"The man I've been hired to investigate."

"When are you planning to do this?"

"Tonight," I said. "As soon as I get my car."

"You don't think I should go with you?"

"Wouldn't make sense. He might talk to me if I go about it the right way. I mean, granted, he wasn't around a whole lot but I lived in Van's house. He's never seen you before in his life."

"Will you be safe?"

"Safe as I ever am doing this kind of thing. I'm planning to meet him in a public place."

He looked worried but seemed to know better than to tell me how to do my job.

He dropped me off at my car and gave me a kiss that suggested I should come back to him alive sometime. "Be careful," he said. "Text me when you get home."

"I'll be fine," I said. "I've met scarier murderers than Dr. Van Gasparian."

It was close to midnight when I left downtown, and I hoped Van was still awake. I texted him to meet me at the bar with the mermaids on the walls, and that I'd be there in fifteen minutes.

The place was as empty as the last time, and I sat in the same booth with another pint of Guinness in a dirty-looking glass. My phone indicated that Van had read my message, and given how much he was hiding, I knew he'd have to show. He couldn't afford to ignore a late-night summons from his wife's private eye of choice.

I drank slowly while I waited, mulling over the facts as I knew them, trying to fit them into one coherent story. The loose threads were starting to come together, and my mind buzzed with a final sense of convergence that had been missing when Kizil was my primary suspect. I prepped my phone to record whatever Van had to say. I had a feeling I'd want to have it on tape.

He arrived around a quarter after midnight, in a sweater and wrinkled slacks. He looked alert, but I guessed he'd run out the door as fast as he could manage without freaking out Rubina. He had the nervous air of a hunted man.

I waved him over and he sat across from me, keeping his eyes trained on mine.

"What's this about?" he asked without preamble.

I decided not to keep him in suspense. "I want to talk to you about your gambling addiction."

He blinked. "What gambling addiction?"

"I followed you to Seoul Tokyo," I said. "I know it's not just a Korean restaurant."

"You followed me?" He rose in his seat, his voice prickling with anger. Then he slumped back down. "Oh, God. Ruby."

I didn't confirm his wife's involvement, but I didn't have to. "Tell me about the gambling," I said.

"I need to talk to my wife," he said, gathering himself up to leave. "If I have to have this conversation, it should be with her."

This was true enough, and if his gambling were the end of it, I wouldn't have confronted him directly. But I couldn't let him go now. "We're having a conversation you won't want to have with your wife," I said. "You told me that if it ever came down to it, I should side with Rubina over Lusig. Does that mean you'd like me to tell her whatever Lusig tells me?"

He stopped moving and gave me a long, searching look. "I need a drink," he said, and walked to the bar to get one.

I didn't stop him. Given everything else, falling off the wagon was the least of his problems. And besides, he might talk more easily with some booze warming his gullet.

I watched him take a shot and come back with a tall glass of what looked and smelled like straight vodka. He sat down wearily. "I knew the minute I met you that you would ruin me one day."

"I don't traffic in anything as grand as that," I said. "All I do is turn on the light."

"I knew," he continued, ignoring my wisdom. "God, it was so fucking idiotic to begin with. She knew it was nuclear to send a private eye after Lusig. That's why she didn't consult me. If she'd asked my opinion I would've dissuaded her in a second." He pressed a thumb deep into his brow. "But once she figured out hiring a private detective was something she could do, I knew it was only a matter of time before she put you to every possible use."

"It's not my fault you have a mountain of shit to hide. And honestly, what did you think was going to happen? You're married. Money problems don't stay in the closet."

He took another sip of vodka. "I know. It was only a matter of time until this came out once I started using the joint account."

"Do you have other accounts?"

"We have separate accounts on top of our joint account. I had a trust fund kick in when I turned thirty-five."

"Then why dip into— Right. You depleted it."

His expression was soggy with shame. He added another swill of vodka to the mix. "I grew up wealthy," he said.

"I've gathered."

"I understand that this isn't sympathetic, but I truly did not know that money could be so finite. That everything I had could slip through my fingers so quickly."

"How did it happen?"

"The same way it happens to anyone. I started gambling. I didn't stop."

"When did you start?"

"Not until a couple of years ago. After the house was bought."

"After you stopped drinking?"

He nodded. "It seemed less harmful. We had plenty of money, and I was making more of it every day."

"You said you didn't think you could have a family with an alcohol problem. It didn't cross your mind that gambling might get out of control, too?"

"You're right." He took another gulp of vodka and set the glass down hard. "I'm a failure of a husband. A failure of a father before Alex was even born. Is that what you want to hear?"

"No, I don't care how sorry you feel for yourself. I want to hear what happened."

I waited, and after a sullen minute, he continued. "I heard about this place, Seoul Tokyo. From a coworker. Korean guy with a high-roller dad. He was telling a fantasy story, the kind that happens once in a while if you play regularly enough. Heroic gamble, six-figure payoff."

"How much do you have to gamble to get a six-figure payoff?"

"Six figures. Many, many times." He laughed emptily. "I have stories like that, too. A few of them. Always told myself I'd quit if I was far enough ahead. Never fully believed myself."

"So you got into this place. Became a high roller. And then what, you ended up six figures in debt?"

He nodded and drank. He looked miserable, damp with a nervous sweat.

"But you're still playing," I said. "You're paying for past debts, and still creating new ones?"

"I'm not losing like I used to. If I pay a couple grand a month for a while, I will be in the clear."

"You were hoping Rubina wouldn't notice a couple grand a month?"

"It didn't seem impossible."

"How can you possibly know you'll pay it off if you keep gambling? You spent what must've been a sizeable trust fund. How do you know you won't sink the joint account, hand over the house?"

"I wouldn't do that to Ruby," he said earnestly.

I almost laughed. "You don't seem to have the best self-control."

"They won't take everything," he blurted.

"And who's 'they'?" I asked.

"Do you even have to ask? Some scary fucking people."

"Criminals," I said. "The organized kind."

He nodded. "The casino extended me a line of credit. It didn't occur to me to ask where it was coming from."

"I don't believe that."

"Maybe it did occur to me. But I didn't want to know."

"How on earth do you know they won't take everything?"

"That wasn't an option. So, I struck a deal to stanch the bleeding."

"Jesus. This is some *Godfather* shit," I said. "Tell me how."

"One night I was at the tables, and I got called to the front of the house. This man I'd never met before told me to get in a car. I knew I couldn't say no."

"Who was he?"

"He calls himself Hong. Who knows if that's his real name."

"Korean man?" I felt a twinge of disgust.

"I don't know. Korean, Chinese. Asian, yes. That's about all I know. I don't even know his role, except that he was sent after me."

"Was it just him?"

"No. There was the driver. Boris."

"Hong and Boris," I said, trying out the names. They sounded fake, placeholder aliases for an Asian and an Eastern European. "They just up and introduced themselves?"

"I learned their names later," he said. "Boris, by the way—I know what Boris does. He's pure muscle. I knew that as soon as I saw him. I thought he was going to be the last face I saw on this earth."

"Where did they take you?"

"I don't know where, exactly. They blindfolded me. I thought I was being taken to be executed. I was begging for my life and no one was responding. I almost pissed myself."

"But they didn't execute you."

"No. They took me to a house. When they took my blindfold off, I was looking at what I thought was a crime scene. There was blood on the carpet, and it was leaking out of a dead man."

"Only, he wasn't dead," I guessed.

He looked at me curiously. "You see where this is going, then."

"You got lucky, or unlucky, depending on how you look at it," I said. "The mob was in the market for a surgeon."

He nodded. "I saved that man's life. Who knows if that's a good thing. I never found out who he was."

"And I'm guessing they didn't thank you profusely, forgive your debts, and drop you off to live in peace with your family."

"The way I understand it is they'd been looking for a surgeon they could trust."

"You mean a surgeon they could pinch by the balls when they held him in their pocket. Did they know what you did for a living before they extended that line of credit?"

"Yes," he said. He looked mildly embarrassed, and I pictured him pulling rank at a card table, demanding the respect due to his prestigious profession.

"So you became the mob doctor. I'd think that's a full-time job. Is it not?"

"No. Emergencies only, and not all emergencies. Only injuries they don't want taken to the hospital," he said.

"Injuries that imply criminality."

"It wouldn't help anyone if they started to overuse me. As it is, I've already had to leave an overnight shift without any notice. That kind of thing draws attention. No one wants me drawing attention, at work or at home."

"You, least of all."

"Me, least of all." He stared at his glass and took a long sip.

"Have they ever had you kill anyone?" I asked.

He wiped his mouth and curled his upper lip in a display of disgust. "Good God, no. I'm a doctor."

"We're well beyond the scope of the Hippocratic oath here. Doctors have easy ways to kill people. I had to ask."

"I would never do something like that," he said.

I wondered if he'd convinced himself I wouldn't ask about Nora. "Did you ever see anyone they'd hurt?"

"I tried to learn as little as possible about what they did, who they hurt, if they hurt anyone at all."

I gave him a skeptical look. "You think it's likely people are shooting at them and they're not shooting back?"

"Whatever they're doing, I don't see it."

"Nothing? In over a year of working intimately with a bunch of straight-up gangsters?"

"Nothing."

"And now, what? You keep working for them until you die?"

"I don't know," he said. "I need another drink."

He walked over to the bar, a slight wobble in his step, and came back with another tall one.

"So," I continued, "at what point did you decide it was a good idea to have a child?"

"Never. But Ruby was insistent, and I'd held her off for too long already. I couldn't say no without explaining, and then I would've risked losing her altogether."

I felt my first throb of real sympathy for Van—it hadn't hit me until now that he was deeply in love with his wife. It vanished the next instant.

"You're a cold-blooded man, Van," I said. "Did you even want Lusig? Or did you just know you couldn't afford more rounds of IVF?"

He didn't answer for a long time. He looked at his upturned hands, studying them with the earnest inquiry of a palm reader. They were capable surgeon's hands, hands that Lusig had desired, had described as compelling. Hands that had taken what could never be given back.

"I don't know. There is no okay answer to that question," he said. "I love my wife. Other than with Lusig, I have been faithful to her."

"Sure, you've never cheated on her, except with her cousin, who you were trying your best to impregnate."

"I wouldn't have done it if I didn't care about this pregnancy. It could have been okay. Lusig would never have told her. And Lusig knew why we were doing it, too. She wouldn't have slept with me if it weren't for Ruby."

"Neither of you were doing Rubina any favors. Lusig wanted to sleep with you. She just needed a reason to abandon her loyalties. And I'm sure you didn't mind sleeping with the nubile little cousin, either. But Van—I didn't ask you here to talk about your personal life."

Fear crept across his features as he watched the set of my face. His eyes froze in their sockets, their dark brown grown glassy as his pupils spread black.

"You're a killer, Van."

The bar seemed to go quiet around us, though no one was listening in. I waited for him to deny it, but he didn't say anything at all.

"I know Nora Mkrtchian went looking for you," I said. "I talked to someone at Seoul Tokyo who said she was asking about you the night she disappeared. Hours after anyone else is supposed to have seen her."

He started to say something, but drowned it with vodka instead.

"The management knows she was there, and they seem to want to keep things hushed up. Not great for business to bring homicide police down on a mob-run casino."

I sipped on my beer while I waited for him to react. He didn't—he seemed to be watching me instead, abject but expectant, as if he were interested in seeing what might happen next.

"She wanted your help, didn't she? She was being hounded by a man who wanted to hurt her, and she went on the offensive. But she couldn't do it alone, and the men in her life, the ones who loved her, weren't going to help her go after him. She looked to you because she had more to hold over you than love. She had knowledge. She had the power to destroy you." The story unrolled in my head as I spoke, the connections I'd been missing snapping into place. "And she knew more about you than even Lusig, didn't she? She wasn't blind to you at all. She found out about your gambling. She found out you were mobbed up."

I kept my eyes glued to his, and slowly, painfully, his face lost its rigidity and gave way to anger, sadness, and underneath it all, resignation. I waited, and this time he spoke.

"She wanted me to help her solve a problem. That's what she said."

"Her stalker."

He nodded.

"She wanted you to put the scare in him. Threaten him. Beat him." I remembered her anger, her fear, the way these feelings had pulsed through my body as I looked for her, chasing her to her destiny. "She wanted your help getting rid of him."

"She was acting crazy," he said. "Completely insane. You should have heard her. She was talking about an execution."

"She wanted you to take him out personally?"

"Either that or get someone else to do it. She kept saying, 'I know you know people,' like I could just speed dial a hit man for her." He spoke with a show of moral disgust that I was supposed to share. I didn't exactly condone Nora's attempt to line up Kizil's murder—an attempt that paid off, I had to note, in the end—but, given what happened to her at the end of that conversation, I couldn't muster much fellow feeling with Van.

"You could have helped her," I said. "I don't think you refused out of any moral compunction. But she threatened to tell Rubina about you and Lusig. She knew, and she would always know. So you killed her."

"I didn't know what I was doing," he said, pleading. "I didn't see that I had any choice, do you understand? You get to a point where you don't have options, and you kick into survival mode. It's almost . . . physiological. You get cornered. You lash out."

"No, drop this 'you' bullshit. You're talking about *you*. You're talking about what *you*, Dr. Van Gasparian, did when you were cornered. This isn't a thought experiment. This is what happened. Tell me, what happened in survival mode?"

He grabbed at his drink and glugged it down like water from a long-sought oasis.

"I can't say this out loud."

"She had you in a corner."

He nodded.

"You did the only thing you could."

He nodded again.

"You murdered her."

"It was an accident," he objected, a thin whine in his voice.

"Convince me."

He looked around the bar. No one was paying any attention to us.

He began in a whisper. "I just wanted her to shut her mouth. I . . ." He faltered and I waited a long time for him to go on. Then he reached across the table and sealed my mouth with one hand. "I put my hand to her mouth, just like this, and I held it there. I kept holding it there. And then, the way she looked at me." He withdrew his hand and cradled his head, remembering against his will.

"You couldn't stop," I suggested, breathing deeply.

"I couldn't. There was no turning back, do you understand? She would have ruined me."

He finished his drink in one last thirsty gulp. It didn't matter, anyway. He could sober up in prison.

"Where is she?" I asked.

"I don't know," he whispered, slotting his head between his hands.

"Don't fucking lie to me, Van. This is over. Tell me what I need to know."

"I don't know!" He was still whispering, but his voice was raspy and emphatic. "I didn't get rid of her."

"Your friends. Hong and Boris," I said.

He nodded.

"So, never mind a little gambling debt. You now owe the mob for a covered-up murder. The only ways out of this pickle are death and prison."

"You think I don't know that?"

"God," I said. "Poor Rubina."

He perked up at her name, his eyes burning red and wet. "You can't tell her," he said.

"This is not a secret you get to keep, Van."

"It was an accident!"

"Then you'll get convicted of manslaughter. Doesn't change that Nora died at your hands. This is not a family matter. This is a criminal case, Van. You understand that, right?"

"I know," he said, grabbing his head. "I know that. I know it's all over now. I'll go on trial, my face will be in the papers. I'll die in prison."

"I doubt it," I said. "It looks pretty bad, I'll give you that. You don't get to keep your life as is. You killed someone. You don't deserve that. But my guess is you'll take a plea, and I'll bet it'll be a sweet one."

"What makes you say that?"

"They don't have a body, for one thing. That makes it hard to prove anything beyond reasonable doubt. But also, you have information that they want."

He gulped, visibly, his Adam's apple like something stuck in his throat. "I don't know anything."

"Sure you do. You have connections to some of the shadiest people in L.A. The kind of people it takes teams of police years of hard work to track down. You know the names and faces protected by other names and faces."

"They'll kill me."

I shrugged. "You knew that might happen the minute you got in bed with them. Anyway, that's your problem. All I'm trying to say is it's not the end of the world."

"But my wife—"

"Yeah, your wife's going to find out. There's no way around that."

He stared at his empty glass. "Just do me this one favor," he said, subdued.

"Maybe," I said. "Depends what it is."

"Let me tell them."

"Them?"

"Ruby and Lusig. My family."

I thought about it. I wondered if he could look them in the eye and confess. It sounded a whole lot harder than walking into a police station.

"Okay," I said. "If you have the balls for that, I'll hold out."

It was strange, really, that I had any sympathy for this man. He was a murderer, yet he had been a murderer for as long as I'd known him. We'd lived under the same roof, and though I had no love for him, I had started to think of him as a reasonable, ordinary human being. I'd seen things about him that were interesting and true, that were a part of him apart from the desperate man who had killed an innocent woman. I couldn't make the switch to seeing him as a stranger. It didn't matter how little he deserved my compassion.

Still, I didn't need to sit with him a minute longer. I swallowed the rest of my drink and left.

I checked my phone as soon as I got in my car. Rubina had texted me four times, asking me to follow Van. I'd have to wait to get back to her. I made sure the interview had recorded. It was all there—a thirty-five minute audio file with a full confession, ready to go.

I didn't know how long Van would take to come clean with Rubina and Lusig. I couldn't wait overnight to get the recording to

Veronica. It was too big to e-mail her from my phone, but she'd have it before bedtime. At least before my bedtime.

I was relieved in a cowardly way that I wouldn't be the one to tell Lusig. I knew she was torn by her desire to know, but I couldn't help feeling she was better off in the dark. She'd entangled her life with Van. She'd trusted him. Maybe she'd even loved him. I couldn't imagine how she might react.

And then there was Rubina. Poor Rubina. I didn't even know where Van would start. What was worse, from a wife's point of view—the seduction of a loved one or the murder of an acquaintance?

I kept trying to picture the scene of this confession as I drove home. I couldn't do it. It was inconceivable.

I was turning onto my street when I realized—it was never going to happen. Van had doubled down.

At first I thought I'd run over a pothole. There was the loud pop, the sudden lurch, the same disorientation of being thrown while stable. I cursed and started to pull over. The car limped as I drove, dragging its busted tire like a mangled foot.

Then lights came on behind me, high beams come to life out of darkness, flashing to get my attention. I became sharply aware of the emptiness of the street. All this nightmare needed was a full moon and a sudden rain.

I reviewed my impressions of the last fifteen seconds. Had I heard a gunshot? I became sure that I had.

The car behind me continued to flash its lights. I couldn't see much else. Not the driver, not the number of passengers, not even the make of the car. The dark and the light were blinding.

I took a deep breath, then another, making an effort to convince my body that I was in control. It helped. I made a mental list of immediate objectives: First and foremost, escape if possible; if I couldn't outrun dedicated pursuers with a gimp car in a dark city, then the next best thing was to ensure my release.

I turned on my hazard lights and crept along the side of the road, slowing enough to indicate that I was rolling to a stop. I could tell from the sound and feel of my car that the back left tire had been blown to burnt rags. The road scraped against what remained, and I felt the rough, dry impact grate like nails on a swallowed chalkboard.

As the car rolled I got my phone out and called Veronica, pleading out loud for her to answer.

She picked up after the fifth ring.

"This better be good." Her voice was hoarse and groggy.

"I found out what happened to Nora."

I heard her scrambling to rise on the other end of the line. I had her attention. "Tell me."

"She's dead. Killed by a man named Van Gasparian."

"Gasparian? Isn't that the name of your client?"

"Yeah, her husband. I don't have time to get into it. Listen, I'm in some shit. Where are you now?"

"It's one o'clock in the morning, J.S., where do you think I am?"

"You live in Eagle Rock, right? If you leave now, you can get to Echo Park in twenty minutes?"

"The fuck's going on?"

"I have a confession to Nora's murder on tape. It's on my phone. I wanted to send it right away but it's too big."

"Can't you Dropbox it or something?"

I almost laughed. "No, not now. I have to concentrate on getting away from whoever just shot out my tire and is trying to get me to stop."

"Where are you?" Her voice was taut. She wasn't wasting any more time.

"I'm basically home, in Echo Park, on Santa Ynez. I'm going to try and get down to the lake, but I might not make it." I only had two downhill blocks to go to Glendale Boulevard, which was a much busier street than mine, but I doubted I'd be allowed to get that far without a fight.

I heard the sound of a door slamming behind me. There was no longer any distance between my car and the one behind it. I'd slowed down enough that the pursuer could get to me on foot. "Come quickly. Bring friends," I shouted into the phone.

I hung up. Veronica would come. I didn't have time to dial 911. I slammed on the gas.

The engine roared, but after an energetic twenty-foot sprint, it was clear I wasn't outrunning anyone. It didn't help that the car behind me was still moving. There were at least two people coming for me.

Chaz always insisted we didn't need to carry guns. I'd disagreed in theory, but I'd never gotten around to getting the permissions I'd need to have one on the job. I kept a Taser in my glove compartment, but it wouldn't do me much good with two attackers and a busted car. All I could hope to do was to Taser the guy on foot, and piss off him, the driver, and whatever other goons they had in tow.

I went back to my cell phone. I might have time to dial 911.

But now there was a face at my window.

It belonged to an Asian man with a shaggy black beard shot through with a dozen strands of white. He was about forty-five, with coarse skin and narrow eyes. Chinese, I thought instinctively, though I couldn't say why. On another street, at another hour, I might have thought he had a kind face, gentle and a little doughy, soft in the cheeks. But even Mister Rogers would have put the fear in me under these circumstances, and this was not Mister Rogers. This had to be the man Van knew as Hong.

He tapped at my window and I tried to think of a way to avoid rolling it down. My tire was busted, but I was inside, everyone else was out. I didn't want to create another breach.

He sighed loud enough for me to hear through the glass. When he tapped again, the sound was heavier. I looked back up. He was tapping with a gun.

I rolled down the window and waited for him to speak.

"You seem to have a flat tire, miss," he said, finally. His voice was smooth and calm, with the hint of an accent carried over from a childhood in another country.

"It's a little late for that script," I said.

"I guess you're right." He laughed, congenial and maybe a little embarrassed, as if I'd pointed out that his fly was open. "I'm not here to change your tire," he said.

I didn't say anything.

"Why don't you get out of the car?" he suggested, casually aiming the gun at my throat.

I obeyed. It was clear in any case that the car was not going to get me out of there.

The other car had stopped behind mine. It was a Crown Victoria with a dull blue paint job, nondescript aside from a family resemblance to a police car. Another man was emerging from the driver's seat. He was big. The kind of big that suggests oafishness, thoughtless physical power—the childish strength of Lenny Small, the servility of Pinky to the Brain. He wore a scowl on an Eastern-European face, his eyebrows thick and blunt. Boris.

"This isn't exactly a fair fight," I said, echoing Hong's reasonable tone. "I mean, there are two of you."

"I'll make you a deal." He gestured at his sidekick with a long thumb. "If you want to challenge us in hand-to-hand combat, you can fight him while I watch."

I entertained a brief fantasy of kneeing his balls and running away, but I knew there wasn't anything in it.

"You might be interested to know that I've already called the police," I said instead.

The men looked at each other. "I'd like to take a look at your phone," Hong said. I gave it to him and he thumbed the screen, finding my call history. "No 911 call."

"No, but check the time stamp. I called someone, didn't I? I can assure you I wasn't ordering pizza."

"Veronica Sanchez. Girlfriend of yours?"

"You could say that. She's also a homicide detective."

He thrust his tongue into a cheek, causing the beard beneath it to bristle. "Yeah? And what'd you tell her? Couldn't have had much to say about us."

He had a point. I couldn't have seen much before he approached me, and I was off the phone by then. I thought for a few seconds, about whether it would be wise to tell them I had police coming.

Hong might as well have read my mind. "Are they coming here?" There was no trace of fear, or even anxiety, in his voice.

I didn't say anything, and he laughed, softly. "It doesn't matter," he said. "We're not staying, either way."

Raw panic ran through me, and I remembered other times when I'd been packed into strange cars by dangerous men. It was a scenario that never seemed to end very well.

"It's over for Van Gasparian," I blurted out. "I told my friend he killed Nora Mkrtchian. I got that from his own mouth, and he might not have told you this, as he didn't know, but I recorded his confession."

He stared at the phone in his hand. "On this thing?"

I nodded. I was about to tell him that I'd already sent it to the police when Boris took the phone from his hand and smashed it on the pavement, crunching it under a heavy-soled dress shoe.

There went Van's confession. I wasn't likely to get another, even if I did make it out of this night alive. I felt sick to my stomach, like my computer had crashed and swallowed my thesis. Only the recording was a bit more important than schoolwork.

I kept my face as calm as possible, then morphed my expression into a smile. On the bright side, the giant's big move had strengthened my bluff.

"If you'd waited one second, you might've spared the effort and saved me a few hundred bucks," I said. "I already sent it to the police."

Until a couple years ago, when I started this business, I'd always thought of myself as a bad liar. It was a skill I'd never put to the test in any serious way, and I just assumed, that given what I thought of as my forthright, bullshit-free nature, I would be unable to utter falsehoods without my better self getting in the way—if not by stopping me altogether, at least through a quiver in my voice, or a conscience-driven facial tic. If anyone had ever asked me, I would have said I was a terrible liar, and it would have been a standard humble brag, a baseless nod at my own integrity.

Then one day, I started lying. Not pathologically, not when I could avoid it. But I compromised, and there was no way to take that back. I had my reasons, and in my softer moods, I let myself think they were good ones. The end result was no less dirty for my attempts at rationalization. There was a big lie to start, and it created the need for smaller ones. I told them to people I loved, to people I respected.

I hated it. It made me vile; it changed me. But in a way it brought me closer to the truth of me. I learned one thing, anyway—it turned out I was a great liar, probably always had been.

Hong stared at me for a full fifteen seconds, reading my face for a flinch or a tell. I didn't give him anything. When he was finished, he smiled. His eyes narrowed even further, nearly disappearing amid a mirthful network of wrinkles.

"How did you do that?" he asked. He sounded genuinely curious.

I shrugged and hoped he'd defer to my millennial savvy. "Sent it to the cloud. You can do that from any smartphone. If your friend hadn't brutalized mine, I could show you."

"It's convenient," he said, smiling steadily, "that I can't call your bluff." He gave his partner a strong pat on the back. It was less congenial than it was a threatening show of power, and it pushed the giant man in my direction.

Anger flashed across his face as his footing faltered. He recovered quickly and walked right up to me, then smacked my face with the back of his hand.

The shock of it almost dropped me. In my short career as a private investigator, I'd been grabbed, dragged, and held at gunpoint. I'd even been knocked out with a blow to the back of my head. But I'd never been confronted with anything as straightforward and openly violent as a hand to the face.

The pain was stunning, bright and magnificent—it filled my whole head, from the ringing in my skull to the pulse in my lip to the tear in my cheek, where one jeweled finger had made first contact. My hands shot up to my face to assess the damage. The fingers at my cheek came away wet with blood.

"No cause for that," said Hong. He checked the time on his phone. There was a picture of a golden retriever on his lock screen. He was a regular sweetheart, this Hong. "We'd better get off this street, though. We can continue this conversation in the car."

Boris grabbed me by the shoulder with enough force to tack me up on a wall. Hong walked ahead and we followed him to the Crown Vic. Hong didn't look back. Boris had me under control.

He only let go to shove me into the backseat of the Crown Vic. I registered a throbbing soreness in my shoulder as I scanned my surroundings and noticed the car door was unlocked. I ran some quick calculations as Boris took the driver's seat. Speed and distance and odds of survival. There wasn't a straw to grasp at in sight. I let my head fall back against the seat.

"Where should we go?" Boris asked Hong.

"Echo Park, Echo Park . . ." He snapped his fingers. "Let's go to that staircase," he said brightly, as if he'd thought of the perfect spot to get lunch.

They didn't bother to blindfold me, and I took this as a bad sign. Boris drove silently while Hong fiddled with his phone. I willed myself to peek at his screen, which was how I learned he was playing *Angry Birds*.

He didn't look up until Boris stopped the car a few minutes later. We were still in Echo Park, on one of the hilly streets scattered with old apartment buildings. Hong got out first and Boris followed, dragging me with him.

The street was dark and the buildings around us looked unoccupied, blind. We were parked at the foot of a long concrete staircase that ran up the hillside like a dirty zipper. There were dozens of these staircases speckled around the Eastside, free gyms for morning joggers that were empty at night. This one was more isolated even than most, with nothing but ground and grass on either side. It was a nice spot to get up to no good. Hong did a lap up and down the stairs—making sure, I guessed, that there weren't any high school kids fucking on the landings. When he was almost back to our level, he waved us over, saying, "The coast is clear."

There was a good chance I'd punch my ticket on this stairway, and I tried to make each step last as long as possible, trying to force time to expand to fill the needs of my mind, to allow for an arrival at a final kind of peace. It didn't work.

When we reached a high enough landing, Hong sat at the top of the steps and gestured for me to sit next to him. I obeyed, and felt Boris standing behind me like a pillar ready to fall down.

"What did Van tell you?" Hong asked.

"He told me what happened to Nora," I said. "He told me he had friends in dark places who owed him a favor."

"A favor?" A note of contempt crept into his tone. The first hint of unpleasantness in his demeanor so far.

The irritation felt like a step in the right direction. "Would that be a mischaracterization of your relationship?"

He smiled wide. "What did he say about these friends?"

I thought about our conversation, about the gambling operation in Seoul Tokyo Grill, his role as surgeon to the mob. Hong and Boris, named and described in recognizable detail.

The recording was pure gold. It incriminated not only Van, but a whole ring of gangsters who had come in touch with him. I felt a powerful sense of loss.

"Nothing," I said, affecting suppressed exasperation. "He was vague. He kept saying he'd get killed if he said anything."

The giant made a gruff sound of approval, and I saw Hong flinch at the elbow, as if he might want to jab him in the ribs.

All at once, the panic and desperation screaming in my head subsided into something quieter, something a little more relaxed and muffled. I saw my situation at a short remove—the distance between a player and her chessboard. I was in check, but not checkmate; I could force a draw with an ugly move. My split cheek throbbed with a vivid red pain. It was distracting, even in this moment, and I thought of the bleak lessons of 1984, the impossibility of heroism in the face of prospective pain.

I'd been gearing up for a bargain from the moment my tire blew out.

"But it's only a matter of time before the police get to him," I said. "They'll arrest him. Tomorrow definitely, maybe even tonight. They'll take him away from his family, charge him with murder."

Hong was listening. There was a thoughtful, attentive look in his eyes that allowed me to keep on going.

"And what do you think he'll do when he's hauled in? How confident are you in his loyalty? He's just a doctor. He's not one of you."

I felt Boris's eyes on me as I spoke. I knew he couldn't dispense with me until Hong said so.

"Someone like Van, he doesn't feel like he belongs in prison. He can't imagine it. He doesn't have the right constitution. You think if he has a bargaining chip to stay out, he's not going to use it?"

"That rat," Boris said. He sounded as angry as if my prediction had already come true. "I never did trust him."

"This was a good idea when Van called you, okay? I'm a loose end. You get rid of me, Van walks, at least for now. Nora stays buried. You get to keep your surgeon. But the situation is different now. You seem like a levelheaded guy," I said to Hong. "You must recognize that."

He smiled. "You're a smart girl, I have to give you that. But the way I see it, all that's changed is that there are now two loose ends."

"Let me go," I said, keeping my voice as calm and rational as possible. "You have no use for me. I won't hold any of this against you. And even if I do, what am I going to do about it? I don't know the first thing about you."

"You could be lying about that," he explained. "You could cause us trouble."

"She knows about the barbecue spot," Boris put in, ever helpful.

"It's too late to keep Seoul Tokyo out of this. Van didn't have to give that up when I talked to him—I already went there and asked him about it on tape. And look, I understand I've caused some inconvenience here, but there's no real upside to getting rid of me. You don't want the trouble that comes with murdering an innocent Korean girl. You'll get heat from the cops. Speaking of which, it can't be too long now before they pick up Van," I said, looking straight into Hong's eyes. "So isn't there somewhere else you need to be?"

Hong held my gaze without fear or anger, but a building intensity. I didn't breathe until he broke away, what felt like minutes later.

He stood up, knees creaking, and patted Boris on the back. "Come on," he said.

"We're leaving her?"

"Don't sound so disappointed, my friend," he said, looking at me one last time before heading down the stairs. "We can always come back."

I sat in the stairwell for a long time after they left, trying to breathe and collect the pieces of myself that had fled in the panic of a brush with death. I closed my eyes and started to imagine my funeral— the mournful faces of my scattered friends and family, Lori heartbroken, my mother destroyed. I had to stop when I got to the speeches. There wasn't a person in the world who could eulogize me properly, who knew me well enough to encapsulate who I was, what I would leave behind.

I'd just put a target on Van Gasparian's head. He might have been a murdering scumbag who'd tried to do the same to me, but I knew there was nothing noble about what I'd done. He was a husband and a brand-new father, and I'd orchestrated his execution.

I couldn't tell anyone what had just happened. I would live out my life in the loneliness of an undetected killer. I thought about crying, then decided it was time to go home if I had nothing better to do than feel sorry for myself. I needed a drink and a cigarette, badly.

I walked down the staircase, back to dim-lit Los Angeles, the life and landscape I'd almost left behind. It held darkness, ugliness, corruption, and sin, but the choice was never clearer than in the moment I grabbed it—life, in all its horror, was a better devil than death.

I walked home through Echo Park, feeling the soreness in my shoulder, the wretched reliable thumping of my pulse. I took my time. I followed the sounds of the living night to my front door.

Sixteen

❦

Veronica once told me that in order to become a homicide detective as a gay Latina, she had to be twice as good, twice as diligent, twice "the man" of every other cop in the LAPD, even as jealous colleagues tracked her rise with disdain and mumbles of affirmative action and PC bullshit. Which was how she'd gained a reputation as an abrasive, ball-busting hard ass, despite what I had always suspected was a pretty compassionate core.

And now, Detective Veronica Sanchez was rising from the curb in front of my apartment, arms open and shouting my name.

"Juniper Song. Holy shit."

I let her hug me and spoke into her hair. "I thought I said to bring friends."

"I did. I let them leave a while ago." She laughed. "You're a piece of work, you know that? I've been worried sick about you."

"Want to come in?"

She followed me to my apartment, where I poured out two glasses of rye and lit a cigarette.

"What the fuck happened to you?" she asked, taking her drink without further comment.

"I got kidnapped," I said. "These two men, they took me up a deserted staircase and we had a nice talk about whether they should kill me."

"Are you okay?"

I shrugged and took a deep drag off my cigarette, letting the smoke go in a long white spiral. "I'm shaken up, but glad to be alive."

"These men—was one of them Van Gasparian?"

I shook my head and steadied myself. "No. They were the men who murdered Nora Mkrtchian."

Somewhere in my subconscious, I'd committed to this lie the moment I traded Van's life for mine. If he survived the night, I could reevaluate, but for now, I would start the work of sanitizing his legacy. If Rubina and Alex had to lose their husband and father, they could at least remember him as something short of a murderer. I felt I owed him that much.

Veronica narrowed her eyes over the rim of her glass. I knew my new story would be a hard sell. "Really."

"Van has a gambling problem," I started. I would hew close to the truth to burnish the lie.

I filled her in on Van's descent into debt, as well as how Seoul Tokyo BBQ really stayed in business. I told her about Van's indefinite gig as a mob surgeon, bound to the men who'd almost killed me.

"These men, they have names?" she asked.

"Sort of," I said. "Hong and Boris."

There was a chance that Hong would find out I'd given their aliases to the police, but I couldn't withhold everything from Veronica—I felt guilty enough as it was. I also doubted this would come back to me. There was no way Hong and Boris were their real names, and if the LAPD did find them, it wouldn't be off of my information alone.

"Hong and Boris. No last names." Veronica snorted. "Please tell me they at least have distinctive facial tattoos."

I described the pair as well as I could, while Veronica shook her head.

"We'll check out the barbecue joint," she said, "but I'll tell you right now, I doubt it'll lead straight to your guys."

"Why not?"

"What were you, born yesterday?" She chuckled. "I have a lot of choice phrases for you, but 'born yesterday' has never been one of them."

"You'll have to share your list sometime. For now, humor me?"

"You should hear Arturo talk about this," she said. "It is fucking difficult to catch mobsters. They're organized. They have experience. They know how to clean up after themselves."

"I doubt Hong and Boris are the top guys or anything. They're probably just triggermen. Boris, in particular, didn't seem all that bright."

"You don't have to be a genius to get away with murder," she said. "It's a skill like anything else. You just need to know how to use it."

"Maybe you'll find them, maybe you won't. But you're closer now than you were ten minutes ago."

"We haven't talked about the murder," she said, her tone colored by an unsettling note of amusement. "Tell me exactly how and why these goons offed your girl."

She knew I was lying, on top of which I knew she knew, and she knew I knew. But I plunged on. She couldn't prove it, and I'd stick to my story from now on.

"She found them through Van," I began. "She wanted to go after Kizil, and she thought they might help. She wasn't planning to pay them, so she tried a little light blackmail. She overplayed her hand."

"You got this from Van?" she asked, leaning back in her chair.

I nodded. "I told you I recorded him. But that's gone now. Boris destroyed it."

"Why did they let you go?"

"I convinced them they had nothing to fear from me. I didn't know anything about them, really, and I said it wouldn't be worthwhile to kill me. I also might've mentioned I had just placed a call to a friend who happened to be a homicide cop."

I willed myself not to drink just to cover the silence that followed. If anyone could deduce the terms of my bargain, it was Veronica, but even she could never prove it.

She sighed. "This sounds plausible and all, except you already told me you had Van Gasparian on tape confessing to the murder."

"I said I had him on tape *telling* me about the murder."

I knew she wouldn't buy this version over the panicked phone call in her memory, but I also knew that she wouldn't be able to play back the audio. If I'd called 911, I would've been recorded, but I'd called Veronica's cell in the middle of the night.

She shook her head. "I don't get you sometimes, J.S. I like you, always have. Always thought maybe we were similar. Me, I like to find the truth in things, and I've lied maybe five times in my life that I can remember, all of them to my mother. It's not that I'm a great woman. It's just that honesty is a virtue that comes easy. It's just not that hard to live life without lying all the time, no matter what anyone says."

"Sure," I said, with a small wink. "Maybe modesty is a little tougher."

She didn't respond to the weak joke. "I don't know why you need to lie. I don't know what you get out of it. I really don't."

I didn't protest, and we passed a few minutes in a fraught, sulky silence.

"Maybe you just have to take me with a grain of mystery," I said with a conciliatory smile.

She laughed harshly and stood up, leaving her drink unfinished on the table. "Well, I'm glad you're okay," she said.

"Me, too." I stood up to follow her to the door.

She put her hand on my shoulder and patted it three times,

somewhat begrudgingly. "But don't call me again just to bullshit me. I'm not up for playing your fool."

I slept poorly and went into the office the next morning after a hot cup of coffee with a little pour of rye. Part of me thought I deserved a day off after the night I'd had, but I knew I had to call Rubina. I had little desire to talk to her, but I had no choice. I guessed she'd been calling my dead cell phone all morning, maybe all through the night, too.

Chaz and Arturo were both in, and my heart cracked at the sight of them. Here were my colleagues, two good men who trusted me, and I'd shown up with another pack of lies on my back.

"Why do you look like you slept in a chimp cage?" Chaz asked. Arturo rolled his chair to his door to get a look.

"Had a rough night," I told them. "But the case—the big one? It's over. I'll explain later. I need to call my client."

I pulled Rubina's phone number and dialed from my desk.

"Where is he?" she asked immediately.

"Back up," I said. "You mean Van?"

"Didn't you get my messages?" She sounded frantic. "He left the house late last night, and he never came back."

"Oh, no." I checked my voice for insincerity and felt immediately slimy. "He left to meet with me."

"What? Why didn't you tell me?"

"It was urgent. Listen. I figured out what Van's been up to, and it's nothing good."

I gave Rubina the same story I'd handed to Veronica, and in the retelling, I started to think about how easily it could have been true. Van's gambling, Van's mob connection—none of that could be hidden. I could only spare him his last inch of humanity, and even that only in the eyes of others.

By the time I was finished, Rubina was sniffling, controlling her tears with careful measured breaths. "They were going to kill you?" she asked, wanting to disbelieve. "Oh, God. Do you think they—" She stopped. She was willing me to interrupt her.

"Where's his car? Weren't you tracking it?"

"At the Mermaid Lounge," she said. "He used to drink there all the time."

I pictured Van drowning his miseries after I'd left, hoping to forget he'd killed Nora, that he'd sent two dangerous men to kill me. He must have stayed until closing—just enough time for Hong and Boris to get from Echo Park to Glendale. I wondered what went through his head when they greeted him outside.

"You should report him missing. The police will find him."

"Like they found Nora?" she asked bitterly.

She had a point. If the police hadn't found Nora, I doubted they'd be able to find Van, either. He would become one of the vanished, the indefinitely missing, and Rubina would live her life in haunted uncertainty, even if he were presumed dead. I couldn't tell her that this was better than the truth.

"I'm sorry, Rubina." I didn't know what else to say.

I stayed on the phone with her for another fifteen minutes, answering questions and talking softly, waiting, scared for her to blame me. When I hung up, I was exhausted.

Chaz and Arturo were both in their doorways, wearing looks of open horror.

"You got all that?" I asked rhetorically.

I called Rob, later than I'd meant to, to let him know I was alive. We agreed to meet up later, and I tried to summon the usual excitement. It was muted, but to my relief, it was still there. Life went on, I knew, and I had to be grateful—for each day, each burst of feeling, and each person in it important enough to lie to.

Epilogue

❦

In the end I told the whole truth to the one person who needed it—my friend and fellow sinner Lusig Hovanian.

She moved back in with Rubina, to help her cousin manage her confusion and grief as well as her baby. I stayed away from that house, but talked to Lusig almost every day.

On April 24, the centennial of the Armenian genocide, the memorial Nora Mkrtchian had fought for went up in a public park in Glendale. Thayer White had dropped EARTH's lawsuit after Kizil's murder heightened public attention, and EARTH itself seemed to dissipate, its unscrupulous battle lost. Over a month later, there were no leads on Kizil's killer.

I skipped the centennial gathering, where Lusig and Rubina rallied with the L.A. Armenian community, baby Alex held close between them. Nora's death was still not a public fact, but she was remembered at the centennial, along with the memorial she'd fought to support. I went to pay my respects a week later, accompanied by Lusig.

The memorial was maybe ten feet tall, much smaller than the monument I'd imagined. I had to wonder what all the fuss had been about, how this single statue could rouse the temper of an entire nation. It consisted of two bronze pillars leaning toward each other, their posture describing humanity. I bent down to read the inscription at the foot of the memorial:

I SHOULD LIKE TO SEE ANY POWER OF THE WORLD DESTROY THIS RACE, THIS SMALL TRIBE OF UNIMPORTANT PEOPLE, WHOSE WARS HAVE ALL BEEN FOUGHT AND LOST, WHOSE STRUCTURES HAVE CRUMBLED, LITERATURE IS UNREAD, MUSIC IS UNHEARD, AND PRAYERS ARE NO MORE ANSWERED. GO AHEAD, DESTROY ARMENIA. SEE IF YOU CAN DO IT. SEND THEM INTO THE DESERT WITHOUT BREAD OR WATER. BURN THEIR HOMES AND CHURCHES. THEN SEE IF THEY WILL NOT LAUGH, SING AND PRAY AGAIN. FOR WHEN TWO OF THEM MEET ANY-WHERE IN THE WORLD, SEE IF THEY WILL NOT CREATE A NEW ARMENIA.

"That's William Saroyan," Lusig said. "He was Nora's favorite novelist."

"It's a powerful quote," I said, straightening up.

She smiled sadly. "You know, this is my fourth time here this week."

"Wow, really?"

"I guess I'm starting to accept that she's gone. And this is where I come to see her."

I nodded. "Makes sense. She fought hard for this."

"It's not just that. Nora's parents won't give her a funeral. They won't accept that she's gone."

"She's their daughter and there's still no body," I said. "Can't really blame them."

"Oh, of course I don't blame them. I'm just saying, I know she's dead now, and this is the closest thing she'll get to a grave."

We stood in silence for a while then walked around the park. It was a Saturday afternoon, warm and beautiful, and we were the only people treating the park like a cemetery. Families picnicked and dogs chased Frisbees. There were children everywhere, zipping around and running past the memorial without the slightest idea why it was there.

"Ruby might call you," said Lusig.

"What for?" I asked.

"She's making herself crazy about Van. She won't accept that he can't be found."

"Tell her I can't do it. Tell her those mobsters scared me off."

"I'll tell her, but I don't know. I feel terrible for her."

"Me, too."

We circled back to the memorial and Lusig sat down, leaning her back against it.

"You did the right thing, you know," she said.

I laughed. Over the last few weeks, I'd come to terms with the decisions I'd made at the end of this case. They'd blended into my past like all the other things I'd never thought I'd get over, all the shit I'd forgotten to keep feeling bad about. Still, I knew too much to fool myself. "No, I didn't."

"It was you or Van, and Van was the murderer. And at the very least, it was decent of you to lie for him."

"I wonder if the LAPD would agree. Or Mr. and Mrs. Mkrtchian."

She shrugged. "Van's dead. He wasn't going to stand trial. And as for Nora's parents—without a body, telling them wouldn't have made a difference. I've told them about Hong and Boris, and they won't buy it."

"Maybe because it's bullshit. Maybe because as far as anyone can tell, Hong and Boris are figments of my imagination."

"In any case, you've spared Ruby. You've spared Alex. You've spared a shiny new child from a legacy of guilt."

I pointed behind her. "She says, leaning against a hotly contested genocide memorial."

"Okay, I see the irony there, you fucking smart-ass." She smirked and looked behind her, touching the bronze. "Speaking of children—"

"Were we?"

"—now that you have all this free time, do you think you'll track down your eggs?"

"Are you going to maternity test Alex?"

"Jesus, no."

"It won't kill you not to know?"

"I can't say I'm not curious, but I think I'll have to deal."

I leaned back on my hands, cracking my knuckles. "I feel exactly the same way."

"Everything's a mess all the time, isn't it?" She sighed and rested her head against Nora's memorial, turning lazily to me.

I met her eyes and smiled. A current of joy bubbled through me, unexpected, and subsided just as quickly, leaving a lingering coolness, temporary serenity.

I tore up a handful of grass and scattered it back on the ground. "It is what it is, I guess. Might as well get used to it."